AN EXCLUSIVE FAMILY BOOKSHELF
2-IN-1 EDITION

A CALL TO HONOR

✩ ✩ ✩

THE COLOR OF THE STAR

GILBERT MORRIS

AND BOBBY FUNDERBURK

✩ ✩ ✩

COMPLETE AND UNEDITED EDITIONS

SINCE 1948, THE BOOK CLUB YOU CAN TRUST

All Scripture quotations, unless otherwise noted, are taken from The King James Version.

First combined Hardcover Edition for Christian Herald Family Bookshelf: 1994
Library of Congress Cataloging-in-Publication Data

Morris, Gilbert.
    A call to honor / Gilbert Morris and Bobby Funderburk.
      p. cm. — (The Price of liberty series : #1)
    ISBN 0—8499–3494–X
    I. Funderburk, Bobby, 1942- . II. Title. III. Series.
PS3563.08742C28   1993
813'.54—dc20   92–44517
                                                 CIP

Printed in the United States of America

GILBERT MORRIS
AND BOBBY FUNDERBURK

A CALL TO
HONOR

WORD PUBLISHING
Dallas · London · Vancouver · Melbourne

All Scripture quotations, unless otherwise noted, are taken from
The King James Version.

Library of Congress Cataloging-in-Publication Data

Morris, Gilbert.
    A call to honor / Gilbert Morris and Bobby Funderburk.
       p.   cm. — (The Price of liberty series : #1)
    ISBN 0–8499–3494–X
    I. Funderburk, Bobby, 1942– . II. Title. III. Series.
PS3563.08742C28   1993
813'.54—dc20   92–44517
                                                                   CIP

Printed in the United States of America

To Helen
Wife of my youth—
I'm glad we're together on the pilgrimage
through the Lamb-white days
that lead to Life.

Bobby

CONTENTS

Part 1

LIBERTY

1

BEN

*S*hut up, boy!" Earl Logan snarled at his son as the two of them rattled along the gravel road in his rust-speckled pulpwood truck. "A man's gotta have a little fun in his life!"

"Yes sir." Ben saw the fires of anger banked in his father's dark eyes and clamped his lips together.

Logan took a cotton bag of Bull Durham from the pocket of his khaki shirt with his left hand, opened it with his teeth, and dumped a line of tobacco on the cigarette paper he held in his right hand, resting on the steering wheel. Taking the string in his teeth, he drew the bag tight and returned it to his pocket. He licked one side of the paper, rolled it together, twisted the ends, and placed the cigarette between his lips in one smooth motion.

That's one thing he can do right, Ben thought bitterly. *Maybe we ought to put it on his tombstone: "Rolled a Good Cigarette."*

Taking a kitchen match from his pocket, Logan flicked it into life with his thumbnail, waited for the swoosh of flame and smoke to die down, and lit his cigarette. "Now, like I was sayin', I'm gonna stop at Shorty's for a couple of cool ones. Then I'll be on out to the woods to help you finish up in an hour or two." He inhaled deeply, letting the smoke flow from his nostrils.

Ben looked at the scratched and dented syrup bucket that held their cornbread and baked sweet potatoes. "I kinda figured you'd be stoppin' here when you said we'd go to town for a Coca-Cola to go with our dinner."

Logan turned toward his son, his eyes squinting from the smoke that drifted up from the cigarette between his lips. "You gettin' smart-alecky with me, boy?" he demanded, a threat in his husky voice.

"No, sir," Ben said quickly, returning his father's stare. "I just knew what you had in mind. That's all." Ben watched the muscles working in his father's jaw, half-expecting a backhand across the mouth—but it never came.

Logan bounced over the rutted, hard-packed ground in front of Shorty's Bar, pulling underneath a gnarled cedar tree. He killed the engine then turned toward his son, staring at him through the wavering trail of blue-white smoke, the cigarette dangling from his lips. "A man's just gotta have a good time now and then, son. You'll understand when you get a little older. Now, you wait here. I'll git you an R.C. Cola."

Ben sat on the grease-stained seat of the truck, his feet resting on a tangle of chains on the floorboard, but said nothing. He had a bitter thought of his mother's long day that began before sunup and lasted well into the night. *I reckon women don't ever need to have a good time*, he thought sourly.

Something passed between them during these moments—this father and son. Earl Logan had the sudden feeling that if he left the truck something vital would be lost—forever. He looked at his son, into the boy's gray eyes—light as an eagle's in his dark face—then abruptly came to a decision. Moving his foot toward the starter, he paused—then turned sharply around on the seat, kicked the door open and stepped out of the truck.

Shorty's had once been a storage shed for hay. When Ike Prather felt it looked too dilapidated to have in his pasture, he'd told Shorty he could have it just to get it out of his sight. Shorty took him up on it and moved it to the little plot of ground outside of town. The smell of hay that still lingered after so many seasons was the best part about the place. Backed up to a kudzu-covered bluff, it had a dirt floor and two benches out front so the customers could enjoy the fresh air on hot evenings. The only indications that it was a place of business were the Pabst Blue Ribbon sign to the left of the door and the green metal Lucky Strike circle with white lettering on the right.

Occupying the bench under the Lucky Strike sign was J. T. Dickerson. His suit was expensive and well cut ("No off-the-rack threads for J. T. Dickerson!"), but it was twenty years old and shiny with wear. The shirt collar was yellowed and frayed, and the tie looked as though it had been pulled from the back pocket of a diesel mechanic.

Logan swaggered over to the bench, rolling another cigarette. Grinning down at the rumpled figure, he drawled, "J.T., I 'member when you used to hang out at the country club. Shorty's is a long step down, ain't it?"

J.T. stood up and looked around him, his rheumy brown eyes wide in mock alarm. "Good gracious! I must have taken a wrong turn. This definitely isn't Pine Hills."

"You took a wrong turn all right," Earl said, flicking the match with his thumb, "first time you turned into Grady's Liquor Store."

Combing the long greasy hair out of his eyes with his left hand, J.T. smiled his crooked smile and collapsed on the bench. "Right you are, Earl, right you are. It's not so bad though when you adopt an existentialist point of view. One lives a life of the mind, learns to embrace all forms of human behavior. Even sobriety—in moderation of course." He took a battered silver flask from his inside jacket pocket, unscrewed the top and took a long pull.

"With all yore fancy talk, you're still just a worthless drunk, J.T.," Earl snapped, propping his foot on the bench.

J.T. screwed the top back on the flask, slipped it back into his pocket, and turned his sad brown eyes up toward Earl. "I prefer to think of myself as perniciously enamored of leisure and drink."

"You plumb crazy, J.T.," Earl grinned, drawing hard on his cigarette. He glanced at two cat squirrels chasing each other in a spiral down a white oak. "Seems like it was last week you was handin' off to me on the two yard line or chunking a long one on third and ten. Have to give it to you—you could really hum that ol' pigskin! I don't reckon you can even pick one up now."

J.T. leaned over and scratched the ears of a bony blue tick hound that lay next to the bench. The dog looked up with eyes that matched J.T.'s and moaned with pleasure. "Those were the days, Earl," J.T. said softly, looking out across the rolling pasture on the opposite side of the road, "those were truly the days—

> Smart lad, to slip betimes away
> From fields where glory does not stay"

"What's that, J.T.?" Earl demanded, leaning closer. "I didn't git that last part."

J.T. rubbed his eyes with both hands and came back to the present. "Nothing, Earl. Just somebody who had sense enough to do it right—a 'Townsman of a stiller town.'"

"You gittin' loonier ever day, J.T.," Earl said, shaking his head slowly from side to side.

From inside the bar drifted the sound of Jimmie Rogers singing "Peach Pickin' Time in Georgia." Someone began shouting and cursing loudly, the noise all but drowning out the sound of the music.

Earl glanced toward the open door. "Whut in tarnation is he hollerin' about?"

"Moon? Oh, he's been carrying on like that since he delivered Shorty's load of liquor without benefit of federal stamps," J.T. shrugged, looking back over his shoulder.

"Whut's his problem?" Earl asked, shifting about uneasily and flicking his cigarette into a mud hole next to the rickety building.

"The plight of the moonshiner, Earl," J.T. said, glancing at him with a malicious smile. "It seems that while Moon Mullins, master distiller, has been making his nightly runs—as are sometimes necessary in his time-honored profession—something has gone amiss."

"Will you speak English for once in your life, J.T.?" Earl grunted, picking up a rock and flinging it at the squirrels who were still playing in the big oak.

"Some scoundrel has been frequenting his home to win the favor of his winsome wife," J.T. replied fulsomely, leaning back against the sun-bleached boards of the building.

"Winsome wife! That woman weighs two hundred pounds if she weighs an ounce!"

"I believe I heard your name being bantered about in there earlier, Earl," J.T. grinned. He was an idle shape as he leaned back against the faded boards. Yet despite the scruffy appearance, there remained a trace of the man he had once been. Under the puffy face lay the solid line of jaw that had been firm and handsome, but the years had leached him of most of his good looks. His mind, once brilliant and sharp, was now foggy, dulled by a thousand bottles of bootleg whiskey, though he was still sharper—even in his gin-soaked condition—than some of the lawyers and politicians who sneered at him.

At that moment, Leon Mullins came weaving out of the darkness of the barroom. He steadied himself with one hand on the door facing, squinting into the bright sunshine. As his eyes came into focus, he turned them on Earl.

Everything about Leon was sharp—except his wits. His thin whitish hair was combed straight back from his low forehead but stood up in back where the comb never reached. People said he was too dumb to know he had hair on the back of his head. With his beady eyes, long pointed nose, and tiny ears, his face had the appearance of a plucked woodpecker.

Leon drew himself up to his full five-foot-six-inch height and took a shaky step into the sunshine. "Earl Logan, you ben messin' wif my wife!" he screeched in his keen little voice.

"You're drunk, Moon," Earl said, waving his hand. "Go on home and sleep it off before you git in trouble."

Leon was a meek man, but he carried a load of courage in his veins and a pearl-handled switchblade in his back pocket. "I'll show you who's drunk, you two-bit Romeo!" Leon pressed the button on the handle of the knife and the six-inch blade glinted in the sunlight. He took two wobbly steps toward Earl.

Logan spread his feet apart and went into a crouch, moving lightly on the balls of his feet. "Now Moon, you put that thing back in yore pocket! You gonna git hurt!"

Peering at the world through a red haze of anger, Leon had forgotten that his adversary was six inches taller and outweighed him by seventy pounds. Thin lips trembling, he took two steps forward and thrust the knife toward Earl's barrel chest.

Earl brushed the knife aside with a sweeping movement of his left arm, planted his foot and came up from the hip with a right hook, his horny fist catching Leon squarely on the jaw. The light went out instantly in Leon's eyes as his head snapped backward, his body lifting in the air and landing in a crumpled heap on the hard ground. He lay there in the hot sun, the back of his head lying in one of the big ruts of Shorty's parking lot, the muddy water plastering down his hair so that it matched the part he had combed.

"Splendid—just splendid!" J.T. shouted from his bench. "I knew you could take that hulking brute of a man!"

Earl glowered at him. "It ain't funny, you winehead! What if he's hurt bad?" He knelt beside Leon, lifted his head from the water and dragged him over to the bench opposite J.T.'s. Leon moaned softly as Earl stretched him out on the rough wooden surface.

"I believe our fallen hero will live to cross the Styx another day," J.T. announced, taking his flask out.

"Yeah, I reckon he's all right," Earl agreed. He turned and walked over to where the knife lay shining in the sun, picked it up, and returned to the bench.

"*Victori praeda*," J.T. said, lifting his flask toward Earl and taking a quick swallow.

"Whut're you babblin' 'bout now?" Earl demanded, turning the knife over in his hands.

"To the victor—the spoils," J.T. answered. "For valor on the field of battle you get the knife and the wife."

Earl Logan flushed. He took a step toward J.T., his right hand knotted into a hammer of a fist, the left clutching the knife. J.T. smiled serenely at him. Taking a deep breath, Earl looked down at the moaning form of Leon Mullins, a trail of blood seeping from the corner of his mouth. He plunged the knife through the middle of the Pabst sign and snapped the blade off. Spinning quickly, he flung the handle high into the air like a center fielder throwing to home plate. Arcing end over end, it flashed in the sunlight, disappearing into the tall grass on the other side of the road.

"The lad must be proud of you, Earl," J.T. said slyly, "after such a display of chivalry."

Earl looked toward his son, having forgotten he left him sitting in the truck. Suddenly he was angry and embarrassed and called out harshly, "Whut're you starin' at, boy? You got work to do!"

Ben got slowly down from the cab of the truck, slamming the door behind him. He walked across the parking lot, passing in front of the three men—prone, seated, and standing. *Gettin' drunk ain't enough for you—you gotta chase another man's wife!*

"Don't believe what this dumb moonshiner says, boy—" Earl shouted at his son. "There ain't a lick of truth to it."

Ben stared coldly at his father and kept walking, carrying the syrup bucket with the lunch he would eat without an R.C.

"I'll be there in a hour to help finish up—two at the most," Earl called out.

Ben glanced over his shoulder at his father. *Sometime between midnight and dawn—that's when you'll show up!* Anger was raw and bitter in his throat, but he kept his face impassive as he turned and walked away from the scene.

"You keep yore mouth shut about this, boy! You hear?"

Walking along the side of the gravel road toward the heavy work that waited for him a half mile away, Ben heard the faint sound of Jimmy Rogers spilling out of the side window of Shorty's:

> I'm a thousand miles away from home
> Waiting for a train.

* * *

I'd rather die than do this for a living! Maybe I'd drink like Daddy does after thirty years of this!

Ben slouched along the dirt road that led to his house, his scuffed, high-topped brogans kicking up small clouds in the warm brown dust. Wearing only faded and threadbare overalls, he carried two double-bit axes over his right shoulder and gripped the handle of a crosscut saw in his left hand, the other end plowing a furrow as it dragged along behind him. His tanned arms and shoulders were corded with the smooth muscle of youth, his slim hands belying the strength in them.

I knew he was gonna do this as soon as he started bein' nice to me this morning—leave me to finish all the trimmin' while he goes into Shorty's to get liquored up. How am I ever gonna keep up in school? Two days he's kept me out this week!

The Georgia sun had lost its thin white summer hue and was taking on the pale gold of September as it slipped down behind the crooked tin fence that enclosed Creel's junkyard. As Ben walked from the shade of a sweet gum tree that grew beside the road, the sunlight struck him, shining on his hair, black as a raven's wing. Frowning at the ramshackle clutter of other people's castoffs, he continued toward home.

Yes sir! Garden spot of Liberty, Georgia. I know I'm almost home when I see Creel's Empire—a real-life Camelot right here in the rural South. Maybe it's where we belong—the whole family. Just a bunch of rejects and misfits!

17

As his home came into sight, Ben felt a weariness overcome him that was born of more than the bone-grinding work of cutting pulpwood. Dropping the saw and axes at the side of the road, he slumped down under a towering pine, enjoying the sharp clean scent rising from the bed of needles at its base. As he gazed down the hill where the road ended and his front yard began, a sadness, dark and undefined, settled over him like the dusk settling in the pine barrens beyond his home.

He looked at the unpainted shotgun house with its sagging front porch and torn screen door—at the rusty Model T, its axles resting on concrete blocks. *Gonna fix that motor first thing Saturday mornin'. Be like new when I finish.* He had heard his dad say that for as long as he could remember. He stared at the tattered clothes hanging on a wire strung between two Chinaberry trees in the side yard and thought of the rich green expanse of grass and shrubs and trees that led to the white-columned mansion where Debbie Lambert lived. Debbie—with her pale yellow hair and blue eyes—made his knees go watery every time he saw her walk across the school ground.

A heavy sadness seemed to harden and weigh on him, and he felt that longing common to boys standing on the front steps of manhood—for that one thing to lead them through those fearful, uncharted spaces of the flesh and of the spirit. A flash of motion caught Ben's eye, and he watched a blue jay lift from the roof of the house in the slanting amber light and—like a final, shining hope—it disappeared into the dark woods beyond the yard.

"Come play with me, Ben!" Micah called out from the tire swing hanging from a high limb of the old walnut tree. Children had played around it and in it so much it was almost like a member of the family. The ground beneath it and the bark of the tree were worn smooth from decades of young climbers whose families had rented the house. It stood like an avuncular sentinel between the house and the deep woods, an object of permanence in a world of change.

Ben smiled affectionately at his six-year-old brother who jumped out of the swing and came running up the hill toward him. He had the same hair and eyes as his dad, was chunky and round-faced, and would one day have the bulky muscles of his father. "Can't do it now, Micah," Ben said. "Got to get cleaned up and do my homework."

"Aw shucks," Micah whined, looking at the ground. "Just for a little while!" he pleaded.

Ben relented, pushed him for awhile in the swing; then the two of them played chase until Micah climbed the tree out of reach.

"That you, Ben?" he heard his mother call from the kitchen window at the back of the house.

"No ma'am," he answered, walking toward the back porch. He smiled and had his fun with her, saying, "It's Mr. Clark Gable. I heard way out in Hollywood you was the prettiest gal in the southern part of these United States, and I come to see if you'd be in my next movie."

"You cut out your foolishness and get cleaned up for supper, young man," Jewel laughed. "Everbody else is finished."

"OK, but this is serious business," Ben said over his shoulder, walking out to the well. "I'm gettin' awful tired of looking at that ugly ol' Carole Lombard."

Ben walked the well-worn path from the back steps to the well where a one-quart Mason jar sat on a small shelf he had nailed to the well post. Lowering the long, narrow galvanized bucket into the well, he heard the flat hollow splash far below and listened as it gurgled full. Then he wound it to the top, the rope wrapping smoothly around the wooden spool and spinning through the creaking pulley. Tying off the wooden handle of the spool, he grasped the bucket and poured the Mason jar three-quarters full of the sweet, cool water.

Savoring this simple pleasure every time he drew water from the well, Ben looked at the clear liquid, felt the smoothness of the jar, and drank slowly with the coolness spreading outward from his throat and stomach. Sometimes he imagined himself in London, nursing a pint of bitters and watching ships from all over the world ply the fog-shrouded Thames. Another time he would be in Paris, drinking wine at an outdoor cafe while the mademoiselles in the latest spring fashions strolled along the boulevard, skirts blowing about their long legs.

As he stood there savoring the cool water, it was typical that his mind would leave the squalid surroundings of Liberty, Georgia, taking flight for one of the colorful and romantic spots he'd absorbed from the world of books. There was little of the romantic in his appearance, but in his spirit he had the dash and verve of a d'Artanan, the daring of the Deerslayer. Perhaps it was this ability to submerge himself in the world of romance that kept him from bitterness. It was, however, this same trait that made him at times seem forgetful and even slow of thought.

The sun had dropped from sight, its rays from below the horizon striking a few wisps of clouds scattered across the darkening sky, turning them the color of ripe peaches. As Ben finished drinking the water, he heard the sound of his mother's radio through the kitchen window:

I'll be seeing you in all the old familiar places.

And the longing returned with a cold, terrible aching in his chest that caught at his breath.

"Ben Logan, you get in here right now, or I'll throw your supper to the dog!"

"We ain't got a dog, Mama," Ben yelled, hurrying toward the back door. "Remember? Daddy ran over him last week."

After he had washed off in the pan on the back porch shelf, Ben sat at the white-enameled, metal table before a plate of blackened peas, fried salt pork, cornbread, and sliced onion. He hadn't realized how hungry he was until his mouth and stomach began sending out distress signals.

"Sorry all you got to drink is well water, Sugar," his mother said from the kitchen sink, wiping her hands on her apron. Her soft gray eyes looked enormous in her thin face, and when she smiled, she tried to hide a missing front tooth, lost to one of Earl's drunken rages. "The little ones drunk the last of the milk."

"Aw, this is fine, Mama," Ben replied, attacking the food with his knife and fork. "You've got to be the best cook in the county. Why, this tastes good as steak and gravy any day!"

After the supper dishes were washed, Jewel took the cathedral-shaped radio into the living room, and the children gathered around the dial's soft amber glow. Dinah was sitting beside her mother on the couch. At fourteen, she had her father's eyes, but her mother's figure and temperament. Pete, at thirteen, was an older version of Micah. The two of them sat on the cracked linoleum floor.

"You comin', Ben?" Jewel called, adjusting the knob on the radio. "The program's 'bout to start."

"Can't, Mama," he answered from the kitchen. "Got to do an oral report for school tomorrow."

Jewel appeared at the kitchen door. "Maybe you're workin' too hard, Baby. I never saw anybody read so much—even when it's not homework. Come sit with us a spell."

Ben looked at his mother's face in the harsh glare of the bare seventy-five-watt bulb hanging from the ceiling on its cord. He remembered how glossy her brown hair had been only a few years ago and how it glistened in the sunlight. Now it was dull and flecked with gray. The threadbare house dress she had made from flour sacks hung on her spare frame with the same dull lifelessness.

Despite all the torment Ben had seen his mother go through, to the extent of ruining her health, he knew she had a strength far greater than her muscular, blustering husband. In her deep gray eyes there was a calm acceptance of all things and a separate joy that Ben could never understand. "Mama, I've missed so much school my grades are awful," he said. "This report's *got* to be good!"

"What's it about, son?" Jewel asked, looking over his shoulder at the magazines and newspapers.

"It's for history class," Ben replied, thumbing through one of the *Life* magazines. "Current events. I'm gonna call it *How Long Before Hitler Attacks America?*"

"Why, son—that won't happen!" Jewel gasped. "Mr. Roosevelt just wouldn't stand for it!"

Jewel returned to the living room and "The Amos and Andy Show" while Ben turned to the copies of the *New York Times* and *Life* magazines he had borrowed from the school library. Looking through the newspapers, Ben couldn't help but linger over the exotic advertisements from the big city—Ozzie Nelson and his orchestra, featuring vocalist Harriet Hilliard, at the Strand Theatre, Broadway at Forty-seventh—Macy's, the world's largest department store, Thirty-fourth and Broadway, boasted of a solid maple dog bed with a real innerspring mattress (for Park Avenue pups) that cost $2.79. He looked at the clothes and the movies and the latest books, then shook his head impatiently. *Well—enough of this! Time for work.* As Ben perused the war news, he heard snatches of the radio program from the other room interspersed with squeals and giggles and healthy laughter.

On August 24, Nazi foreign minister Joachim von Ribbentrop and Soviet Premier Vyacheslav Molotoff signed a ten-year nonaggression pact while Communist Dictator Joseph Stalin looked on.

"Good moanin', Kingfish . . . Um, ah, hello dare, Andy."

On September 1 at 4:45 A.M., with no formal declaration of war, Germany invaded Poland.

"You is right, Kingfish. I is regusted wid banks! I needs to investigate my money in a good business."

On September 3 at 6:10 A.M., New York time, Prime Minister Neville Chamberlain, speaking from the Cabinet Room at 10 Downing Street, announced that Great Britain and France were at war with Germany.

"Now you talkin', son, and de business you is lookin' for is my uncle's coffee plantation down in Rio de Geronimo . . . Is he honest, Kingfish? . . . Aw yeah, son. De boy a war hero! He won a bronze star wid fig leaf clusters on de thing!"

Half listening to "Amos and Andy," Ben had finished gathering the information he needed and began writing the introduction to his oral report. Taking his pencil firmly in his hand, he wrote carefully: *President Franklin D. Roosevelt says he believes that he can keep us out of the war. I don't!*

When the other children were in bed, Jewel came into the kitchen. Pouring the last of the coffee into a chipped white cup, she sat at the table with her son. "I drawed you some bath water earlier," she said. "I 'spect it's set in the sun long enough to be warm."

"Thanks, Mama," Ben replied. "I'm 'bout finished here. Why don't you go on to bed?"

Jewel Logan took a deep breath and leaned back in her chair, both hands clasping the cup. "Reckon I'll wait up a spell for your daddy. Maybe he won't be much longer."

"Mama, I'm sorry 'bout this," Ben said, gathering up the magazines and newspapers. "I tried to get him to stay out of that place, but he had his mind made up."

Jewel looked into Ben's eyes, so like her own. The other boys were heavy and dark-eyed like their father, Ben being the only one to take after her side of the family. Almost six feet tall, slim and broad-shouldered, she thought him very handsome. "It ain't your fault, son. When Earl acts as happy as he did this morning, I know what he's got in his mind to do that afternoon. Reckon he managed to scrape together a few dollars somehow. You go on and have your bath now. I'll go to bed directly."

"Why do you stay with him, Mama?" Ben asked suddenly, standing up with his stack of magazines and newspapers. The question had been in him for a long time, but never had he voiced it. Now there was a hint of pain in his face as he fixed his eyes on his mother.

Jewel turned her tired face up toward her son. "He wasn't always like this—" She stopped as if she had said too much, and realized the impossibility of explaining the thing to Ben. Abruptly she turned and left the room, and Ben—disturbed by the scene— walked slowly out the back door.

Later, outside in the cool night air, Ben sat in the galvanized washtub, gazing up at the vast scattering of stars across the black dome of the sky. He hated to go inside to the little room that was built as a pantry off the back porch which now served as a bedroom for him and his two brothers. There was just room enough for the three old army cots they slept on, a few clothes hanging on nails, and the odds and ends all boys manage to collect—a slingshot, a football, a few comic books, and some hand-me-down toys.

Ben saw the light go out in the kitchen. A few minutes later, he heard his mother praying as she knelt by her bedside next to the open window. Her voice was not loud but filled with an intensity that troubled Ben.

"Oh, God, we praise Your mighty name. Worthy is the Lamb! Hallelujah to the Lamb of God! Thank You, Jesus!" She always prayed for her husband first, then all her children by name, then so many others. Sometimes she spoke in a language Ben could not understand.

How can she pray for a man who treats her like Daddy does? Since he could remember, Ben had gone to sleep listening to the sound of his mother's praying. It was always a source of wonder and comfort to him. He lay back in his warm bath in the cool night, listening to his mother's prayers and looking up at the high, shining heavens.

2

LOVE FINDS ANDY HARDY

*M*oney. *There was money everywhere! Ben had never seen so much money! Nickels, dimes, quarters—even fifty-cent pieces and silver dollars! All shiny and new—scattered over the school ground—under the huge live oaks in front of the three-story red brick building—around the bike rack and the stone benches—along the sidewalks—everywhere!*

Ben was filling the pockets of his overalls as fast as he could. The glittering coins overflowing, spilling through his hands onto the ground in a silver, tinkling cascade. He was thinking of his mother's face—the surprise and the joy—when he brought home that blue flowered dress with the white lace trim he had seen her admiring so many times in the window of Hightower's Department Store.

Then he noticed—no one else even bothered to look at this ocean of money that covered the school ground. The other children were walking through it—laughing, talking, jostling each other—like it wasn't even there. Then he heard the laughter! They were all staring at him, pointing at him and laughing so loudly the sound was like a tide of laughter washing over him. And he saw Debbie Lambert's face—twisted in the cruelest laughter of all—

Then he found himself sitting on the ground—wood chips spilling from the pockets of his overalls—wood chips covering the school ground like a blizzard. Nothing but wood chips! He looked again at Debbie as she turned with the others and walked in slow motion away from him, all moving, as if underwater, toward the school building, leaving him sitting alone in the pile of wood chips. From some great distance, he heard the steady knell of his father's axe—ringing in the heavy air.

Ben awakened with a start. The dream was strong upon him still—more real than the morning. He still seemed to hear the mocking laughter of his schoolmates—and see the contempt on Debbie's face and, above it all, the sound of the axe echoed. Drawing the quilt his mother had made for him around his shoulders, he enjoyed the last few moments in bed, trying to forget the nightmare.

The raucous cawing of a crow from a tall pine at the edge of the woods pierced the silence of dawn. "There's my alarm clock," Ben said out loud.

"You finish that work yesterday, boy?" His father poked his head inside the door, a scowl on his face, then disappeared.

"And there's the grandfather clock—" Pete whispered from the cot next to him.

Ben chuckled softly to himself. "Yes sir," he called to his father. "I got it all done."

"Well, then, git out here and draw me some water," the growling continued. "This bucket's plumb dry."

"Yes sir," Ben replied, folding his quilt carefully and laying it on the cot. He had picked the pattern out for it when he was a small child, and it was his most prized possession. He remembered pointing to the page in his mother's pattern book. "Grandmother's Flower Garden," she had said. "Why that's a fine choice, Ben!"

She had intended to make one for all the children, but his father's drinking had taken a bad turn shortly after that, and she never could seem to find the money to buy the material. It was one of the major disappointments of her life, as she wanted all her children to have one to remember her by.

Slipping on the khakis his mother had pressed the night before and his school shoes, Ben stepped onto the back porch. His father was leaning on the shelf with both elbows, head drooped between his shoulders. *I hope your head busts open!* Ben thought, grabbing the bucket and heading for the well.

The sun had turned the eastern sky the shade of faded rose petals—dew glistened with a borrowed color in the early light. A breeze, freshening from the west, touched his face like the hand of a young girl. The coolness would last another hour. *This is the best time of day. Don't let him spoil it for you—forget about him and enjoy it.*

After the rest of the family had cleaned up, Ben poured the last of the water from the bucket into the pan and then washed his face, neck, and hands. He smelled the freshly baked biscuits and the bacon frying—heard his mother stirring the pot of grits—the table sounds of his brothers and sister—savoring the moment. As he was combing his hair in front of the mirror that hung on the porch post, the news broadcast came on. The president was speaking.

"This nation will remain a neutral nation. . . . I have seen war and . . . I hate war. . . . I hope the United States will keep out of this war. I believe that is wise."

That's smart, President Roosevelt, Ben thought. *But that crazy German Führer's gonna drag us all into it!*

Then came the distinctive voice of Winston Churchill, the old "English Bulldog." "I cannot forecast to you the action of Russia. It is a riddle wrapped in a mystery inside an enigma."

Ben stayed on the small porch a moment longer, enjoying the freshness of the morning as the commercials flowed from the radio:

Try Heinz Fresh Cucumber Pickles and you too will say, 'What food these morsels be!'

The U.S. Government has helped farmers raise finer tobacco—and the better grades go to LUCKIES!

After Ben heard his father wolf down his food and leave the kitchen, he went in to breakfast.

"Always the last one," his mother admonished gently, spooning steaming grits onto his plate next to the bacon and biscuits. "No eggs today. This'll have to do you."

Ben inhaled deeply. "Why, Mama, who'd want anything better'n this?"

His mother smiled and returned to her dishpan.

Micah and Pete were shoveling their food down while Dinah ate sparingly, sitting primly erect. "You two boys are gonna have bellyaches if you don't slow down," she warned.

Pete looked up from his plate. "Just don't wanna end up a beanpole like you."

Dinah lay her fork on her plate and pressed her napkin to her lips—she was the only one in the family to use one. "Not much chance of that. You already look like Spanky in the *Little Rascals.*"

"And you look like Olive Oyl!" Pete shot back.

Micah never raised his head from his plate.

An announcer was praising the benefits of Ironized Yeast on the radio. "Thousands of girls today feel themselves unwanted—"

"Better listen to this, Sis," Pete said.

"—many lack feminine allurement," the announcer continued. "They are too thin and angular. Their complexions may be blemished, lacking in natural bloom."

Pete looked up from his eating once again. "Shoot! I bleeve the ol' boy knows you, Sis!"

Dinah sniffed and ignored him.

"—blossom forth with new, enticing natural curves, new normal beauty of skin, new pep and ginger that often bring instant popularity!" the voice concluded.

"That's you all right," Pete nodded. "Enticing natural curves—you could sure use some of them!"

"Mama, make Pete hush!" Dinah cried.

Pete grinned his big grin, white teeth flashing. "You better get down to Ollie's Drugstore now. Tell him you got a real emergency. Maybe it ain't too late."

"That's enough, Pete," Jewel said sternly, the clatter and splash of the dishwashing never slowing.

The newscast came back on: "The huge German army—some say as many as fifty-six divisions—continues to overrun Poland. The flat, fertile fields provide ideal conditions for the Germans to field test their new blitzkrieg—lightning war."

Ben was more convinced than ever that Hitler would eventually go to war with the United States.

"Warsaw is completely cut off and appeals daily by radio broadcast for aid from France and Britain."

Micah finally looked up from his plate, rubbing his round belly with both hands. "That sure was good, Mama."

"Well I'm glad you liked it, son," Jewel said, collecting the rest of the dishes from the table.

"Moscow has voided her nonaggression pact with Poland stating that, 'A Polish state no longer exists,' and the Red Army is moving in 'to protect White Russian and Ukrainian minorities in Poland.'"

Ben leaned back in his chair with a thoughtful look. "This country's in trouble and don't even know it."

"I reckon President Roosevelt told you that last time ya'll had a visit, huh?" Pete grinned.

"I been studyin' about this, Pete," Ben shrugged. "This Hitler is as greedy for other countries as some men are for money. They never get enough to make 'em happy."

"Well I'm studyin' about important things like who's gonna win the World Series," Pete replied. "With DiMaggio hittin' like he is, Cincinnati ain't got a chance. He's battin' .381!"

Jewel left her dishes and stepped over to Ben's chair, placing her arm on his shoulder. "You worry too much, Baby. Them countries is on the other side of the ocean. They ain't got nothin' to do with us. Don't fret yourself about it."

As Jewel prepared the children for school—handing out lunches, tucking in shirts, collecting books—a recording of Hitler's emergency morning session of the Reichstag at Berlin's Kroll Opera House came on the radio.

The rhythmic, fanatical chants of "Sieg heil! Sieg heil!" were heard in the background. Hitler screamed his litany of grievances against Poland and her treaty partners and promised there would be a war to the finish. "I have put on my old soldier's coat," he shrieked, "and I will not take it off until we win victory for the Fatherland!"

As the English translation was being read, a thundering chorus of "Sieg heil! Sieg heil!" almost drowned out the speaker.

*　*　*

Two blue jays were having a screeching contest in the crown of an ancient oak while the Logan children walked down the narrow dirt road toward town. As the rising sun struck the highest branches of the tree, the blue-and-white birds were bathed in a green-gold light.

Ahead and to the left, an even narrower dirt road wound out of the woods. Waiting at this modest intersection was Rachel Shaw. She was the same age as Dinah and had a mass of rich brown curls that hung to her shoulders, framing a oval-shaped face that was lightly dusted with freckles. Her nose was straight and slim like Ben's, but her mouth, unlike his, was small. People said it looked like Shirley Temple's.

"Hi, Rachel," Dinah called out. "You ready for that English test?"

"I reckon so," Rachel responded, but her eyes were on Ben. "How can anybody learn that old Charles Dickens though? It's so boring!"

29

"Ben helped me this week," Dinah said proudly. "He's a real expert on Dickens."

"Is that so?" Rachel asked, her eyes still on him.

Ben noticed that her lavender and green dress was too small for her—faded and slightly frayed from two years of the wash tub and clothes line. Preachers didn't make much money, especially Pentecostal preachers like her daddy, Brother Samuel Shaw.

How can I tell her I love Dickens because he wrote so much of poor people who were, in a lot of ways, like my own family? I also love stories about King Arthur because they're so different from my own life—full of mystical, heroic characters like Merlin and Lancelot! What do I care what a skinny fourteen-year-old girl thinks anyway? They're all just silly kids!

Reading was a coveted and valuable part of Ben's life, taking him to other worlds by the only road he could travel. "Just something to pass the time," he replied. "Dinah talks too much."

"I think you're smarter than you want people to know, Ben Logan," Rachel said, her hazel eyes finding his.

Pete laughed out loud. "I believe this girl's gone cow-eyed over you, big brother."

Ben flashed his gray eyes at Pete who, knowing what that look meant, dropped the subject and walked on ahead with Micah.

In a few minutes they reached the first houses on the outskirts of town—modest frame structures painted white, with front porches and a few trees. Many had vegetable gardens in back and some had enough in cultivation to be called small farms. Usually an old car sat in the yard. Dogs came out from under them to wag their tails in greeting or bark warnings that their yards were forbidden territory.

As the youngsters entered the town proper, the dwellings became more substantial. The streets were lined with stately shade trees—live oak, maple, and elm—and the yards were spacious and well landscaped with azalea, gardenia, crepe myrtle, and flowers of all kinds. White picket fences, as well as a few built of stone and wrought iron were commonplace, and the houses were large— some with two and even three stories—and had wide porches, second-story verandas, and lattice work. Late model cars gleamed in driveways and under carports.

"Boy! Look at that!" Micah said, pointing to a shiny blue car in a driveway behind an iron piked fence. "They must have just bought it yesterday!"

"That's a La Salle," Pete said offhandedly. "That's what I'm gonna buy when I start my own business."

"Your own business!" Dinah exclaimed. "You can't spell *cat*—and you're gonna run a business? Better put more time on your lessons or you'll be lucky to have a bicycle!"

"Oh yeah!" Pete countered. "You just wait and see! Books ain't everthing."

Dinah ignored him and turned to Rachel. "Did you see the new movie at the Rialto. It's called *Love Finds Andy Hardy*, and it's the most precious thing! Anyways, that's what Rae Spain told me. She saw it last Saturday with her mama."

Rachel started to answer, but Dinah, carried away by the story, continued breathlessly.

"Well, it seems that Andy has a date with his girlfriend, Polly, who has to break the date and go out of town. Andy's friend Beezy goes on vacation and asks him to 'date up' his girl, Cynthia, so she won't run around on him. Then Andy falls for Cynthia and forgets Polly. In the meantime Andy dates Betsy, who is a neighbor's visiting granddaughter. Cynthia likes to smooch so much Andy is afraid it'll harm his health, but Betsy is falling for Andy and . . ."

"Slow down," Rachel interrupted. "How in the world do you remember all that?"

"If it's about smoochin'," Pete said, "she'll remember it."

Dinah gave him a dirty look and returned to her story. "Now where was I? Oh, yes. Betsy gets Andy to take her to the dance and she sings so well—Betsy's played by Judy Garland you know—that she and Andy lead the grand march. It finally ends when Betsy goes home and Polly and Andy get back together."

"That sounds like a nice story," Rachel said. "But Daddy won't let me go to the movies."

"Why not?" Dinah was chagrined. "There's nothing wrong with Mickey Rooney. He's like a member of the family—not like that Clark Gable at all."

"What do you mean?" Rachel asked.

"You mean you haven't heard about what he said in *Gone with the Wind?*"

Rachel shook her head.

Dinah's face glowed with anticipation. "Well, it probably won't come to a hick town like Liberty for a couple of years, but Eddy Lambert and Taylor Spain went to Atlanta where it's playing, and you'll never believe what they said about it."

"I guess you're right," Rachel said, watching Ben walking along in front of her.

Dinah stopped, took Rachel by the arm and looked furtively toward her three brothers. Placing her mouth an inch from Rachel's ear, she whispered for a few seconds.

Rachel gasped. "I don't believe it! Dinah, you shouldn't be repeating such things!"

"Well, it's the truth," Dinah said haughtily, hugging her books and tilting her chin upward. "After all, Rachel, this is 1939. We're not in the Dark Ages."

* * *

Ben moved through the morning as if in a misty dream. He was bone tired from the last two days' work with his father. His mind had apparently gone on strike, refusing to accept any new information. The clamor and confusion in the halls—shouting, laughter, and banging of lockers—merged somehow into the classroom, where it seemed that his teachers were speaking some ancient language that became extinct with the dinosaurs.

He stared above the blackboard at the portraits of Washington and Lincoln flanking both sides of the schoolhouse clock—at the somber expressions—at the eyes that saw something others could not. *They sure don't look very happy. Guess they had their troubles back then just like we do now.*

Math was especially difficult, where, even on a good day, Ben thought Miss Simpson might as well be teaching from a soundproof booth for all the good it did him. If things weren't complicated enough, Debbie Lambert sat right in front of him, her soft blonde hair flowing and bouncing with every move she made. It mesmerized him, which was the state he was in when he heard the sound of Miss Simpson's voice—like fingernails on a blackboard—like a cat with a stepped-on tail.

". . . and if you are paying attention, Ben Logan, then I apologize," she said, looking around with a smug smile, her tall angular form dominating the room.

"Sorry," Ben mumbled, knowing he was in for it now, but not especially concerned. His weariness had done that much for him.

"No apology for you I'm afraid, Mr. Logan."

Miss Simpson allowed the class to laugh a few seconds—then cut them off with a wave of her bony hand, which was sprinkled liberally with liver spots.

Debbie turned her head quickly to see Ben's reaction, and he felt his face go hot.

"Would you take your homework paper and put problem number eleven on the blackboard, please?" Miss Simpson said, her long curved nose tilting at a forty-five-degree angle.

That ol' biddy knows very well I haven't been here for two days. Ben looked at her—then down at his desk. "I—ah. I'm afraid I wasn't able to do it, Miss Simpson."

"Out galavanting around somewhere I would imagine," she declared, as if he had been on a two-day drunk instead of swinging an axe or manhandling one end of a crosscut saw.

Ben said nothing.

"Well, young man," Miss Simpson said evenly, returning to her desk—high-topped shoes thudding on the polished floor, giving voice to an anger that was concealed by the tone of her words. "There are consequences for slovenly behavior!"

Ben smiled inwardly as she made a production of opening her brown, hard-backed grade book. *She thinks she's Moses coming down Sinai with the stone tablets!*

"We'll just have to put a little zero by your name here in *the book*," Miss Simpson said, pen in hand. Then she stood, holding the book face outward in both hands for all the class to see the power at her command.

Ol' bat needs to be in an insane asylum instead of a classroom! Ben began to drift inside himself. He smelled the chalk dust, the wax on the pine floor, and the not unpleasant mixture of perfume and Vitalis hair tonic. The morning breeze was stirring the first fallen leaves of autumn outside the window with a dry sibilant sound. Debbie's hair moved slowly before him, waving and shimmering like a straw-colored cloud. He saw himself touching it—running his fingers through it—felt it caressing his face all through a soft, starry summer night.

* * *

· "What're we havin' today, Taylor?" Keith Demerie asked, standing in line under the covered walkway that led from the school building to the cafeteria. Conversation hummed around him, but his rich bass voice rose above it. His father, Senator Tyson Demerie, had helped him train it for public speaking, hoping that this robust, big-framed son would follow in his footsteps.

Taylor Spain looked through the wire-mesh reinforced glass of the door to the blackboard that hung on the wall inside the small entrance way to the cafeteria. "Meatloaf, mashed potatoes, and spinach," he answered back over his shoulder.

"Oh, Lord! Why didn't I go home for lunch?" Keith replied, rolling his blue eyes upward. His movements were theatrical and almost feminine, in spite of his six-foot stature and jutting chin. He wore a gray linen sport jacket and navy tie. "Got to play the part," his father had often told him.

Debbie Lambert and Peggy Jackson, who were standing near Keith, giggled and reprimanded him.

"Oh, Keith," Debbie said, slapping him lightly on the shoulder, "you'd complain if we had pheasant under glass!"

"That's right," Peggy enjoined, "You can't be too particular. You didn't get to weigh two hundred pounds by skipping meals."

Keith brushed his thick blond hair back from his face, his wrist a tad too loose. "I can see I'm in the company of common folks."

Ben listened to this conversation as he walked with Jack Clampett, the night marshal's son, along the outside of the main cafeteria line. Inside, they stood with a few other children—dressed in khakis, overalls, and hand-me-down dresses—at the small counter near the end of the serving line to buy their half-pint bottles of milk for a penny. Mrs. Waters, the plump gray-haired lady who served the milk, always had a big smile for them and made Ben feel better.

"Wouldn't mind having some of that meatloaf," Jack said, as they sat at a table near the back entrance. He was as spare and sallow as his father and, like Ben, was dressed in khakis. The pleated gabardines and tailored sport shirts of the "Haves" were just another line on the wish list for the "Have Nots."

Ben opened his brown lunch bag, taking his wax-paper-wrapped sandwich and leftover biscuit out and placing them on the table. "Mama's is a lot better," he said, remembering that she hadn't fixed meatloaf in months.

"You got baloney and mustard again?" Jack asked, eating his two homemade cookies first.

"I like it." As Ben ate he looked across the cafeteria at Debbie, Keith, and the others who were ignoring their heaping plates of food in favor of animated conversation. It was not far from his table, but they might as well have been on the moon for all the chance he had of joining them. *I believe it's closer to Atlanta than over there where they are!* he thought bitterly.

After carefully folding the brown bag and wax paper, Ben put them in his back pocket and left with Jack. As they walked across the school ground, Jack saw another friend of his and, with a quick good-bye, went running off.

Ben moved casually toward the group he had been watching in the cafeteria. Debbie and Peggy were sitting on a stone bench under a spreading live oak with Keith, Taylor, and Doak Myles, whose father was Dr. Amos Myles, sitting on the grass near them.

"Hello, Ben," Doak smiled. "Come on and join us." He was slim and dark like Ben, fashionably dressed in a white shirt and blue-and-gray school sweater, although he was rushing the season. Ben liked him. Doak was the only one of the "Haves" he felt truly comfortable with.

"Thanks." Ben sat on the grass between Doak and Taylor Spain, whose wavy brown hair framed his classic good looks—classic except for a terrible case of acne. His father, Morton Spain, who practiced law, could afford the best doctors, but even they had been unable to cure it. Ben was careful not to stare at him, knowing how sensitive he was.

"I think *Our Town* is the perfect choice for our fall play this year," Debbie said, crossing her legs and pointing her saddle oxford at Keith. "It's never been done, it's romantic, and there's almost no scenery to worry about."

"Think you can find time from those critical cheerleading duties of yours to play the lead?" Keith responded, grinning slyly at Taylor, who lowered his head, chuckling softly.

"Cheerleading *is* important!" Debbie said heatedly, her blonde hair swirling as she tossed her head.

"Calm down," Taylor intoned. "We're all for school spirit— rah-rah—hail-hail Liberty High. What we've got to do now is find someone for that last part."

"He's right," Doak said. "The Stage Manager is a critical role. And he's got to have a good memory with all those long pieces and no one to take a cue from."

"How about Ben?" Debbie chirped, uncrossing her legs and placing her feet primly together. "He's smart."

Ben was staring at Debbie's slim calves flowing upward from the white bobbysox. "I—I don't know if I can or not," he stammered. "I've never done much acting."

"Sure you can do it, Ben," Peggy chimed in, her freckled face pale beneath her curly red hair. "I remember when you memorized the "Rime of the Ancient Mariner"—the whole poem! This should be easy if you can learn that dreadful ol' thing!"

"Ben, you've just *got* to try out," Debbie cooed, leaning over and taking his hand in both of hers.

Ben felt his heart doing backsprings. He lost himself in those cool blue eyes. "Well—if you think so. I guess I can at least try out for it."

Debbie quickly released Ben's hand, her point won. "Well, that's settled. What time are you coming by Friday night, Keith?" She rubbed the top of his shiny penny loafer slowly with the sole of her shoe. "I can't *wait* to go for a ride in your daddy's new convertible!"

3

A MOON PIE AND
AN R.C. COLA

*T*he harsh clanging of the bell ended a hundred conversations at once, drawing the scattered children of Liberty from all parts of the school ground as surely as salmon are drawn to the pools and backwaters of their birth. They trusted the people who rang the bells and made the speeches and wore the uniforms. It was a rare person who didn't feel that sudden racing of the blood when the bells of America called.

Mrs. Ora Peabody could have passed for Santa Claus's wife if she had worn red velvet dresses trimmed with fur and lived at the North Pole—which is where Ben wished that she lived instead of Liberty, Georgia! But she had never been north of Asheville, and her plump and benign appearance dissembled a sometimes caustic nature.

Euliss, her husband of thirty-seven years, was crippled in a logging accident shortly after their marriage, and it fell to her lot to teach American history to the children of Liberty, a boring, thankless job—to her way of thinking—that, on occasion, brought to the surface her fractious ways.

"Well, class," Mrs. Peabody began, folding her plump white hands together on her desk blotter, "today Current Events is scheduled, and I'm sure we'll have some very interesting reports."

There was a low murmuring and a few stifled snickers around the classroom.

"Who'll be first?"

A shuffling of papers—coughing and clearing of throats—scraping of desks on the wooden floor.

"Come, come, students," Mrs. Peabody snapped impatiently, rising from her desk to stand before them.

Eyes turned downward or looked toward the bank of windows that ran the length of the outer wall.

"I'll do it!" a perky voice cried.

"Fine, Debbie," Mrs. Peabody nodded, returning to her desk. "At least there's *one* prepared in the class." *Nit wit, that is! If your father didn't own half the town, I'd tell you, too!*

Holding her neatly typed notes, Debbie Lambert stood next to the desk, licked her full red lips and began. "Classmates," Debbie lilted, "my Current Events report on Brenda Frazier was such a big hit last year—well, I just decided to do it again this year."

Muted groans and eye rolling broke out in the room.

Debbie turned toward her teacher. "After all, she still makes the newspapers, Mrs. Peabody," she pouted. "That makes it a current event, doesn't it?"

Mrs. Peabody beamed up at the wholesome face. "Please continue, Debbie." *Hartley Lambert must have packed your head with sawdust from his lumber mill! I know it was empty when you were born!*

"Well, Brenda Frazier is just the most beautiful creature in this country, that's all," Debbie trilled, "and if any of you've seen her Woodbury Soap ads you know that's the gospel! She practically rules 'Cafe Society!' They say places like the Stork Club and El Morocco actually pay her just to be *seen* at their best tables. She was the Glamour Girl of 1938, and as far as I'm concerned the one for this year, Cobina Wright Jr., is just a Plain Jane next to Brenda . . ."

Ten minutes later no one was bothering to stifle their yawns and some had lain their heads on their desks. Mrs. Peabody appeared to be in a mild coma.

Debbie didn't seem to notice as she bore down for the big finish. "And if all *this* wasn't enough, she's a simply marvelous poet! Just listen to her "Glamour Girl Serenade."

> I'm established now for '38
> With the title of glamour and reprobate.
> I've won a position in *Vogue* and *Harper's;*
> For a hundred bucks I'll advertise garters.
> I grit my teeth and smile at my enemies;
> I sit at the Stork Club and talk to nonentities.

Debbie returned to her seat amid the applause and whistles of her classmates.

"Perhaps we should speed things up a bit," Mrs. Peabody said, penciling Debbie's grade into her book. "Keith Demerie, would you like to share your report with the class?"

"Yes ma'am, I'd be happy to," he smiled, always the politician.

"No longer than five minutes—*please!*"

"Yes ma'am," Keith answered, striding heavily to the front, a three-by-five card clutched in his thick right hand. "My Current Event report is on sports. You might call it a sort of sport report."

Giggles and guffaws broke out in the room.

"That's enough, class," Mrs. Peabody said, holding one hand toward them like the pope in St. Peter's Square. "Keith, if you don't mind, leave the comedy to Fred Allen."

"Yes ma'am," Keith responded contritely. "The Yankees and the Reds are gonna play in the Series. It's DiMaggio, the leading hitter going against Paul Derringer, the leading pitcher. I predict Dimaggio'll be too tough for him. Bobby Riggs, the Wimbledon champion, leads the U.S. Davis Cup squad against John Bromwich and the Aussies."

"Keith," Mrs. Peabody interrupted, "is there no exposition to your report?"

"I'm afraid I've been kind of short on time—getting ready for the big game with Pine Mountain, you know."

"Well, there's something to be said for brevity, I suppose," Mrs. Peabody said, glancing at Debbie Lambert's glowing face on the front row. "Please continue."

"I predict that Tom Harmon of Michigan will win the Heisman Trophy this year," Keith said, slipping his three-by-five card into the pocket of his jacket.

"That's it?" Mrs. Peabody asked.

"Yes ma'am."

"Well, you may be seated," she continued, "and thank you for the sports roundup, Keith." *You big clumsy sycophant—if the senator didn't get so much state money for the school, the coach wouldn't let you carry the water bucket!*

Keith walked to his desk among shouts of "Just brilliant" and "Splendid performance."

"Ben Logan, you're next."

Ben, looking at his notes, bumped into a desk on the way to the front of the room. The giggling subsided as he took his place.

"President Franklin D. Roosevelt says he believes he can keep us out of the war in Europe. I don't!" he began, looking around just above the heads of his audience.

Mrs. Peabody turned her head slowly, glaring at Ben. Some of his classmates were open-mouthed.

"When Hitler said, 'I have put on my old soldier's coat and won't take it off until we have won victory for the Fatherland,' I believe he meant more than just victory over Poland—I believe he meant the whole world."

Mrs. Peabody's face was clouding over.

"Hitler's nonaggression pact with Russia is just a ploy. It's so he won't have the Eastern Front to worry about now. After he's got Poland, he'll go for the Low Countries—then France, Britain—who knows? He'll attack Russia when the time is right and . . ."

"That's enough, young man!" Mrs. Peabody blurted out. "Are you aware that the American people are sending thousands of letters to the president asking him to keep us out of war?"

"Yes ma'am," Ben replied sheepishly. "He got a half-million in a single day."

"And he said this nation will remain a neutral nation? Isn't that correct?"

"Yes ma'am."

"Well perhaps you're privy to information that the rest of us don't have—or maybe you have visions!"

Muffled laughter.

"No ma'am. Just the newspapers and magazines and what I hear on the radio," he mumbled, looking at the class—then at the floor. "But Hitler seems to think he's some kind of god with this 'Master Race' and all that. It just looks—"

"Next thing, you'll be telling us those Japanese that are causing so much trouble on the other side of the world are going to attack us, too!" Mrs. Peabody interjected.

Ben continued to look at the floor.

"You may as well finish," Mrs. Peabody sighed, shaking her head slowly. "But in future reports, you would be well advised to stick to the facts and leave conjecture to the politicians. They get paid to make fools of themselves."

Ben stumbled and stammered his way through the rest of his report, knowing that all the information he had so painstakingly put together meant absolutely nothing now. As he made his way back to his desk, there was an oppressive silence in the room.

When the bell rang, the students filed by Mrs. Peabody's desk, picked up the folded slips of paper with their grades on them—then moved into the bedlam of the hallway.

"Hey—I got a C+!" he heard Keith Demerie shout. "Not bad for five minutes work!"

"Well I made a B," Debbie Lambert said haughtily. "Shows what you can do when you put some study time in, Keith."

Ben jammed his slip into his back pocket without looking at it, walking away from the others without a word.

* * *

Three Corners Grocery stood on a wooded interstice where the road to the Logan home joined the highway. Constructed of rough-cut one-by-twelve planks, it boasted of a gravity-fed Texaco pump—a Grove's Chill Tonic sign, vowing to combat malaria, colds, chills, and fever—a red-and-white proclamation that Coca-Cola was "Delicious and Refreshing"—and nonstop gossip.

The ubiquitous wooden benches rested on hard-packed gravel against the front wall, between the two doors. One of the doors was screened, leading into the store proper. The other opened into a lean-to, built onto the side of the store, where the feed was stored. Smaller signs—Nehi, R.C. Cola, Prince Albert, and others—were tacked at random in the spaces between and flanking the doors.

As he crossed the two-lane blacktop, Ben caught sight of the ancient twin pines that rose straight and true on either side of the store, their tops swaying slowly. He smelled the scent of distant rain, listened to the high, strange music of the trees—like some arboreal string section riding the wind. And he remembered something that had happened a long time ago:

The smell of rain was heavy in the air that day as Earl Logan lifted his son down from the cab of the mud-spattered pulpwood truck, placing him on his shoulders, rough hands gripping the slim brown legs. "Don't let the ol' hoss buck you off, boy," he yelled, jumping and whirling toward the store.

Ben laughed and giggled, gasping each time his father made a sharp turn. "More! I wanna ride more!" Ben wailed, when his father swooped him off his shoulders and onto the gravel outside Three Corners.

"Ol' hoss is tired, boy," Earl smiled. "Let's git us a cold drink. You want a NuGrape?"

"Yes sir!" Ben yelped, running for the door just as the first drops hit the dusty ground. "I can beat you, Daddy!"

"You better run fast, young 'un! Here I come!"

Inside the dimly lit store, Ben leaned over into the drink box, lifting a NuGrape from the ice cold water. "I can open it myself, Daddy! Watch!" After several tries, the top popped off the bottle and clicked into the holder on the side of the box.

"I like them R.C.'s myself," Earl said, pulling a dripping bottle from the box and drying it on his shirttail.

Ben took a big swallow of his drink, thinking that nothing in the world could ever taste better.

"You wanna do mine for me?" Earl said, handing his bottle to Ben. "Don't know if I'm strong enough."

Ben set his bottle on the floor and opened his father's drink on the first try. Beaming, he handed it back to him.

"You a strong 'un, boy!" Earl said, feeling his son's bicep.

Ben stood at the counter while Morgan Clark, the owner, rang up the ten cents on his cash register. Ben thought that fifty-nine-year-old Morgan Clark—with his light gray eyes, white hair parted in the middle and combed back, bushy white eyebrows and white handlebar mustache—must look the way God would if he shaved his beard off.

The bell chinged as Ben watched the black numbers on their white cards spring up in the little window of the bulky register. He heard the two nickels clink into the drawer as it quickly slammed shut.

Packs of Camels and Lucky Strikes were neatly stacked on the shelf behind Mr. Clark along with Baby Ruths, Hersheys, other candy bars, and packs of gum. High on the top shelf, Ben saw a rubber ball. In his eyes, it was beautiful—a thing of wonder—shiny and blue and perfectly smooth. It was something out of a dream that you could only long for, disappearing each time you reached out to touch it. He stood there enraptured, gazing upward toward the blue ball.

Ben heard the sound of the cash register—saw twenty-five cents appear in the window. Mr. Clark climbed three rungs of a step ladder, reaching, it seemed, up to heaven (where Jesus lives, Ben thought) and brought *the ball down. Ben saw the ball extended toward him in Mr. Clark's hands, like an offering—unbearably bright and shining. (A gift from Jesus, he thought.) He stood there, unable to move.*

"You want that or not, boy?" Earl snorted. "I reckon Mr. Clark'd put it back fer us."

Ben set his NuGrape carefully on the counter. Reaching out with both hands, he accepted the wondrous gift. As his hands touched its cool, smooth surface, the storm hit—with a howling wind and the thunderous roar of heavy rain on the tin roof.

Under the shed that ran the front length of Three Corners, Ben and his father waited out the storm. Ben played with his ball while his father sat on a bench talking to a skinny little man with a sharp face. He saw the man pour a clear liquid from a mason jar into his father's empty R.C. bottle, wondering what it was. And he wondered why the man didn't comb the back of his hair.

The memory broke away from him as Micah sighed, "I shore am thirsty!" He was tagging along behind the other children as they ambled along in front of Three Corners. "I'd give a purty for a big R.C.!"

Pete walked next to Dinah and Rachel, waiting for an opportunity to fling his darts into any opening in their conversation. "Ask yore big brother," he called over his shoulder. "He's the only one of this bunch who ever has any money."

Micah ran past the three of them, catching up with Ben, who had wandered ahead of the others, lost in thought. "Ben! Ben!" he pleaded. "Can we get a R.C.? Please, can we?"

Ben thought of the two quarters in his pocket that he had earned working with his father this week. *I guess I can get that book another time—if he pays me.* "I don't see why not," he said. "If a rich man like me can't spend money on his own brother, ain't much to him is it? How 'bout a Moon Pie to go with it?"

"Oh boy!" Micah shouted back at the others. "Ben's buyin'!" And he sprinted toward the store.

The three boys were sitting on a bench in front of Three Corners, drinking R.C.'s and eating moon pies. Dinah and Rachel were browsing around inside.

"Ben, you reckon we could go see that new cartoon show that's coming next month?" Micah mumbled, his mouth full of the gooey marshmallow Moon Pie. "I think the name of it is *Snow White and the Seven Warts.*"

"That's *dwarfs*—not *warts*, Micah," Ben laughed. "Dwarfs are very small people."

"Oh!" Micah said, taking a big swallow from his R.C. "Well, anyway, I think it's a real good show. Everbody says it is."

"If we can scrape together enough money—maybe so," Ben smiled. "Have to wait and see."

Micah seemed content with the answer and took another big bite of his Moon Pie.

Ben took a swallow from his moisture-beaded bottle, set it on the bench, and took the folded slip of paper from his back pocket.

"I can't wait to listen to 'The Lone Ranger,'" Pete said, chewing slowly. He swallowed and held his bottle like a microphone. "A fiery horse with the speed of light, a cloud of dust, and a hearty—" Pete held the bottle in front of Micah's face.

"Hi-yo Silver!" Micah yelled.

"From out of the past comes the thundering hoofbeats of the great horse Silver. The Lone Ranger rides again!" Pete shouted into the bottle, as he stood to his feet.

Micah jumped up, spilling R.C. on his shirt.

"Come on, Silver!" Pete mimicked the voice on the radio. "Let's go, big fellow!"

"Hi-yo, Silver! Awaaaay!" Micah screamed into the bottle, jumping up and down.

"You boys want to quieten down a little out here?" Rachel admonished as she emerged from the store. "You sound like a bunch of wild Indians!"

"No! Cowboys!" Micah said, holding his bottle like a saddle horn. "I'm the Masked Rider of the Plains!"

"Settle down, partner," Ben called from the other end of the bench, holding his thumb and forefinger together and turning the knob on an imaginary radio. "Click. Show's over."

Micah returned to the bench and his forgotten Moon Pie.

Rachel saw Ben staring at a slip of paper he held in both hands and sat next to him on the far end of the bench. "What's that, Ben?" she asked, trying to sound casual.

"Nothin'," he grunted, crumpling the paper and thrusting it into his back pocket.

Rachel was silent.

Ben noticed the hurt look on her face. "Sorry," he said. "It was my history grade. D-."

"Oh, I'm so sorry, Ben! I know you worked real hard on it too. Dinah told me."

"What's the difference?" Ben asked bitterly, looking at the thunderhead rolling in from the northwest.

"Ben," Dinah said, moving her hand toward his shoulder, then returning it to her lap, "sometimes teachers make mistakes. They're not always right."

Ben looked into Rachel's clear hazel eyes. "Maybe so. But they always have the last say-so on the grades. Right or wrong don't change that a bit."

"You gonna try out for the play?" Rachel asked, hoping for a more pleasant topic.

"I might," Ben replied, standing and putting his hands in his pockets. "Maybe for the Stage Manager."

"Oh, you'd be perfect for that!" Rachel exclaimed. "You've got a wonderful voice, and you could memorize the lines easy as anything. I hope you get it."

"Way my luck's runnin', don't count on it."

"I'll ask God to let you have it, Ben," Rachel said evenly, standing beside him.

"I reckon God helps those that help themselves," Ben laughed. "That's what the Bible says, ain't it?"

"No, that's in Aesop's fables," Rachel corrected. "The Bible teaches that God helps those who *can't* help themselves! Jesus said that *His* strength is made perfect in weakness."

Ben touched Rachel's soft hair—then ruffled it gently. "You're a funny one, Rachel," he laughed.

Suddenly the wind hit and the rain came rattling across the tin roof like a shower of stones. A cold spray blew under the shed, sending Rachel scurrying for the front door of the store. "C'mon Ben," she called. "You'll get soaked out here."

Ben glanced at her, then stepped through the doorway of the dark storage shed to his immediate left. He breathed deeply the rich, earthy smell of the feed, sitting on one of the sacks and leaning back on a stack behind him. Remnants of old spider webs hung limply in the corners near the ceiling.

Through the door Ben could see the gray sheets of rain as they came sweeping across the fields and roads, shimmering in the pale light—the trees swaying and bending in the wind—limbs breaking loose and sailing like leafy kites with their strings cut.

Breathing again the smell of feed, damp earth, and old timbers, Ben felt strangely calmed by the power and rage of the storm. The wind moaned in the eaves like some restless spirit seeking refuge in the old building. He sensed somehow that another storm was coming—one so extravagantly more terrible than this one.

Ben lay his head back on the rough surface of the feed sack, listening to the storm gradually exhaust its fury. A metronomic drumming on the roof above him became all that he could hear. He drifted in a half-dream—listening to the soothing sound of the rain, seeing again the wondrous, gleaming blue ball.

4

DEBBIE

A soft slapping sound from the hallway caught the attention of the two men and the two women having their morning coffee. Their conversation lulled as they waited for the man who made the sound. Although he looked nothing like a raven, this was his nickname—the tap, tap, tapping from Edgar Allan Poe's poem of the same name, somehow became associated with the *slap, slap, slapping* sound his right foot made when it hit the wooden floors of the school building.

Wearing a brown tweed jacket, the man who entered the teacher's lounge was stiletto-slim. Of medium height, he had soft, light-brown hair that was unfashionably long, touching his ears and the collar of his shirt. His large eyes—the color of old pecan shells—dominated his face with its small nose and full lips above a softly rounded chin.

"Morning, Leslie," Miss Madge Simpson—who actually *did* resemble a raven—said.

"Morning, Miss Simpson," Leslie Gifford replied, continuing toward the coffee pot that sat on a scarred table in the far corner of the room—his left arm swaying loosely—damaged by the polio that had ravaged the muscles of his right leg.

Alvin Ditweiler folded the *Liberty Herald* carefully, laid it on the table in front of him, then sipped his coffee noisily from a heavy white mug that bore his initials. A miniature version of Babe Ruth, with his barrel chest and spindly legs, Ditweiler had the same open, honest face of the baseball player. "Morning, Leslie," he grunted, as did Ora Peabody and Bonner Ridgeway, the football coach.

47

Leslie returned their greetings, pulling out a chair and seating himself at the table. "What's the news?" he asked, as he sipped his coffee and glanced at Ditweiler.

"Well, they let Al Capone out of prison," Ditweiler rumbled, tapping on the newspaper with a stubby forefinger, "but it says here the ol' boy's got third-stage syphilis—so I reckon it won't make much difference one way or the other."

"Please, Mr. Ditweiler—" Ora Peabody scolded, "can't we discuss something a little more pleasant?"

"Sorry, Ora," Ditweiler mumbled, burying his nose in his coffee mug. *Always got to stick my big foot in my mouth!* he thought sourly.

Ditweiler felt inferior to most of his teachers as he only graduated from junior college, securing the principal's job twenty-five years ago through connections on the school board. Feeding his cows and chickens—following his mule behind a plow with the rich smell of freshly turned soil strong around him—hoeing his purple-hull peas and tomatoes—these were the things he took joy in, but the principal's job gave him the status that his wife, Doreen, felt was so necessary for her happiness.

"How about the war, Ora?" Ridgeway interjected, his voice gravelly from years of shouting on the sidelines of high school football stadiums. "Hitler instead of Capone."

"Well, at least there's an ocean between us," she agreed. "I feel contaminated just being in the same country with that awful Sicilian monster!"

Ridgeway leaned back in his chair, light glinting from his slate-gray eyes and off his forehead, where the close-cropped blond hair was thinning. "We might as well talk about Hitler while he's still around. After this business with Poland is over, he'll just fade away. A flash in the pan—that's all he is."

"I don't think so." Leslie Gifford sipped his coffee, his serene face turned toward the burly, tanned coach. "The man's a megalomaniac. He'll never be satisfied."

Ridgeway turned his steely gaze on Leslie Gifford. *What could any woman see in him? The face of an angel. Ha! Just a big sissy!* "You got any facts or just an opinion?"

"History for one thing. Hitler fits the mold," Leslie replied calmly. "Then there's the Siegfried Line."

"What about it?"

"It's designed for offense—not defense, like the Maginot Line of the French."

Ridgeway's face reddened slightly. *You think you're so smart!* "Well I think he's just a banty rooster struttin' around in his own little barnyard! See what happens if he tries something with France! They've got something more than horses and lances to go against his tanks with! Them poor Poles are still fightin' in the eighteenth century!"

"The world hasn't seen anything like the blitzkrieg before," Leslie said as if to himself, looking beyond Ridgeway to a slender poplar swaying in the morning breeze. It always looked so out of place to him among the moss-bearded oaks, standing like stoic old men about the school ground. "And very few men are as ruthless and full of hate as Adolf Hitler."

"Oh yeah! Well this country—"

"Please, gentlemen!" Ora Peabody interrupted. "Enough of violence! We have more important matters to discuss! Now who shall we consider for the part of the Stage Manager? Leslie, you always seem to take the lead with the school plays."

Leslie turned his eyes from the view outside the window, from an uncertain future to an all too certain present—toward Ora Peabody. "Of the ones who've tried out so far, I think Ben Logan would probably be the best choice."

"You must be kiddin'!" Ridgeway growled. "Keith Demerie is *perfect* for the part! He's got a voice you could hear plumb to the other end of the county!"

Ora Peabody turned her benign expression on the coach. "I'm afraid volume is not the only requirement for the part, Mr. Ridgeway. Keith does have an excellent speaking voice, but his memory may be—shall we say, somewhat limited? Any suggestions other than Ben Logan? What do you think, Mr. Ditweiler?"

Alvin Ditweiler went to the school plays as part of his job obligations, dozing through them most of the time. He proceeded cautiously. "Well, I have confidence in Leslie's opinion—not that I don't in yours, Coach—but this isn't the gridiron and you never help with the plays anyway. Besides it wouldn't look good if we gave all the best parts only to the children of families with money."

"That's good thinking, Alvin," Madge Simpson agreed, with a toothy grin. "We wouldn't want anyone to think money has any influence over what happens in *this* school system."

Ditweiler cleared his throat, squirming slightly in his chair. "Yes, well, there are children out there we've got to educate now," he proclaimed. "We've got until Friday to decide on who plays what part." Taking a final swallow of coffee, he rose and plodded heavily out of the room.

"Well, reckon I'll get on down to the gym," Ridgeway grunted, pushing his bulk out of the chair. He looked directly down at Leslie Gifford. "Time to make men out of some boys that don't quite know if they're ready for it yet."

After he had left, Ora Peabody took out her gold-flaked compact, applying a touch of rouge to her already pink cheeks. "Don't let him bother you, Leslie. Bonner thinks if a man doesn't growl and beat his chest like a bull ape several times a day, there's something wrong with him. Been like that since he was a boy."

"Many things bother me, Mrs. Peabody," Leslie said, the scent of her compact reminding him of his mother. He rose awkwardly from his chair, shifting his weight to his good left leg. "Bonner Ridgeway doesn't even make the list."

The two women were quiet as Leslie Gifford left the room, not knowing how to respond.

"Well—he certainly has a knack for ending conversations," Madge Simpson offered.

"Yes—he does," Ora Peabody agreed as the soft slapping sound faded away down the early, empty hallway.

* * *

Silent as the last star of morning, the great barred owl lifted to its daytime home in the top branches of a hickory tree, rising from the forest floor. Soon he was as lost in the dreams or dreamless sleep of animals, as the star had been in the first blaze of sunlight. Below, in the clearing, the coal oil lamps were still shining through the windows of the tar paper shack.

"Good groceries, Esther!" Samuel Shaw said to his short dark-eyed wife as he spooned oatmeal into his mouth. His tall lanky frame spoke of a lifetime of too much work and too little rest, but his face still had a youthful glow about it—light blue eyes bright beneath his corn-silk yellow hair.

"You'd say that if I filled your bowl with corn shucks, Samuel," Esther sniffed, brushing her dark hair back from her round face. "Wish we had some meat to go with it. Maybe after Sunday meetin' somebody'll have a piece for us. Lord knows it's been awhile since we got a pounding from the congregation."

"They do what they can, Esther," Samuel assured her. "And what they can't provide—the good Lord will. Besides, I'm hauling with Earl Logan today. Might make as much as four dollars."

Esther continued around the table filling the bowls of her children. Tom, at sixteen, tall like his father with the same hair and eyes, a quiet boy, began eating without a word.

"Thanks, Mama," twelve-year-old Toby said, his blue eyes turned upward toward his mother. "I could eat the whole pot this mornin'!"

"I reckon you could, son," Esther agreed, running her fingers through his bright red hair. "Don't know where it goes, though. You're skinny as an ol' stray cat!"

Esther filled Rachel's bowl, watching her soft brown curls catch the light from the coal oil lamp. *She gets prettier every day.* "Eat up, child. You'll be late for school."

"Yes, Mama," Rachel replied. "Mama, you know what I prayed for while Daddy was saying the blessing?"

"I can't imagine," Esther smiled. "But whatever it was, you had plenty of time to talk to the Lord about it with one of your daddy's blessings."

"Well, I've got a lot to be thankful for," her husband laughed, looking up from his bowl and waving his hand about the table. "Just look at my beautiful, healthy family."

"Now, Rachel, what favor did you ask of the good Lord?" Esther inquired, placing the pot back on the stove. "Tom, I need some stove wood chopped when you get in today."

"Yes ma'am."

"Toby, you stack it for him."

"Aw, Mama!"

"Sorry, Rachel. What were you telling me now?"

"Well, Mama, there's a school play comin' up," Rachel said eagerly, "and I prayed that Ben would get this important part that he wants. He'd be so good in it."

51

She loves that boy—or thinks she does. Wish he'd come to church a little more. "Why, that's mighty thoughtful of you, Rachel. I'm sure he'll get it with you praying for him."

"I'm sure too, Mama!" Rachel agreed.

* * *

If I can just get the Stage Manager part, I'll be able to see Debbie at rehearsals—and maybe other times too! Maybe even go to her home! Who knows? Ben thought—unaware that he himself was the object of Rachel's thoughts.

His hair is so beautiful—all soft and shiny black—and I love the way it curls behind his ears, Rachel thought, dropping back behind the other children and walking next to Ben. "Guess what I did, Ben?" Rachel blurted out, more loudly than she intended.

Startled, Ben turned toward her, irritated at having his daydreams of Debbie interrupted. "I don't know, Rachel. Something to do with church I bet."

"No, but it's something real special," she assured him. "I prayed for you to get that part in the play."

Her hair sure is pretty this morning—all soft and shiny and curly. Too bad she doesn't have nicer clothes, like Debbie. She'd be real pretty. "I 'preciate that, Rachel. I doubt I got much chance though with all them rich kids tryin' out for it. Seems like they always get just about anything they want," he sighed.

As he walked onto the school ground, Ben noticed Debbie Lambert getting out of her daddy's long, green Packard.

"Oh, Ben! Ben Logan!" Debbie trilled, hurrying across the school ground toward him.

Ben felt that his throat was thickening, tightening. He found it difficult to breathe and his knees were almost too weak to support him. *Oh Lord! She's so beautiful! Take your time—try not to say anything too stupid.*

"Ben," Debbie said as she approached him, slowing down, her jade green skirt swaying with the motion of her hips. "You're just the man I'm looking for."

Man! Ben thought. *She called me a man! Oh, Lord, please don't let me mess up now!*

"We need to talk about the play," she said, glancing at Rachel with annoyance. "I'll simply *die* if I don't get the part of Emily!"

"I—ah—I'm sure you'll get it, Debbie," Ben stammered, averting his eyes from Debbie's lilac blouse.

"Well, I hope so," Debbie pouted, looking at the ground, then at Ben, her head tilted slightly. "Emily's supposed to be pretty, and I'm just ever so plain."

"Oh, no, Debbie! No, you're not!" Ben said quickly. "You're just about the prettiest . . ."

"And if you don't get the part of the Stage Manager . . . ," Debbie interrupted herself, straightening the collar of Ben's shirt—made by his mother from a flour sack. "I don't believe I've ever seen a shirt like this before, Ben. Wherever did you buy it?"

"Uh—I don't remember," Ben lied.

"It's surely—different," she observed, releasing the collar like there might be a bug lurking beneath it. "Well, no matter. Like I was saying, if you don't get the part of the Stage Manager, then . . ."—Debbie paused for effect, tilting her chin and staring directly into Ben's eyes—"then I just might drop out myself!"

"Don't do that, Debbie!" Ben pleaded, his brow furrowed with anxiety. "The play'd be a flop without you!"

"Oh, I'm sure you'll get it," Debbie said, sufficiently satisfied with Ben's reaction. "Then we'll be able to study our parts together. Wouldn't that be fun?"

Ben thought of being with Debbie in her huge, beautiful house. Then he remembered the wondrous, blue ball. *It'd be just like getting the blue ball all over again! That's how good it would be!* "It sure would!" he agreed.

Debbie took Ben's arm, guiding him toward the school building, glancing over her shoulder at Rachel with a toss of her blonde tresses. "The play's going to be on a Saturday right before Christmas this year," she cooed, "with a party afterward. We won't have to go home 'til who knows when."

"Would you go with me?" Ben blurted out, without thinking. "That is—if I get the part."

"Oh, I think that would be grand!" Debbie exclaimed. "We'll have such a glorious time!"

Rachel stood on the curb under a spreading live oak, forgotten by the couple, walking arm in arm away from her. She glanced at her threadbare dress, her figure still more girl than woman—at her hands, red and chapped from washing clothes in the huge iron pot behind her house. She longed for the familiar things of childhood, fighting those strange stirrings in her breast that always seemed to leave her unsatisfied. *Lord, what's the matter with me?*

As Rachel gazed across the hard-packed school ground toward Ben, she saw Debbie speak briefly to him, then hurry away, catching up with Keith Demerie as he gained the front steps of the building. As they entered, she was clinging tightly to Keith's arm. *Oh, Ben, Ben! Are you really that blind?*

* * *

I love this place, Ben thought as he entered Ollie's Drugstore. *It's so cool and bright and clean!* He walked across the black-and-white tiled floor to the marble-topped counter where two half-eaten sundaes were melting in their glass dishes, cherries resting brightly in the vanilla ice cream.

Sitting on one of the stools, he looked around the drugstore—the five tables in front near the plate glass window, with their round marble tops matching the counter, and wire-backed ice cream parlor chairs neatly in place—the three wooden booths along the far wall—the jukebox against the back wall, its bubbles moving in a slow, silent dance of color—the Coca-Cola and Borden's Ice Cream signs. In Ben's mind, it was an empty and quiet perfection. *I could spend the rest of my life here.*

Spinning the cushioned seat of a stool around and around on its shiny metal pole, Ben waited for Ollie Caston to appear from somewhere in the labyrinth of rooms in back where he warehoused his stock and filled prescriptions. The high-pitched squeaking sound of the counter stool soon got the results Ben wanted.

"You rang, sir?" A pale man in his mid-thirties stepped through the door holding a mortar and pestle, his clear brown eyes catching the light from the front window, crew-cut brown hair, his round face glowing with humor. He wore his usual white shirt with the sleeves rolled to the elbows, black bow tie, and white apron that reached his knees.

"Hey, Mr. Caston," Ben smiled. "I saw your *Help Wanted* sign in the front window."

"Very observant of you," he replied, grinding the mortar with the pestle. "Hand lettered. Did it myself."

Ben was silent, a puzzled look on his face.

"Anything else?" Ollie asked, grinding the white powder.

"Well, I, uh . . ."

"You want the job. Am I right?"

"Yes sir."

"Good," Ollie nodded, stopping his grinding and looking closely at the mixture in the mortar.

"I never know how to take you, Mr. Caston," Ben said, resting his elbows on the counter.

"Take me just about any way—except seriously, Ben," he smiled. "Life's too short for serious."

"I'll work hard, Mr. Caston," Ben added, knowing that behind the humor of Ollie Caston was a shrewd businessman who worked a fourteen-hour day.

"I know you will, Ben," Ollie agreed. "That's why you got the job. Now let's seal the bargain."

"Sir?"

"What'll it be?" Ollie smiled. "I'm buying."

Ben pointed at the bowls next to him.

"Chocolate sundae, eh? Good choice," Ollie grinned.

They sat together at the last booth—Ollie sipping a fountain Coke and Ben giving his full attention to the sundae. Ollie slipped from the booth and dropped a nickel into the jukebox.

"You'll help out around the store some," Ollie said, sliding back into the booth. "Clean up the place, work the counter once in a while, keep the shelves stocked. But your main job will be delivering prescriptions," he continued, sipping his Coke. "You do have a bicycle, don't you, Ben?"

"Yes sir."

Ben devoted himself to his sundae, listening to the words drifting from the jukebox—something about three little fishes. It made no sense, sounding like baby talk, but Ben was so happy, he liked it and sang along with it under his breath.

". . . And dey fam and dey fam all over de dam."

5

YOU MADE ME LOVE YOU!

*I*t's a real frog strangler out there, ain't it, boy?"
Morton Spain's fifty years had not been kind to him. Even in the
dim light of the back portico of his mansion on Peachtree Boulevard, Ben noticed Spain's red-rimmed eyes with pouches under
them, purple-tinted and permanent. The loose, wrinkled skin
under his neck hung above a round paunch that dwarfed his
thin shoulders and chest.

*Always feels he's got to talk "white trash" to me or anybody else
that's poor,* Ben thought, remembering the perfect diction Spain
always used with his friends. "A regular deluge, Mr. Spain," he
countered, leaning his bicycle against one of the columns that
were miniatures of the huge white ones on the front of the
house.

"I hope you remembered those headache powders for my
wife," Spain said, nervously smoothing the few strands of graying
black hair that covered his bald head. "Twenty-two years old and
she gets a headache nearly every night!" he muttered sourly.

"Got 'em right here, Mr. Spain," Ben said, lifting the lid of the
wooden box that was mounted on the handlebars and front fender
of his bicycle. He reached inside and handed Spain the white paper
bag, noticing the slight trembling of his hands.

"Good—good!" Spain said, handing Ben a ten-dollar bill. He
stood there awkwardly, his thin white fingers crinkling the paper
bag, brow furrowed above the dark eyes.

Ben was making change when he remembered. "Oh, I'm sorry,
Mr. Spain," he said, rummaging around in the box. "Ollie, uh—I
mean Mr. Caston gave this to me just as I was leaving."

Spain's face brightened.

57

Ben lifted a second bag from the box, holding it up to the dim yellow light that shone down from the back entrance way. "Here it is. This one's for you."

"Thanks, Ben," Spain said, snatching the bag and turning around abruptly. "You're a good boy."

"You're welcome, Mr. Spain."

Spain was halfway up the flight of concrete steps when he turned, looking down at the boy who stood dripping in the dull yellow raincoat. "Wait just a minute, Ben," he remarked offhandedly. "I'll have Angela bring you some hot chocolate."

Listening to the flat sound of the rain on the flagstones, Ben sorted through the deliveries he had left, shivering slightly when an errant gust of wind found him underneath the portico, stinging him with a cold spray. *Five bags left to deliver and four of them go to Senator Demerie's house. Seems like the more money you have—the more prescriptions you need. Looks like rich people would be healthier—get to see a doctor any time they need to—sure eat and dress a lot better than most of us in this town. Well—I guess it don't bother Ollie none. They'll spend their money somewhere. Might as well be his place.*

"Oh, Ben!" Angela Spain called out in her breathy voice from the entrance way at the top of the steps. She pushed her long, dark brown hair back from her face, clutching her silk robe at the waist.

Ben noticed the high arch of her eyebrows and the incredibly long lashes. "Yes, ma'am," he answered, closing the lid of the box and stepping from the shadow of a column.

"You come right up here and get dried off before you catch your death!" she ordered. "That dreadful husband of mine should have better manners than to make you wait out here in this storm! Hurry up now! I won't take no for an answer!"

"Yes, ma'am."

"Hang your raincoat in the mudroom here," she said, pointing to a darkened room to the left.

Ben found a hook just inside the door and complied. "Sorry I got your floor muddy," he mumbled uneasily, looking at the mess he had made on the tile.

"Don't worry about it," Angela Spain said absently, with a flick of her painted nails. "The maid'll clean it up tomorrow. Just leave your boots right there."

Ben slipped the rubber boots off, looked around and set them in a corner. As he turned, a white towel hit him in the face. "Uh!" he grunted, snagging it with his left hand.

"Good reflexes. I like that in a man," Angela Spain grinned slyly. "Follow me." She spun quickly, her white silk robe billowing out, revealing a glimpse of the pale green nightgown beneath it.

Ben followed her down a dimly lit hallway, the gleaming hardwood floor glass-smooth through his damp socks. Oil paintings in heavy gilt frames lined the walls, the ancient faces in them gazing at Ben as if he were an intruder. From somewhere near the end of the long hall, the sound of piano music drifted in waves through the scented air. *Stardust,* Ben thought. He had heard it a hundred times on his mother's radio in the window of her tiny kitchen. Without the words, the music seemed austere, haunted—as if longing for the warmth of a human voice.

"Well, are you just going to stand in the middle of the hall all night?" Angela Spain admonished.

"Sorry," Ben said, following her through a doorway on the left, next to a huge mahogany hall tree.

They entered a small, carpeted alcove that overlooked the back yard. A window seat with wine-colored velvet cushions lined the three walls beneath a bay window, matching curtains pulled back and tied at the corners. Raindrops glinted in the light from a tiny crystal chandelier, sliding in erratic patterns down the glass as the wind gusted under the eaves.

Angela Spain grabbed the towel, tousling Ben's hair with it. "Sit down and dry your hair, Ben," she teased, tossing the towel on the window seat. "You look like a drowned cat!"

"Guess I do," Ben admitted, sitting down and draping the towel over his head, rubbing it briskly with both hands.

Angela Spain stepped out of her green satin slippers, leaving them next to Ben. "Hot chocolate OK?"

"Uh—I reckon so," Ben nodded. "Where's Mr. Spain?"

"Where he always is I suppose," she sighed. "In his study. Law is a boring profession, Ben. Constantly digging through those musty old books or hanging around the courthouse to see some judge. Not glamorous at all—like I thought it would be."

"I bet he makes a lot of money though," Ben remarked bluntly, looking about the room.

Something flickered in Angela Spain's violet eyes as she looked directly at Ben, her left hand caressing the base of her throat. "You cut right to the heart of it don't you, Ben?"

"I'm sorry," he confessed, doubling his hair drying efforts. "It's none of my business."

"Be right back," she said, turning quickly, the robe flowing outward from her body.

Ben caught glimpses of her small white feet beneath the robe as she moved silently across the carpet.

The wind was dying—a steady rain falling in thin silver cords, bending slightly as the last breezes touched them. The sound of the piano through the open door was faint and distant like a dream of music, like a dream of stardust.

Something cold—almost palpable touched Ben, causing him to tremble in the warmth of the room. *Why should I leave?* he thought, looking at the slow steady rain. *I'll just drink my hot chocolate. Maybe by then the rain'll be stopped. I'm not doing anything wrong!* The music stopped and, as if signaling the start of some domestic struggle, a metal pan clinked onto the burner of a stove.

The warmth and scent and comfort of the room suddenly felt oppressive. Ben grew uneasy and finally stood up and rustled into the heavy raincoat. Leaving the house, he threw his leg over the bicycle and rode along the flagstone path at the back of the house. *Hope she don't get mad cause I didn't wait for the hot chocolate.* The rain had stopped—the trees dripping softly onto the stones.

Something caught Ben's eye and he glanced to his right. Angela Spain was framed in the bay window. She lay on her left side, elbow bent, supporting her body. Her pale right arm curved down her hip, the slim fingers pointing gracefully toward her bare feet. As she smiled, Ben thought he heard music begin. *Maybe I'll go back—just listen to the music for a little while.* He thought of his mother, heard the sound of her prayers as he drifted into sleep each night. Turning from the window, he rode away down the narrow path.

* * *

"Come on, Baby," Jewel Logan pleaded, looking at her son's books and papers scattered over the white, enameled tabletop.

"Fred Allen's gonna be on Jack Benny's show tonight. It'll be real funny. Come listen to it with us."

"I'd love to, Mama," Ben replied, taking notes from a newspaper, "but I've got to do another report for Mrs. Peabody's class. You know how the last one turned out. Rachel can listen with you and help me study my part in the play later."

"I'm sure glad you got that part," Jewel said earnestly. "I know it's real important to you."

"Well, Rachel said she was prayin' for me," Ben smiled. "So I guess I got her to thank for it."

Rachel leaned against the door post behind Jewel Logan, a grin spreading on her face. "Don't thank me, Ben," she blushed. "Thank God. He answered my prayer."

"That's right, child," Jewel agreed, nodding her head toward Ben. "The good Lord got that part for you sure as I'm standin' here! I hear the program comin' on, Rachel."

The Jell-O program, coming to you from the Grand Ballroom of the Hotel Pierre, starring Jack Benny, with Mary Livingstone, and Abe Lyman and his orchestra.

Ben leaned back in his chair, listening to Jack Benny sing "Love in Bloom" to his screeching violin accompaniment.

"Whoever's strangling that cat had better cut it out. The guy with the foghorn's gotta go, too."

"Well, as I live and regret there are no locks on studio doors . . . if it isn't Fred Allen! . . . What's the idea of breaking in here in the middle of my singing?"

"Singing? When you set that croup to music and call it singing, you've gone too far!"

"Now look here, Allen, I don't care what you say about my singing on your own program, but after all, I've got listeners!"

"Keep your family out of this, Benny."

"Well, my family likes my singing . . . and my violin playing, too."

"Your violin playing! Why I just heard that a horse committed suicide when he found out your violin bow was made from his tail."

Chuckling softly, Ben listened to the shrieks of laughter from the living room. *Why can't I think of funny things like that to say? I bet*

Debbie would notice me then. Well, this is fun but it ain't gettin' my history report done.

Ben returned to his note taking.

"FDR and the Alphabet Agencies. 1933-1939 . . ."

* * *

Moonlight streaming down through the trees cast the narrow dirt road into deep shadow. The cry of an owl, carried by the night wind, blended with the rustling of the leaves. Ben and Rachel walked side by side, listening to the dark music around them.

"I sure appreciate your helpin' me, Rachel," Ben offered. "I'd never learn this without you."

"Sure you would, Ben," she protested mildly. "I think you could do just about anything—if you put your mind to it."

Ben seemed not to have heard her. "Rachel, do you think Debbie really likes me?"

Rachel thought of all the boys she had seen Debbie with these first few weeks of school and how she had treated them all just the same. "I don't know."

"Well, she said she'd go to the cast party with me after the performance," Ben declared seriously. "Don't that mean she likes me? You're a girl. You oughta know about these things."

"Maybe she does, Ben," Rachel suggested. "I haven't been around those rich girls much."

"Yeah," Ben mused. "Seems like they're a lot different."

"You like workin' for Ollie?" Rachel asked, trying to change the subject of the conversation.

"Sure do," Ben affirmed, thinking of the clean smelling drugstore. "He's a fine man. I can't seem to make enough money though. Been saving for a new suit to take Debbie to the party, but most of my money's been goin' to pay for groceries or clothes for the kids. Pete's medicine is pretty expensive too."

"I think his cough's gettin' worse," Rachel said. "Every time he laughed hard tonight he ended up in a coughin' fit."

"Yeah. He don't let on much, but I can tell it's gettin' to him," Ben agreed. "He's gonna have to go back to the doctor if he don't get better soon."

"Well, here we are," Rachel said as they walked into what

passed for her front yard. "You want a glass of water or something? It's a long walk home."

"No, thanks," Ben replied, handing Rachel her books. "It ain't that far and anyway I got to start my paper route in the mornin'. Can't be late the first day."

Rachel stood on the single step that gave access to her front door, still having to look up to meet Ben's eyes. "You're workin' too much, Ben. You look tired all the time."

"Don't have much choice," he shrugged. "Somebody's got to pay the bills. 'Bout the only one Daddy's payin' now is Shorty's. Don't want his liquor cut off."

Rachel watched Ben as he crossed the yard, heading for the dark road through the woods. The owl flew above him in the gossamer moonlight, casting a shadow across his path as it glided silently through its nightly rounds.

6

"THE BIG 'UNS EAT THE LITTLE 'UNS!"

You crazy to be workin' so hard, boy," Sonny Mullins drawled, leaning his bony frame against the brick wall at the back of Ollie's Drugstore. Taking his comb from his back pocket, he ran it through his greasy, whitish hair, a few drops of oil beaded near the hairline of his low forehead. "There's easier jobs to be had. And makin' a lot more money than you'll ever see haulin' medicine around town!"

Ben glanced at him as he loaded prescriptions into the delivery box of his bicycle, parked in the alley under the eaves of the drugstore. At eighteen, Sonny was a twenty-year-younger version of his uncle, Leon Mullins.

"What kind of work?" Ben asked, arranging the white bags and boxes by address.

"Easy work."

Ben paused, holding two bags over the delivery box. "Sonny, I been up since four o'clock this morning—deliverin' papers, tryin' to learn something in class when I could barely stay awake—I ain't got time for no riddles."

Sonny turned his R.C. up to his mouth, holding it like a jug of moonshine, forefinger wrapped around the neck of the bottle as it lay along the side of his hand and arm, draining the last drop. "Does that tell you what I'm talkin' 'bout, boy?"

Ben glared at Sonny and stepped through the back door into the stockroom to get the remaining prescriptions. In a few moments he returned, holding the refilled cardboard box and arranging the last of his deliveries.

Sonny dropped his bottle on the hard-packed dirt of the alley with a hollow thud. "Everbody sees you ridin' that bike all over town, Ben," he grinned.

Ben ignored him.

"You shore are touchy lately, boy," Sonny continued. "I'm jist tryin' to *help* you."

Finished with his loading, Ben stepped through the door with the empty box.

"Anyhow," Sonny said, taking a pack of Camels from his shirt pocket and tapping one free. "It'd be easy for you to make a few *extra deliveries* without nobody bein' the wiser."

"The cook at the jailhouse don't fix nothin' but hard cornbread and watery beans, Sonny."

Scratching a kitchen match on the brick wall, Sonny lit his cigarette. "Me and Uncle Moon is too smart for the law around these parts, boy," he coughed.

"Where were you last Christmas, Sonny?" Ben asked. "Didn't see you at the lightin' of the town tree."

"That was jist a mess up! Ain't no way it could ever happen agin!"

"Not interested," Ben said flatly.

"You'll come around," Sonny replied, reaching into his back pocket again for his comb.

As he walked away down the narrow alley toward the street, Ben called out, "Sonny!"

"Yeah."

"Comb the back of your hair. It's stickin' out."

Ben sat down in the gritty alley next to the back door of Ollie's, slouching against the wall. *Four o'clock and I'm worn out. Maybe I can finish up in a couple of hours. Soon as I get the money to buy that suit, I'm gonna slack off a little. Can't take a girl like Debbie to the party lookin' like a hick.*

From the front of the building, Ben heard the sound of cars passing on Main Street, the hum of tires on pavement lulling him into a comfortable drowsiness. The clock on the courthouse square knelled a somber four o'clock, the last stroke dying away in the distance like a fading memory. Inside the drugstore, someone dropped a nickel into the jukebox.

You made me love you.
I didn't want to do it; I didn't want to do it.
You made me want you,
And all the time you knew it; I guess you always knew it.

Judy Garland—from Broadway Melody *last year. Wish I could'a seen that one!*

You made me happy; Sometimes you made me glad.
But there were times, dear, you made me feel so bad.

I wonder if everybody feels bad sometimes—when they really like another person. Rachel never makes me feel bad . . . never makes me feel real good either, not like—

Give me, give me what I cry for;
You know you got the brand of kisses
That I'd die for.
You know you made me love you.

"Ben," Ollie Caston called from the back door, looking at the bicycle to his right.

"Over here, Mr. Caston," Ben answered, squinting up at his boss, his eyes crinkled from half-sleep.

"Mmmh," Ollie grunted, startled. "You look worn out, Ben. Maybe I'd better cut back on your hours."

Ben scrambled to his feet. "Don't do that, Mr. Caston," he pleaded. "I'm all right."

"You almost forgot Pete's medicine," Ollie said, handing the dark brown bottle to Ben. "By the way, how's he feelin'? Medicine helpin' that cough any?"

"I guess so," Ben replied, holding the handlebars of his bicycle. "Seems to be doin' some better."

"Ben?" Ollie said in a serious tone.

"Yes sir."

"Was that Sonny Mullins I heard you talkin' with out here a few minutes ago?"

"Yes sir," Ben nodded. "I didn't quit though. I kept workin' the whole time he was here."

"That doesn't bother me," Ollie assured him. "You're as good a worker as I've ever seen. But a man—if you could call him that—like Sonny Mullins is nothin' but trouble."

"Don't worry, Mr. Caston," Ben said, throwing his leg over the seat of his bicycle. "I got too much work to do to be hangin' around with the likes of him."

"Good," Ollie smiled.

"Oh, Mr. Caston," Ben called back as he rode away. "Take Pete's medicine out of my pay again."

"OK," Ollie nodded sadly.

* * *

"Here we are, Ben," Leslie Gifford said, pulling his black Ford coupe into the long paved driveway that formed a semicircle in front of the Lambert's antebellum style home. "A bit ostentatious, don't you think?"

"A bit what?" Ben asked, staring at the huge white columns that ran the length of the portico.

"Ostentatious," Leslie repeated. "Look it up. You need to know that word if you plan to travel in these circles."

"I didn't know it would be so *big!*" Ben admitted. "Never seen it up close before."

"Well, it was nice of Debbie to ask the cast members over to work out the fine points of the play," Gifford said.

"Who all's comin'?" Ben asked, looking out over the expanse of landscaped greenery that stretched to Peachtree Boulevard.

"Just a few that play main characters," Gifford replied. "Taylor and Doak—oh, yes, let's not forget that stalwart patron of the performing arts, our beloved principal, the late Alvin Ditweiler."

"And a good time was had by all," Ben laughed, remembering the principal nodding off on the front row of the auditorium.

"You know your lines yet?" Gifford asked, sifting through some papers in his brown leather briefcase.

"I think so," Ben replied earnestly. "Been studyin' night and day."

Gifford looked up at the honest intensity in Ben's face. *Boy's got guts!* he thought, as he remembered seeing Ben riding down the street in front of his house before sunrise, throwing newspapers onto the lawns. "This part really means a lot to you, doesn't it?"

"It's the most important thing in my life right now—just about," Ben admitted. "Hope I do a good job with it. I'd hate to let everybody down."

"Hello, Mr. Gifford—Ben." Wearing a white blouse with lace-trimmed collar and sleeves and pleated navy slacks, Debbie Lambert stood at the massive front door of the house. She greeted them with a smile. "You two come on in."

They were ushered into a high-ceilinged foyer with a slate floor, two massive church pews, and a suit of armor—complete with broadsword and helmet. Following Debbie down a long hall, Ben noticed the landscapes and portraits on the walls—each illuminated by its own shaded light. *That's more lights than I got in my whole house!* Ben thought.

"Right in here," Debbie said, opening a door on the left. "We're getting together in the sitting room."

"Hey, boys," Alvin Ditweiler called from across the room. He was seated in a Queen Anne chair balancing a demitasse of coffee on a tiny saucer. His blue serge suit was slightly wrinkled—a trace of dried cow manure along the edge of the trouser cuffs. "Ya'll come on over and have a shot of this coffee."

Ben followed Leslie Gifford across the room, sitting next to him on a love seat across from his principal. Debbie was pouring from a silver coffee service at a sideboard gleaming with china cups, saucers, and a matching tray of sugar cookies.

At the far end of the room, a long span of glass looked out on a terrace and pool area. Taylor Spain and Doak Myles stood next to it, looking at an aquarium alive with brightly colored tropical fish. They wore clean, but purposely sloppy Levis with the cuffs rolled up, white socks, and saddle oxfords. Ben glanced down at his heavy-soled black lace-ups and neatly pressed khakis, hoping no one would notice the tiny stitches on the left knee where his mother had mended a tear.

"How do you take your coffee, Mr. Gifford?" Debbie asked brightly, holding the laden silver tray in front of him.

"Black'll be fine," he answered, taking the tiny cup and saucer.

"Cookies? I baked them myself."

"No, thanks," Gifford replied, leaning back, the saucer balanced on his lap so he could lift the cup with his good left arm. "Haven't cared much for sweets since I was a boy."

"Ben?" Debbie smiled, "Surely you want some of my cookies."

"Just black coffee, thanks," Ben said, knowing that if he tried to manage both he'd probably spill the coffee or drop the cookies. "Had a big supper."

"Well, it looks like the gang's all here," Taylor Spain said, strolling over and sitting with Doak Myles on a flowered sofa.

Debbie, after serving them coffee and cookies, sat between them on the couch. "I'm so thrilled to have everybody here!" she beamed. "It's going to be such fun this year."

"I'd like to welcome our newest aspiring actor to the cast," Alvin Ditweiler announced, chewing on a cookie. "I don't believe you've been in any of our plays before, have you, Ben?"

"No sir," Ben replied, smiling at Debbie. "I think it'll be fun though."

"Debbie," Doak Myles said, motioning for her to stand up with him, "we need to get our positions straight when George and Emily are meeting."

Rising from his chair, his tiny cup chinking unsteadily on its saucer, Alvin Ditweiler caught Leslie Gifford's eye, motioning to him. Gifford followed him to the far end of the room, his foot thudding softly on the carpet.

"We've got a problem here, Leslie," Ditweiler declared bluntly, sipping his coffee. "Keith Demerie's gonna play the Stage Manager."

Gifford was silent, his jaw muscles working steadily.

Ditweiler looked at the bright, moving patterns the fish were making in the aquarium. "Did you hear what I said, Leslie?"

"I don't know what's prompted this," he finally replied, "and I don't care what kind of politics are being played. It's too late to change now."

Ditweiler watched the fish, slurping his coffee, cup chinking on its tiny saucer. "Keith's the Stage Manager. That's final!"

"Ben's worked like a miner learning this part, Alvin!" Gifford declared. "It'd break his heart to lose it now—maybe his spirit!"

"You see them fish, Leslie?" Ditweiler asked academically. "Life's like that. The big 'uns eat the little 'uns."

"I don't see them eating each other. They look pretty content to me."

"That's 'cause they're well fed," Ditweiler replied, turning to Gifford, a sly smile on his face. "Like all of us at the school. Well fed! And Senator Demerie's dumping the feed in the tank!"

"I believe there's a little fox in you, Alvin," Gifford said, his face growing dark. "Doreen better keep you away from her hen house."

Ditweiler's mouth smiled—his eyes deadly serious. "Remember, Leslie. The big 'uns eat the little 'uns. And I'm the biggest fish in the Liberty High School aquarium."

Gifford looked at the small group in the sitting area, engaged in animated conversation—Ben explaining something to Debbie, who had the attitude of a supplicant at the altar. *Never saw that boy so happy. Hope he's as strong as I think he is.* He shuffled across the room toward Ben like a wounded warrior bearing bad news from the battlefield.

"Can I pour you another cup of coffee, Ben?" Gifford asked, when there was a lull in the conversation.

"Yes sir," Ben replied, walking over to the sideboard. "What happened to Mr. Ditweiler? He left mighty early."

"He—ah—lost something, I think," Gifford shrugged. *His integrity.* "Don't think he'll have any luck finding it though. Happened too long ago."

"Guess I'll try one of these cookies, too," Ben said. "Something bothering you, Mr. Gifford?"

"Is it that obvious?" Gifford replied, looking into his cup.

As Ben bit into the cookie, he saw Gifford's eyes turn upward. Suddenly the cookie tasted like wet sawdust. He wanted to run from the room so he wouldn't hear.

"I don't know how to tell you this, Ben," Gifford admitted. "Except to just get it over with. Keith Demerie's getting the Stage Manager part."

Ben stood transfixed—gray eyes growing bright. "I—I don't understand. We've got our parts. You said I was best."

"You are, Ben. You are," Gifford assured him fervently. "Sometimes that's not enough. Sometimes things happen that . . . You can still have one of the smaller parts—help out backstage. That's important too! Anyway . . ."

Ben was no longer listening—walking dejectedly away from the sound of Gifford's voice, he found himself looking out at the back yard. The sunlight was failing—the water in the pool taking on a deeper blue as night approached. Ben remembered a few lines from a poem by Housman, because they could have been written about his daddy.

> Ale, man, ale's the stuff to drink
> For fellows whom it hurts to think:
> Look into the pewter pot
> To see the world as the world's not.

"Ben," Debbie said from behind him, softly touching his shoulder. "I'm so sorry. Mr. Gifford told me what happened. It's *dreadful!*"

Ben looked into the deep blue eyes, her smile casting a ray of light into the darkness that engulfed him. "It's not important," he mumbled.

"It is *too* important!" she cried angrily. "No one can do that part as well as you—*certainly* not that big lummox, Keith Demerie! Don't you worry now. We'll find you a nice part."

Ben forced a smile. "Well, guess it's better'n nothin'!"

"That's my boy," Debbie cooed, kissing him gently on the cheek. "Why, I bet you could help me with my part! I'm so awful. I sure need it!"

* * *

"Ben Logan, don't you go stompin' through the house like that!" Jewel Logan scolded. "What's the matter with you?"

Ben was on the back porch when his mother caught up to him. "Nothin', Mama," he replied impassively, listening to the cicada's nocturnal symphony. "It's just—well, things didn't go too good today."

"Well, that's no reason for actin' like this," she admonished. "Didn't you see Rachel in the livin' room? She came to help you with your part."

"Hi, Ben," Rachel called through the screen door. "You ready to study some? You know that part so well, this might be our last night."

"You be nice, son," Jewel Logan chided gently. "Rachel's a good girl."

As the screen door closed, Ben stepped off the porch, walking down the path toward the well. Rachel watched until he lowered the bucket into the well—then followed down the well-worn path. Overhead, a shooting star rushed brightly across the heavens, vanishing silently into the void.

"Ben—are you all right?" Rachel asked softly, watching him raise the bucket of water and pour some into his mason jar.

"No," Ben replied flatly, tilting the jar to his lips, draining half of it.

Rachel shook her head when he offered her some. "Can I help?"

"No," Ben repeated. He drank the rest of the water, turning to face her. "Wish this was some of Shorty's whiskey. That's what I need now!"

"Oh, Ben!" Rachel gasped. "Don't say such things!"

"They took my part away, Rachel," Ben said evenly, taking a deep breath. "They took my part."

Rachel stepped close to him, putting her arms on his shoulders. "Ben, I'm so sorry," she sighed. "I know how much it means to you—how hard you've worked. What was the reason? You got it fair and square."

"Money!"

Rachel looked into his eyes, perplexed. "I don't understand."

"You want anything in this world—you got to *buy* it!" Ben said with absolute conviction. "That's all there is to understand. Looks like all your prayin' didn't amount to much!" he added bitterly.

"I don't believe that, Ben!" she responded fervently. "God gives us only those things that are good for us, even if we can't always see it. Maybe this would have been bad for you in the long run. His love for us—"

Ben walked out into the darkness, away from the sound of her voice. The night wind was cool on his face, bringing with it the smell of leaf mold from the dry autumn woods. *Money! That's what it's all about. Maybe runnin' that bootleg hooch ain't such a bad idea after all!*

7

THE LOVE OF MONEY

Sorry, Ben," Pete coughed. "I didn't mean to wake you up."

Ben sat up in bed, throwing his legs over the side, wrapping his quilt around him against the morning chill. "It's OK. 'Bout time to get up anyway." He yawned, then said seriously, placing his hand on Pete's shoulder, "You're gonna have to go back to the doctor, little brother. You ain't gettin' any better."

"Aw, no, Ben," Pete moaned, covering his head with the blanket. "I ain't that sick. Ask Mama."

"We talked about it last night," Ben went on, fumbling in the dark for his clothes. "She's taking you to see Dr. Myles today. He's a good doctor. Have you good as new in no time."

"Well—OK," Pete mumbled, pulling the blanket from his head. "If you say so."

"Atta boy!" Ben smiled, tousling his brother's dark mop of hair. "Now go on back to sleep. Two more hours before you have to get up."

Reaching inside the wall at the side of his bed, Ben pulled out the roll of dollar bills he kept hidden from his father, remembering the times Earl had come in at night and taken all his money to buy liquor. He slipped the rubber band off and counted out the bills. *Maybe I'll just keep two dollars.* Ben shook his head slowly back and forth. *No, I'll just have to start all over. How am I gonna get enough money to buy that new suit?* Reaching back into his hiding place, Ben found the snapshot. Holding it up to the window next to his cot, in the light from the pale moon settling behind diaphanous wisps of cloud, he could barely make out Debbie's image.

He rolled out of his bed and, after quickly washing his face and hands in the pan on the back porch, went into the kitchen.

"Mornin', Mama," he smiled, sitting at the table. "Kinda chilly out there."

"Mornin', Baby," Jewel Logan replied, setting a steaming bowl of grits with strips of crisp bacon in front of him. "This'll warm your insides."

Ben spooned butter that his mother had churned onto the grits, breaking the bacon into the pale yellow mixture. "Umm—boy!" he said through a mouthful of grits and bacon, "Your cookin' gets better every day!"

"Why, thank you, son," Jewel replied, pouring two cups of coffee. *Always a compliment for his mama. Most thoughtful one of my children.*

"Mama, you don't have to get up with me this early," Ben said, spooning sugar into his coffee. "You look wore out. Sleep a little later."

"I'm fine, son," Jewel said, watching her handsome son devour his food. "'Sides—I like these little mornin' times we have together."

"Me too, Mama," Ben agreed, laying his roll of dollar bills on the table.

Jewel stared at the money. "Son, I can't let you do that. You've spent too much on this family already."

"You know Pete's gotta see the doctor," Ben said, finishing his coffee and standing up. "Anyway, there's plenty more where that came from."

Jewel hung her head, the cup of coffee cradled in both hands. "Maybe your daddy'll straighten hisself out."

"Sure he will," Ben lied. "He ain't so bad. Well, I gotta start chunkin' papers. Let everybody know what Lowell Thomas and H. V. Kaltenborn are sayin' about that ruckus over in Europe."

At school that day, Ben realized that his paper route and job at Ollie's Drugstore would never earn him the money he needed. *Guess I'll just have to tell Debbie I can't make the party. They wouldn't let me near Pine Hills Country Club in these ol' wore-out khakis.* Ben dug in his locker, looking for the texts for his next classes. He felt warm breath next to his ear, a kiss on his neck that tingled down to his toes. Trying to remain casual, he lay the fingers of his left hand against the spot where she had kissed him, and turned to face Debbie.

"You handsome thing. I can't wait to get you alone after that party," she breathed, turning from him, and disappearing into the rush of students in the hallway.

The memory of that moment would haunt Ben time and again—the soft wetness of Debbie's lips against his neck—the fragrance of her—the unbearably blue eyes beneath half-closed lids. A single kiss in that crowded, noisy hallway decorated with black witches and orange jack-o-lanterns—and what happened because of it.

After school, Ben made one stop on his way to Ollie's.

"That you, Ben?" Ollie called out from the soda fountain, hearing the back door close.

"No," Ben said in a gruff voice, "it's John Dillinger! Heard you druggists got more money than the banks. Come to rob you!"

"Well, you'll have slim pickings around here," Ollie called back. "Got a bushel of cold medicine to deliver. Seems like everybody in town gets sick after the first cold snap."

"I'm on my way soon as I get my bike loaded, Mr. Caston."

Ben pedaled down the alley behind Ollie's, turning into the smaller alley between the drugstore and Hightower's Department Store.

"I knew you'd slip off the straight 'n narrow," a voice from behind the board fence between the two buildings jibed. "Jist a matter of time with a daddy like yores." Sonny Mullins stepped through the fence holding the board he had pried loose under one arm and a brown paper bag under the other.

"You keep my daddy out of this, Sonny!" Ben protested. "I ain't nothin' like him."

"The ol' apple don't fall far from the tree, boy," Sonny said in his sharp little voice. "Don't matter none anyhow. I could tell you loved money. That's how come I got this little meetin' place ready weeks ago."

"I don't love money!" Ben snapped angrily. "I just got to have it for something important."

"Don't we all, boy!" Sonny squinted through the smoke from the cigarette dangling between his lips. "Don't we all!"

Ben took the bag from Sonny's outstretched hand. "Is this all?"

"We gonna try you out on two customers. See how you do," Sonny replied, slouching against the wall of the drugstore. "The addresses are taped to the bottles. If they're part of yore regular deliveries—so much the better. You get a quarter for ever bottle you sell. Make more in one day with us than ol' Caston pays you in a week—if you play yore cards right."

Thirty minutes later Ben got off his bicycle at the back door of a clapboard house next to the railroad tracks. Standing on the rickety back porch, he knocked on the unpainted door frame. A face appeared hazily through the screen. "That you, Jack?"

"Yeah," Jack Clampett whispered. "You got the stuff?"

"Yeah," Ben echoed. "I thought they gave me the wrong address."

"Daddy can't afford to be buyin' at the liquor store," Jack confessed. "People found out how much he drinks—they'd get a new night marshal real quick." Jack unhooked the screen, slipped a dollar through and reached for the pint bottle.

"It's two dollars," Ben said, glancing around furtively.

"Daddy gets a special deal," Jack said, waving the dollar bill. "You know—for looking the other way. Sonny jist forgot to tell you. He ain't got the sense God give a tadpole!"

Ben hesitated. "OK, Jack," he said, handing him the flat, brown bottle, "But if you're lying—it's comin' out of your hide!"

Three stops later, Ben found himself spinning along the service alley that ran between the back yards in Pine Hills—so the gentlefolk who occupied the mansions wouldn't be distracted by the commoners who served them. Stopping at a break in the six-foot, neatly clipped hedge that ran the length of both sides of the alley, he noted the address on a small white plaque lettered in blue. Rereading the special instructions attached to the bottle, he thought, *You'd never catch her in Grady's Liquor Store.*

Pushing his bicycle through the narrow opening in the hedge, Ben leaned it against a crepe myrtle and went up and tapped softly on the back door of the pool house. The door opened quickly, a cloud of blonde hair appearing through the screen. Ben said nothing, holding out the pint bottle.

"Ben Logan?" she breathed softly.

"Yes, ma'am."

A white manicured hand with three large diamond rings offered him the two dollars.

"Thank you, Mrs. Lambert," Ben said, turning to leave.

"Oh, Ben," the voice called softly.

"Yes, ma'am."

"I can count on your discretion, can't I?"

"Yes, ma'am."

The hand reappeared holding a five-dollar bill.

"Oh, no, ma'am," Ben protested. "I couldn't take that."

As the door closed, the five-dollar bill fluttered silently to the ground at Ben's feet.

* * *

Rock Hill Tabernacle, the sign tacked to the center pole of the brush arbor proclaimed. It was constructed of a rough framework of saplings with the brushy limbs trimmed off and laid across the roof poles. Sawdust covered the dirt floor. Benches were made of "blocks" (thirty-inch sections of logs) turned upright on the floor and "slabs" (crude boards formed when the bark was sawed away from the logs) laid across them, bark side down.

"Looks like a good crowd tonight, Ben," Rachel said, as they walked with Jewel Logan and the other children toward the brush arbor—cloaked in an amber mantle of light from coal oil lanterns. "God's really been movin' in the services this week. I'm glad you could come."

Ben was looking at the forty or fifty people gathering into the temporary church. They wore simple house dresses and work pants, with heavy, coarse coats of somber colors. There seemed to Ben something incompatible between their smiles and laughter (a kind of undefined joy) and the Spartan lives he knew most of them led. *They're all poor as we are—or worse!*

A few Model A's, Model T's, and two wagons sat in the small clearing. Three saddled horses—one snorting and shaking his head, his breath a plume of white in the chill air—stood at the side of the building, their reins tied to the limbs of a cedar.

Leading the way, Ben took the last seat on the last bench from the front. Rachel sat next to him, then Pete, Micah, and his mother, who sat next to the aisle. At the front, Reverend Samuel Shaw tuned his guitar while his wife, Esther, warmed up on her accordion. The small crowd settled down, the talking gradually subsiding.

"Well, hallelujah!" the preacher shouted, lifting both hands toward the leafy ceiling, the guitar hanging from his shoulder. "Let's give God praise for His goodness and His mercy that endureth forever!"

For ten minutes, the congregation gave thanks and praise to God. Ben felt uneasy and out of place as he watched them raising their hands in the cold autumn air, listening as they offered up cries of "Thank you, Jesus!" and "Worthy is the Lamb!" Some were groaning as if in travail. From his childhood, Ben remembered a passage from Romans and the sound of his mother's voice as she read alone at the kitchen table: "the Spirit itself maketh intercession for us with groanings which cannot be uttered." *I gotta get outta this nuthouse!* he thought, looking wildly around him.

In the midst of the praise service, the preacher and his wife broke into song, accompanying themselves on their instruments. The song was quickly picked up by the congregation.

> Sing the wondrous love of Jesus,
> Sing His mercy and His grace;

In spite of himself, Ben was caught up in the spirit of the music. After two more songs, Samuel Shaw lay his guitar aside and stepped behind the pulpit, constructed of three rough planks made steady by cross braces. "I want to remind ya'll that we're having Thanksgiving dinner on the grounds tomorrow after the ten o'clock service. Bring enough for your own family and one more if you're able. If not, just bring yourselves—there'll be plenty—God's people have never begged for bread."

There was a rousing chorus of "Amen!" and "That's right, brother!" throughout the congregation.

Without further ceremony, Shaw picked up his Bible. Opening it, he began to read. "There was a man of the Pharisees, named Nicodemus, a ruler of the Jews: The same came unto Jesus by night, and said unto him, Rabbi, we know that thou art a teacher come from God: for no man can do these miracles that thou doest, except God be with him. Jesus answered and said unto him, Verily, verily, I say unto thee, Except a man be born again, he cannot see the kingdom of God."

Shaw placed the tip of his forefinger in the Bible, closed it carefully, then began to preach. "How many of you folks was ever born?" He peered out over the crowd, staring at the hands. "Well, that's good. Now, how many of you have ever been born *again?*" He moved away from the pulpit, noted the hands that were *not* raised, and his voice began to rise. "If you've only been born *once*, you gotta' die *twice!*" he cried out. "But if you've been born *twice*, you only gotta' die *once!*"

For twenty minutes the awkward shape of the preacher moved back and forth, his arms often extended toward the crowd, and his face contorted with effort as the words poured out of his mouth. Words of encouragement came back to him from the "amen corner" of the congregation—"Amen!"—"Preach it, brother!"— "Glory to God!"

Finally Shaw paused and looked out over the group. "Now," he said, "why is it that some of you good people ain't never been converted to Jesus? Do you *want* to go to hell? Course not! Nobody wants to burn forever! The Lord's been speakin' to me, and I've got His word for you. Some of you ain't been saved because you're lusting after the world! You want money! You want ease and pleasures! You want to run with the high society folks, and you want to have the things money can buy!"

Ben sat rigidly erect, hands gripping the rough edge of the bench tightly, feeling that every word Shaw spoke was a dart striking his chest.

"Now you may think this is a strange message for a bunch like this," Shaw continued. "Look around you. See any diamonds? Mink coats?"

There was laughter out among the benches, people pointing at each other's clothes good naturedly.

"But let's listen to it again," Shaw suggested, not touching his Bible. "The *love* of money—not money itself, is the root of all evil. How many times have you heard—not *said*, Lord knows none of *us* would ever say anything like this—"

There was some laughter and coughing in the building.

"Heard someone *else* say, 'If I just had the *money*, I could look as good as *her!*' Envy! 'If I just had the *money*, they'd show me a little *respect!*' Pride! 'If I just had the *money*, I could have that *woman!*' Lust! Do you see what I'm gittin' at?"

Ben felt that Samuel Shaw's intense blue eyes were directed only at him.

Shaw gave other Scriptures and examples from both the Old and New Testaments. "Well, let me wind this up with what Peter had to say about it. He's kinda my favorite. Let his mouth get him in a lot of trouble—but he never would give up. Fought the good fight, as Paul would say.

"There was a sorcerer named Simon who bewitched the people of Samaria, saying he was a great man. Well, he saw that when Peter and John lay their hands on people, they received the Holy Ghost. He wanted this power real bad, so he offered Peter money for it.

"Whatta you think Peter told him?—" Shaw asked, pausing. "'Thy money perish with thee, because thou hast thought that the gift of God may be purchased with money.' That's the only things worth havin', folks. The only things that last. The gifts of God! Salvation. Healing. Peace. Joy. Eternal Life. And they're free. You don't need *money*."

Shaw stepped in front of the rostrum, his left hand extended toward the people. "Come to the cross of Jesus. He'll give you everything you need. Come to Jesus. He loves you so much!" He stood there, pleading with his crowd, his eyes filled with compassion. He was not an eloquent man, this preacher, but he had the one thing that many educated men lacked—he loved people, and it showed in every gesture and was revealed in every word!

Ben glanced at Shaw, then upward toward the flickering shadows cast by the lanterns hanging from nails driven into the trees. Lowering his head, he looked at the sawdust floor—felt a pull, a gentle tugging in his chest, almost persuading him to leave the bench. *I'll quit sellin' liquor. I almost got enough money. I can't walk down there! What would people think about me? They'd know I been doin' something wrong! I won't do it any more!* He felt Rachel place her hand gently on his shoulder. Deliberately, he reached up and pushed her away.

* * *

"I'm so sorry, Ben!" Debbie sighed, straightening his tie. "But Daddy says I just *have* to go to the party with Keith Demerie. I simply *couldn't* tell you 'til after the play. I didn't want to ruin it for you. It's just *awful*, I know, but our families have been friends for so long, and . . ."

And Senator Demerie's gonna get that state contract for your daddy's business! Ben thought bitterly.

They were standing at the back of the auditorium after the performance, in the clamor and excitement of the crowd, rushing off to their holiday parties and get-togethers. As they surged through the doors, Ben heard cries of "Academy award actin', Debbie!"—"We'll see you all at the party!"

"Ben, don't look at me like that!" Debbie pleaded, caressing the lapels of his pearl-gray jacket. "You know I'd rather go with you. Why, you're the handsomest boy in this whole school! And this new suit is just perfect for you."

Ben looked at Debbie, radiant in the blue silk gown that perfectly matched the color of her eyes—then at Keith Demerie, standing across the way, his perfectly tailored tuxedo making him look almost trim.

"Now, Ben Logan, you just pull yourself together," Debbie said maternally. "I'm going to personally see to it that you get the lead in the spring play. It'll be just grand when . . ."

Slapping Debbie's hands away, Ben spun around, storming into the rush of the crowd leaving the auditorium. He thought of nothing—saw only a red haze before his eyes. Ignoring the greetings of his friends, he strode away from the raucous throng of party-goers, crossing the school ground through the dry, swishing rattle of the leaves.

Later, he found himself aimlessly wandering the almost deserted streets. Stopping in front of Hightower's Department Store, he gazed stoically at the Christmas scene in the display window. A boy about Micah's age proudly lifted his Red Ryder air rifle while his little sister played with her Shirley Temple doll next to an elaborately decorated Christmas tree. Their mother and father sat on the couch of the sumptuously appointed living room, coffee mugs in hand, smiling at their good fortune.

A brutal wind, spawned in the arctic wastelands of Canada, moaned down the street, striking discord in the strains of "Oh Little Town of Bethlehem." Ben glanced at the speaker above the window, spilling its music into the night. A section of newspaper slapped against his leg, startling him from his reverie. Shivering, he folded his arms across his chest. *A few more deliveries—I could'a bought me a decent, warm coat.*

The music changed—Bing Crosby sang "White Christmas" in his rich baritone. Ben walked with a wooden gait down the street, the music growing fainter, anger roaring darkly in his brain. *Ol' Sonny told me if I stayed with him and "Moon" I'd have my own car, women, whatever I wanted. If a half-wit like him can do it—oughta be easy for me. Besides, I can get Mama some of them things she's been wantin'. That's what I'll do—just stay with it a little while—get some nice things for my Mama!*

He moved down the street, the muted sound of hymns falling on the town. A small girl was staring at a doll in a brightly lit window, singing in a tiny voice, "Jesus loves the little children—"

8

THE ROAD NOT TAKEN

What's troubling you, Ben?" Leslie Gifford asked, watching a black-and-white terrier leave his calling card on a stop sign post, then trot confidently across the street toward town. "You used to be my best student—now you're barely passing. I had hopes of your getting a scholarship—maybe coming back and teaching here someday."

Ben stared vacantly at the hard February light angling through the classroom window. It struck the globe that sat on its walnut stand in front of Gifford's desk, bringing the colors into sharp relief—the backside of the world in shadow. *Surely the darkness shall cover me; . . . but the night shineth as the day: the darkness and the light are both alike to thee,* Ben thought. *Why can't I get these ol' sayings outta my mind? Hadn't heard them in years—but they keep comin' back!"*

"Ben?" Gifford asked softly, leaning forward, arms on his desk. "Do you hear me?"

"What—? Oh, sorry, Mr. Gifford," Ben said absently, glancing at the strange intensity in his teacher's eyes. *Like a mind reader,* he thought. "Guess I'm workin' too many hours. Not much study time."

"Spending your money on clothes, I see," Gifford said, nodding at Ben's new outfit.

"No sir!" Ben shot back. "Just a little bit. Most of it goes to my family."

Gifford lifted himself painfully out of his chair, sitting on the edge of his desk, his crippled right leg hanging over the side at an odd angle. "Ben, those Florsheim shoes you're wearing are their Roan Brown style—calfskin if I'm not mistaken. Cost ten dollars at Hightower's. I know, because I wanted a pair and couldn't afford them. Those wool slacks are tailored and cost almost as much."

Ben stood up quickly. "What're you tryin' to say? I work hard for my money!"

Gifford glanced out the window toward the bicycle rack, then stared directly into Ben's eyes. "Ollie doesn't pay you that much," he said evenly, as Ben looked away.

"What's it to *you?*" Ben protested hotly, glaring at his teacher. "It's *my* money, ain't it?"

Gifford shook his head slowly, then looked up at Ben, who stood rigid and tight-fisted in front of him. "First of all—you look ridiculous dressed like that for school!"

"Whatta' you talkin' about?" Ben snapped, his eyes blazing. "I got the best stuff in the men's department. The man told me it was what they wore on Park Avenue."

"You look like a little boy dressing up in his daddy's clothes—trying to play grownup, Ben," Gifford admonished, a gentle light playing in his strange, sad eyes. "A seventeen-year-old boy masquerading as a forty-year-old businessman. It's not an outfit for school—it's a costume for trick or treat."

Ben's lips grew thin and pale—his eyes narrowed. "Don't you make fun of me!"

"Sit down, Ben," Gifford said casually, turning away—but his right foot hit the floor at a bad angle, the ankle giving way as he slumped to the floor.

Ben moved quickly to help him up.

"Stay back!" Gifford ordered, rolling over awkwardly and pushing himself to a sitting position with his good right arm. "I can handle it myself!"

Watching Gifford struggle to get up, grabbing the edge of the desk with his left hand—the strain showing on his face—Ben felt helpless and embarrassed. *Why does he have to be crippled? Why couldn't it be somebody mean?*

"You can sit down now, Ben," Gifford gasped as he gained his chair. "I won't keep you much longer."

"Good!" Ben said sharply, slumping into the chair. "Ollie's got a lot of deliveries for me to make."

"Who else are you making deliveries for, Ben?" Gifford barked in a tone Ben had never heard him use.

Caught off guard, Ben stared back wide-eyed. "Uh—uh, no-body," he stammered.

Gifford glanced toward the window. "That's your bicycle with the box on the handlebars—isn't it? What's J. T. Dickerson standing there for? Waiting for you?"

Ben got up and walked to the window. His face went pale as he saw J. T. Dickerson lounging against a tree next to his bicycle. "How do I know what that *winehead* wants?"

"I don't think he's waiting around down there for a prescription, Ben," Gifford replied.

Ben sat with his head down, elbows resting on his knees, staring at the floor.

"Debbie's not worth throwing your life away, Ben," Gifford said in an even tone.

Ben's head snapped up. "You leave her out of this! She don't mean nothin' to me!"

Gifford continued as if Ben had said nothing. "She may grow up to be a fine woman—or maybe not—she's got some good qualities. Right now she's just trying any way she can to get the attention she's not getting at home. She's not capable of any kind of commitment to one boy—not now anyway."

"Shut up about her!"

"So there's no use ruining your future," Gifford continued in a steady voice. "Besides, you're going about it the wrong way."

Ben looked up, a quizzical expression on his face.

"Why do you think she was attracted to you in the first place?" Gifford asked, hoping that Ben would see what he was doing to himself. "You wore khakis and flour-sack shirts then."

How could he tell? Ben thought.

"I know what the shirt was made of, because my mother used the same kind of flour sacks." Gifford answered the unspoken question. "But, what Debbie saw in you, Ben, was something none of the boys in that silver-spoon crowd had. Something born of hard work and shouldering the responsibilities of a man. And that rarest of qualities—putting other people ahead of yourself, in spite of the cost."

The anger had gone out of Ben and he listened intently. "I don't understand all this."

"Just think about it for a minute," Gifford said. "What Debbie saw was a sensitive, intelligent young man—someone gentle and kind that she could trust. Now—what have you become, Ben?"

"I don't know. What?" Ben asked wearily, leaning forward on the edge of his chair.

"That's something you'll have to learn for yourself," Gifford said, throwing some papers into his briefcase. "More importantly—be sure it's the kind of man you want to become."

Ben's clear gray eyes brightened with thought. Searching inwardly, he asked Gifford. "There's a poem in that last book you let me borrow about a man walking in the woods and coming to a fork in the road. Is that kinda what you're talking about?"

"That's it exactly, Ben. It's called 'The Road Not Taken,' by Robert Frost. Read it again—several times—memorize it," Gifford said, glancing back out the window. "Now you'd better hurry. I think your customer's getting a little shaky."

And he was! J. T. Dickerson walked back and forth next to Ben's bicycle, rubbing his hands together. His greasy tie hung at an odd angle, twisted around with the label showing. When he saw Ben trotting down the front steps of the school building, he hurried clumsily toward him. "Ah, Ben," J.T. expounded, running his hand through his long, oily hair. "Sound of mind and limb I see. I was afraid some misfortune had befallen you."

Ben walked quickly past him. "You was afraid your supply was cut off, J.T.," he said, not looking back.

J.T. stumbled after him, his wobbly legs barely holding him erect as his foot caught the root of a tree. "You cut me to the quick, son," he protested. "You know I've always been fond of you."

"You never said two words to me until the last couple of months, J.T.," Ben shot back, whirling around. "And don't call me 'son.' I already got one daddy that's a drunk. I don't need another one!"

"Sorry, Ben," J.T. said, trying to catch his breath after his short run. "It's the nature of the malady. I find myself assuming any posture these days—no matter how degrading—for a drink. Even lying, for that next 'snort'—to use the vernacular."

"J.T.," Ben said, tying his books to the small rack mounted on the back fender. "You gotta quit hangin' around me. People are gettin' suspicious. You're gonna get me in big trouble."

J.T. gave Ben a hang-dog look. "You're right, of course. Never could learn to control my impulses."

Ben sat on his bicycle, his left foot on the ground for balance. "I reckon you're just loaded down with money—ain't you, J.T.?"

"I find myself thrown in with a rather impecunious crowd these days, Ben," J.T. said absently, wiping his face with a handkerchief and still breathing heavily.

Ben shook his head, smiling sadly at the wreck of a man before him. "Meet me at the regular place," he said, riding away. "We'll see what we can work out."

"You're a prince, Ben Logan!" J.T. called to him.

As Ben rode toward Ollie's, he remembered one morning last week when he had started out on his paper route and had seen J.T. walking down the highway next to Three Corners. Stopping near the Texaco pump, Ben had told him good morning. He continued along the side of the road, passing within ten feet of Ben, never seeing him. As he walked by, Ben heard him mumbling to himself. "You're a walking misery, J. T. Dickerson. A nighttime, 'fraid of the dark—rambling, shambling—mumbling, stumbling, worthless, midnight sorrow. Do yourself a favor—get a gun and . . . and do . . . what? Have fun—fun with a gun—a gun is fun. . . ." Ben watched him weaving along toward the red glow in the east.

After stopping at Hightower's, Ben rode down the narrow dusty road past Creel's Junkyard, a brown paper package inside his delivery box. He leaned his bicycle against the back porch, listening to the sounds his mother made as she prepared supper.

"I found this on the side of the road, Mama," Ben said, walking in the back door. "Might as well see what it is."

"Why're you home so early today?" Jewel Logan asked, laying her knife among the potatoes she was peeling.

"Just wanted to come by for a minute," Ben said, pouring a cup of coffee. "Can't stay—lots of deliveries today."

Jewel wiped her hands on her apron, sitting down at the table and unwrapping the package. "Land sakes, Ben!" she exclaimed, her gray eyes wide with wonder. "Where in the world did you get the money for this?"

"Ollie gave me a pretty good raise," Ben lied, watching his mother's eyes light up with pleasure for the first time in a long while. *It's worth doin' this to see that smile on her face.*

Jewel held the blue flowered dress up in front of her, hands tracing the delicate white lace trim. "Oh, Ben!" she cried, "I've never seen anything so beautiful. You really shouldn't spend your money on something so fancy though. Maybe I'll just take it back—"

"No, you won't, Mama," Ben protested, sipping the hot coffee. "It's about time you had something nice."

"Well—I'll just put it up and save it for Easter Sunday then," Jewel smiled. "It'll be my special dress."

"Fine with me, 'long as you keep it," Ben agreed, kissing his mother on the cheek. "Gotta get goin'."

"Ben," Jewel said, standing up and placing her hands on his shoulders. "You're workin' too hard. We'll get by without all these things you're buyin' for me and the children."

"You're right, Mama," Ben nodded, setting his cup in the dishpan. "Gotta think more 'bout my education. Another week or two, I'm cuttin' way back on my—deliveries."

*   *   *

"In the Mood" was playing on the jukebox as Ben washed glasses behind the counter at Ollie's soda fountain. He was smiling at the decision he had made, keeping time to the music as he worked. Looking around at the shining floor he had just mopped and the tables and booths sparkling from his cleaning, he thought for the hundredth time. *I love this place. I could spend the rest of my life here.*

"Hey, soda jerk!" Keith Demerie rumbled in his deep voice, walking in the door with Debbie Lambert. "Think you could spare enough time from your housekeeping to fix us a couple of chocolate malts?"

With a quick glance toward Demerie, Ben replied, "Two chocolate malts, coming up," and picked up two clean glasses from the shelf in front of the mirror. He flipped two scoops of vanilla ice cream into each of the tall, silvery containers, squirted chocolate syrup from the dispenser on top of the ice cream and poured in milk. Taking the top off the ceramic crock with Borden's Malt in blue letters on the side, he spooned in the malt. The mixing machine whirred loudly as Ben set each of the metal cups under the bladed shaft.

As Ben bustled around the soda fountain, Demerie stood at the jukebox, his lips drawn back in a half-smile, glancing occasionally over his shoulder at Debbie, who sat at a table next to the front window. When the song ended, "Whistle While You Work" from Walt Disney's *Snow White* began playing as Keith sauntered over to the soda fountain. Looking at Ben, he said, "Take a lesson from the song."

Ben said nothing as he stabbed two long spoons into the malts, walked over to Debbie, and set them on the table.

Demerie followed him to the table. "I'm serious, Ben. You could whistle while you wash the dishes. You know—act like one of the seven dwarfs. I think Dopey would just suit you."

Ben watched Debbie smile—placing her hand over her mouth and looking down at the table—and he saw himself as a kind of insect someone had stepped on. Then he saw nothing!

With a rush of fire in his veins, Ben spun with incredible speed, slapping Demerie across the mouth with the back of his right hand. His lip split open like a ripe plum, spurting blood across the front of Ben's white shirt. As Demerie shook his head, Ben grabbed a handful of hair with his left hand, pulled Demerie down and toward him and drove his hard right fist into the solar plexus.

With a whoosh of air from his lungs, Demerie went down on his hands and knees. Ben grabbed another handful of hair, pulling his right fist back to drive it into Demerie's face, when Ollie Caston wrapped his arms around Ben from behind, dragging him backward, away from his bloodied victim. Demerie lay doubled up on the floor, gasping to draw air into his burning lungs.

"Ben! Ben! Stop it!" Caston shouted in Ben's ear, holding him tightly. "Settle down!"

Ben slowly saw through a red haze, like looking through a glass coated with a thin film of blood. Debbie was kneeling next to Demerie, crying—almost hysterical. Ben felt his body go limp. *I wonder what happened to Keith?* he thought briefly, even though it flashed before his eyes in precise detail. It was as though he had watched himself hitting Demerie—had seen the sadistic smile on his own face.

"Come with me, Ben," Ollie demanded, clutching him tightly

by the back of his neck and pulling him around behind the counter toward the stockroom.

Ben sat on a cardboard box of Hershey's chocolate syrup in the stockroom, head in his hands.

"Ben," Caston began in a calm tone. "I'm gonna try to make this right with Keith and Senator Demerie, but I can't guarantee anything."

"Yes sir."

"I heard him goading you into it," Caston continued, "but that gave you no right to do what you did."

Ben looked up into Caston's clear brown eyes, thinking what a good man he was to work for—how much he enjoyed this job.

"If it doesn't work out—" Caston warned, as Ben looked back at the floor, "I may have to let you go."

Ben glanced out the back door at the little black-and-white terrier, trotting down the alley.

"Now go ahead and make your deliveries," Caston said. "You're still on the payroll."

*　*　*

"This is yore big chance, boy," Sonny Mullins whined, taking a long swallow of his R.C. "Yes sir, you gonna make *big* money from now on—if you do what *I* say!"

"I'm thinkin' about quittin', Sonny," Ben replied, standing next to his bicycle in the alley. "I don't think it's worth the risk anymore. If I got caught, it would just about kill Mama."

Mullins slouched against the fence in his usual position. "Never figured you for a mama's boy, Logan. Guess some fellers can't turn loose of them apron strings."

Ben's eyes narrowed. "You better watch your mouth, you dried up piece of beef jerky! I said I'm gonna *quit* and there ain't a *thing* you can do about it."

"Don't be so all fired touchy, Logan," Mullins peeped, his eyes growing wide. "Can't a feller pick at you a little?"

"I'll finish out the week—then I'm through!" Ben said evenly, stacking the last bottle in his delivery box.

"Well," Mullins squeaked, dropping his R.C. bottle for effect. "How 'bout finishin' up in style?"

"No riddles today, Sonny."

Mullins grinned crookedly. "There's a railroad sidin' twenty miles east of here—you know, jist across the county line where that water tank is."

"I know the place."

"The business is kinda growin'," Mullins said expansively, lifting a pack of Camels from the pocket of his starched white shirt—an oil slick on the collar where he had combed his hair. "Need somebody to drive a carload over there tomorrow night."

"Not interested," Ben said flatly.

"Pays fifty dollars," Mullins smirked, striking a kitchen match on the drugstore wall.

That'd pay off the rest of Pete's doctor bill—plus another month's rent. "One trip—then I'm through," Ben said flatly.

"Figured you'd see it my way," Mullins gloated through the screen of smoke rising from his cigarette.

"What's the plan?"

Sonny pointed at his feet. "Meet me right here at ten. Go drop it off. Come straight back. Whole thing oughten to take no more than two hours—three at the most."

"I'll be here," Ben assured him, riding away on his bicycle, "but this is my first and last trip."

* * *

The darkness gradually began to brighten around the edges, the glimmerings moving together—becoming a painful glare. Ben felt that his skull had been cracked, and he wouldn't move his head for fear that his brain would slide out on the rough concrete floor he found himself lying on. As he rose toward consciousness, the pain seemed to intensify—seemed to be emanating from the harsh white light directly above his head.

Ben rolled over on his side, pain like daggers piercing his head. As he slowly sat up, he saw that he was in a bare room about six feet wide by eight feet long. It had cinderblock walls on three sides—the fourth was made of vertical iron bars with a door of the same construction. A single narrow window opened like a rectangular wound in the outside wall.

"Head feels like it was used for battin' practice, don't it, boy?" Ring Clampett sat in a ladder-back chair, his feet propped on a battered gray table that held a tin-can ashtray, a stained coffee cup, and a ragged copy of the *Police Gazette*. He wore khakis and scuffed brown cowboy boots—a large silver badge hanging from the left pocket of his shirt.

Ben pushed himself over to the wall, leaning back against it and trying to make some sense of the situation. He remembered meeting Sonny at the alley—driving down the back road in the clattering Model T, gravel clanking against its underside. At the county line where two oaks spread their limbs across the road, forming an arch, he saw Ring Clampett parked in his black pickup with the white town marshal emblem on the door.

Then he knew what had happened to him. Clampett pulled him over, making him lie face down in the gravel road while he searched the car. When he opened the rumble seat, he whistled loudly and said to Ben, "Whooeee! They was shore right about you, boy! You got enough corn squeezin's in there to keep me drunk fer a year!" Ben jumped up and scrambled for the woods—and then the lights went out.

"Get yoreself together, boy," Clampett said, a line of tobacco juice staining the right corner of his mouth and chin. "You got a 'pointment with the judge in fifteen minutes."

"Can I use the bathroom?" Ben asked, looking around the tiny room that served as the town marshal's office.

Clampett pointed to the corner of the cell to Ben's right. "You're settin' nearbout on top of it."

Ben's head was clearing—his eyes focusing on a round hole in the floor. Near it a foul liquid was pooled in small hollows of the concrete and the smell of human waste hit him, turning his stomach.

Later Ben walked the half block to the courthouse, hands cuffed behind his back—Clampett close beside him twirling his sawed-off Louisville Slugger like a cheerleader's baton. A heavy mist hung in the early morning air, lending an unnatural quietness to the town. Standing watch over the courthouse on all four sides, the live oaks appeared to be burning with a heavy wet smoke. Ben thought of an execution scene in a novel he had read years ago, where a man was led before a firing squad on just such a morning.

Massive white columns flanked all four sides of the court-house in the style of classic Greek revival architecture. Shadowed by Clampett, Ben climbed the wide stone steps, entering through the carved oak doors into a spacious foyer. They stepped through a frosted glass door to the right, climbing stairs that led to the court-room.

Outside the judge's chambers, Clampett cuffed Ben to a heavy iron ring set into the wall. "Be back in a minute," he sneered, glancing at Ben's manacled wrist. "Don't go runnin' off now."

"Mornin', Judge," Clampett nodded to Morton Spain who sat stiffly behind a huge mahogany desk with a brass plate bearing the name *Garron K. Stone* attached to a small slab of black marble.

Spain patted the few strands of gray and black hair that were combed across his scalp. "I'm only the *ad hoc* in Judge Stone's absence, Ring. I'm not the judge."

"Mornin' then, Ad Hoc," Clampett beamed, gloating over his capacity for learning.

Spain lowered his head, sighing heavily. "You got that Logan boy out there?"

"Yes sir," Clampett replied proudly, jerking his thumb toward the door. "Gonna send him up the river?"

"He's under age, Ring," Spain said, his face clouding over. *If only I could! That white trash son-of-a-drunk! Come sniffing around Angela in my own home!* Remembering his wife's flushed excitement the night she asked Ben in for hot chocolate, Spain felt a burning pain deep in his chest. "He'll pay for what he did to the Demerie boy at Ollie's, though. Rest assured of that."

Clampett smiled ominously, a drop of tobacco juice sliding down his chin. "We ready for court?"

"Bring him in," Spain ordered, getting out of his chair and reaching for the black robe that hung on an antique clothes tree next to the desk. "And Ring—?"

"Yes sir?"

"Leave that club in here. You look like some kind of Alley Oop."

The hearing was so blatantly a "kangaroo court" that Morton Spain could very easily have been awarded "Marsupial of the Year" honors. No bill of information was filed, no access to an attorney was provided, and the charges were not read to the defendant. The trial began as the clock on the courthouse struck the first note on its seven o'clock announcement to the townspeople and ended five minutes later.

Ben sat between his mother and Rachel. Earl Logan had refused to come—his only explanation—"Serves him right!"

"Since I can't put you in the pen where you belong for cheating your country out of its rightful liquor tax," Spain pronounced vindictively, the gavel poised above the bench, "I hereby adjudicate you to be delinquent and place you on probation for an indefinite period, under the supervision of our town marshal, Ring Clampett. Mr. Clampett may impose any conditions he deems appropriate during the course of your rehabilitation."

The gavel came down with a bang, startling Clampett, whose eyelids were already beginning to droop.

"And Logan," Spain said sternly, rising from the bench, "that includes detaining you in the town's holding cell for a period not to exceed forty-eight hours—which is legal for a juvenile as long as he's separate from the adult population."

Spain thought of his wife at home alone, waiting for Ben. "You have an alternative, Logan," he offered. "I'll suspend this judgment for a period of one week to give you time to join any one of the armed services. If at the end of that period, you have not done so— you belong to Marshal Clampett here."

"What does all that mean, Ring?" Ben whispered to the marshal.

Clampett was scratching his head. "I'll explain later, boy," he answered absently, whirling to catch Spain, who was striding out of the courtroom, his black robe billowing out behind him.

9

THE MUTT

Mama—I ain't got much choice," Ben declared flatly, sitting at the white enameled table in the kitchen. "Somebody's givin' orders to Ring, and he's havin' a lot of fun takin' 'em. Just as much as told me I could expect to be spendin' most of my weekends in that holdin' cell of his—grinnin' and tappin' that baseball bat on his hand the whole time he was talkin' to me. Said he'd lock me up if I spit on the sidewalk."

Jewel Logan sat across the table from her son, her face dark with concern. "Oh, Ben!" she sighed deeply. "Why did you ever let that Sonny Mullins talk you into doin' such things? He ain't never been nothin' but trouble!"

"It's not his fault, Mama," Ben confessed, reaching behind him for the coffee pot on the stove. "*I'm* to blame. Nobody *made* me do anything I didn't want to."

"Made you do what?" Pete asked, slamming the back door. "What's goin' on?"

"Hush, Pete!" Jewel admonished, holding her finger to her mouth. "Go do your homework."

"Ain't got none."

Ben finished pouring his coffee. "You always say that, Pete. Your grades say something else."

"That's right," Jewel agreed. "They say you just ain't *doin'* it! Now you go get them books and start *studyin'!*"

Pouring coffee into his mother's cup, Ben said, "Sit down a minute, Pete. He needs to hear this, Mama."

"Aw, I ain't got time for this," Pete moaned. "I wanna go look at my new Superman comic book."

"Won't take but a minute, Pete," Ben said, taking a Baby Ruth from his coat pocket and tossing it on the table. "And quit whinin'. It's time you started growin' up."

Pete's face brightened when he saw the candy bar. He grabbed it, sitting down and tearing the wrapper off. "Whatever you say, Ben. You know I always got time to listen to your speeches. One of my favorite things."

"I can tell," Ben grunted. Then he leaned back, sipping his coffee deliberately. "Pete, I'm joining the Navy."

Pete stopped in mid-bite, his eyes going wide. "What? The *Navy?* Why?" he mumbled through the chunk of candy.

"It's because of what the judge did, Pete," Jewel answered for Ben. "It ain't fair!"

"There's nothing for me here anyway, Mama," Ben said stolidly. "Besides—it might be fun to see some of the world. I hardly been out of this county."

"When you leavin'?" Pete coughed through a mouthful of the candy bar.

"I thought you were over that cough, Pete," Ben said. "You finish takin' that medicine?"

"Yeah." Pete replied, coughing several times more. "Reckon I'm just eatin' too fast."

Ben stood up and looked through the kitchen window. Micah was perched on a low limb of the walnut tree, his back against the trunk, shooting up at an imaginary airplane with his stick gun. Long shadows lay across the yard, reaching toward the woods. "Tomorrow morning," he answered. "Early."

"I wish I'd known you was goin' so soon, Ben," Jewel sighed, getting up from the table and standing next to him. "I could've fixed you a nice goin' away supper."

"It don't matter, Mama," Ben said, kissing his mother on the cheek. "You've fixed plenty of good suppers for me."

"You goin' on a ship?" Pete asked, swallowing the last of the candy bar.

Ben sat back down, his face heavy with thought. He felt a loneliness building up inside but didn't want to show it. "I guess so. Not at first though." He looked solemnly at Pete. "Pete, listen to me."

Pete caught the tone of his brother's voice. "Okay," he answered, folding his hands together on the table.

"I want you to look out for Micah and Dinah," Ben declared softly, looking into Pete's dark eyes. "And don't give Mama no trouble, okay? You do what she tells you."

"Yes sir!" Pete replied energetically, saluting and lifting his eyebrows in mock fear.

"I'm serious, Pete," Ben admonished. "You're gonna have to take over for me around here."

"Aw, Ben, I was just foolin'," Pete replied sheepishly. He turned to Jewel. "You can count on me, Mama."

"I know I can, son."

"Study time," Ben said, pointing out the back door toward their small bedroom.

As Pete went out the door onto the porch, Jewel sat down at the table. Her worn face was tinged with apprehension. She was a woman who had known much sorrow, but losing Ben cut her like a knife. "Ben, you'll run into some mighty bad company in the service," she said gravely. "Stay away from 'em, son! You was brought up to know right from wrong. I know you just about quit your church goin', but if you get a chance—go! It might bring you some comfort. It'll bring me some, knowin' you're listenin' to the Word."

Ben thought of Sunday school classes he had known as a child—the colored pictures of Moses, Samson, and David. He remembered the Christmas his class had built a Nativity scene of popsicle sticks and cardboard, and he had placed the tiny Baby Jesus in his match stick manger. But the bitterness that had built up inside him had formed a wall, and he stubbornly dumped all those memories about God into a big box and closed the lid. "I worked a deal with Ollie, Mama," he said, ignoring her request.

Jewel held her cup in both hands, sipping the coffee slowly. "He always was a nice fellow," she remarked absently, trying to picture those remote, unknown places and people that would have her son.

"I'm gonna have my allotment check sent to the drugstore," Ben continued. "Mama, are you listenin'?"

"Yes," Jewel almost whispered, turning toward her son. "My mind wanders sometimes."

Ben stood up and put his cup in the dishpan. "Anyhow, Ollie said you could pick the check up every month. It'll be just like me givin' you money when I was workin' there."

"That's a mighty fine thing to do, son," Jewel said, her eyes turned upward toward Ben, filled with a deep sadness and an even deeper love. "You always was the most thoughtful of my children."

"Ollie said he'd even cash the check for you. Save you from havin' to go someplace else. All you have to do is sign it. It'll be made out in your name."

Jewel continued to gaze at her son, saying nothing.

"Remember to get the money, Mama," Ben insisted firmly, worried that she seemed so unconcerned. "I didn't tell Daddy nothin' about this. See that it stays that way."

"I will, son," Jewel replied, looking toward the window where a pale orange afterglow was filling the yard. "Ben? Yore daddy wants to take you to the bus in the mornin'."

"Mama, I—"

"He ain't askin' much, Ben," Jewel pleaded quickly.

He looked down into his mother's gray eyes. "All right, Mama. I'll do it for you."

Ben went onto the back porch, opening the narrow door of his bedroom. Pete was sprawled on the middle cot, reading a Superman comic book by the light filtering in from the single small window next to Ben's cot. "That your English book, little brother?"

Pete quickly stuffed the comic under his pillow, opening his history text. "Just looked at it a little bit."

"Forget it for a minute," Ben said, sitting down on his cot. He reached into his hidden compartment in the wall, pulling out a roll of dollar bills and his picture of Debbie. He slipped the picture into his coat pocket and tossed the money to Pete.

"What's this?" Pete asked, staring wide eyed at the roll of money.

"The first of three gifts," Ben replied with a wry smile. "Jesus got gold, frankincense, and myrrh. You get the money, my quilt, and my cot by the window."

"Oh, boy! I can—"

"Settle down, little brother," Ben ordered. "There's twenty-seven dollars there and it ain't all yours. I want you to share it with Dinah and Micah. Stop at Ollie's once in a while and get ya'll a malt or something—maybe a Moon Pie now and then at Three Corners. Make it last as long as you can. And Pete—bring home a loaf of bread, milk, meat—something to help Mama out sometimes."

"You can count on me, Ben," Pete said in his best grown-up voice, holding the money tightly. "Everybody'll get treated right. I won't take more than my share."

"I'm gonna miss you, little brother," Ben said, lying back on his cot, staring at the ceiling.

Pete was silent a moment. "You, too."

* * *

Rachel stood at the intersection where her road joined with Ben's. *Last time I'll meet him here,* she thought—*maybe for a long, long time. I don't know if I can stand not seeing him walking down this road every mornin' with Dinah and his brothers—talkin' with him on the way to school. Oh, Lord, help me! It'll be so lonely here with Ben gone!*

A dull aching began to fill Rachel—heavy and cold, like an iron bar lying against her heart. She felt herself trembling—a weakness washed over her like a warm wave, and she thought she would faint. Sitting under the huge oak, she leaned back against the rough bark and closed her eyes until the feeling passed.

When she opened her eyes, Rachel saw Ben walking toward her, his shining black hair whipped about his face by the March wind. *I love to watch him walk. He moves so easily—almost like a deer. Ben, can't you see how I feel about you? Don't you care about me at all?*

"Hey, Rachel," Ben called out, waving to her. "What in the world are you doin' here?"

Rachel stood up, brushing off her flowered dress—pulling her thin wool coat together with both hands, against the March wind. "Dinah told me you'd be coming back to town," she said. "Something about gettin' your bus ticket."

"Yeah. They didn't have it ready this mornin'," Ben complained, stopping in front of Rachel. "Daddy told me that's the way the military operates. That I better get used to it."

"Why didn't you ride your bicycle in?" Rachel asked, looking into Ben's clear gray eyes. "It'd be a lot faster since you don't have much time left to be with your family."

"I'll never ride that thing again," he said flatly. "I gave it to Pete—after I took that box off."

"Ben," Rachel asked softly, "do you mind if I walk into town with you? We might not see each other for a long time."

"Fine with me," Ben agreed, striding off down the road. "Don't see why you'd want to, though. This wind'll cut you in two. Hope the Navy sends me someplace warm."

"You don't even know where you're goin'?"

"Nah. Navy recruiter said everthing would be in with the bus ticket," Ben answered, striding three steps ahead of Rachel.

Rachel hurried to catch up with him. "Looks like they'd at least tell you what ship you'll be on."

"I won't be on a ship for a while," Ben laughed. "And I don't *care* where they send me—long as it's away from *this* dump!"

"Ben?"

"Yeah?" Ben answered, looking back over his shoulder as Rachel struggled to keep up.

"Could you slow down a little?" she asked, the pace beginning to tell on her.

Ben stopped, allowing her to draw abreast of him. "Sorry, Rachel. Guess I'm just ready to get out of this town."

"I know they gave you a hard time, Ben," Rachel admitted. "But the world's full of people who don't do right."

"Maybe so, but the only ones who ain't doin' me right live in Liberty, Georgia."

Coming to the intersection, Ben glanced at Three Corners, remembering, as always, the day his daddy gave him the blue ball. They crossed the highway, walking by a pasture with guernseys and holsteins bunched together, their backs against the wind that swept across the rolling hills. Sparrows hopped about in the dry grasses, their feathers ruffled against the cold.

When they reached town, Ben walked up to the glass door with *Navy Recruiter* labeled in white. Looking inside, he turned back to Rachel. "Guess he's gone for the day. Said it'd be in the mailbox if he was."

Rachel watched as Ben took a large brown envelope from the blue mailbox with a ship painted on it, next to the door. "Aren't you going to look inside?"

"Nah. Plenty of time for that when I get home," Ben said off-handedly, stuffing the envelope inside his jacket. "We'd better get on home. It'll be pitch dark 'fore you know it."

The street lights were coming on, the town almost deserted. As they walked along the sidewalk next to a white picket fence, the sounds of "I'll Be Seeing You" drifted faintly from a side window of the house. Ben felt an emptiness—dry and sharp as the March wind—welling up inside him. He couldn't have known that it marked the path of his life—that part where childhood ended.

Continuing on through the darkening town, Ben saw something lying in the gutter near the alley next to Ollie's Drugstore. As he got closer, he recognized the little black-and-white terrier that he had seen trotting all over town for years. Limp and lifeless now— crushed by someone speeding home to a hot meal, or to an empty room littered with bottles—he lay like a cast-aside toy.

Ben knelt beside him, touching the white spot on his left shoulder. "He's still warm. Must have just happened."

"Who does he belong to?" Rachel asked, placing her hand on Ben's shoulder and squatting beside him.

"No one—the whole town I guess," Ben said in a somber tone. "Can't just leave him here."

"What'll we do with him then?" Rachel asked. "No place to put him around here."

Ben picked the small creature up, cradling him in his arms. "I'll bury him on the way home."

Rachel looked into Ben's face as he held the terrier, but what she saw was his heart—the heart of someone touched by a loss that no one else had noticed. *I hope nothing changes your heart, Ben.*

Ben stood up, walking over to Ollie's window. Gazing inside he saw the bright mirrored soda fountain with its shining glasses and dishes—the table in front where Debbie always sat—the slow moving colors of the bubbles in the jukebox. He remembered what a good friend Ollie Caston had been to him. *But the deal is done now.*

Twenty-five minutes later, they reached Three Corners. Ben laid the terrier on one of the benches in front of the store and walked around to the side of the store away from the highway. Gleaming dully in the dim light filtering through the store windows, the ground there was hard-packed and greasy from years of oil changes, mechanic work, and tire fixing. Ben found a tire iron leaning against the side of the building, picked it up and walked toward the back.

"What're you doin'?" Rachel asked, hurrying after him, the wind whipping her dress about her slim legs.

"Gonna dig a hole and bury him," Ben pronounced, rounding the corner of the building.

Rachel squatted down beside a pine tree, pulling the hem of her dress down to her ankles, hugging herself to keep warm. "Can you dig a hole with that thing?" she asked into the face of the wind.

Ben didn't answer but brushed aside the leaves with his shoe and began to dig. When he had finished, he walked around the corner of the store, returning in a few moments with the terrier. He lined the bottom of the hole with leaves, lay the small dog inside, covered it with more leaves, then with dirt, packing it with his foot.

Ben stood for a full minute, staring at the freshly turned earth. "He didn't even have a name that I knew of. Everybody just called him *dog* or *pup*. Now here he is layin' out here in the ground— nobody'll even miss him." He stared down at the small mound, grief stirring in him. "You know, Rachel, sometimes I feel I ain't nothin' more than this ol' mutt here."

Rachel stood up and stepped close to Ben, holding his arm. She shivered as the dark wind touched her. "Ben?"

"Yeah, Rachel?"

"You think my daddy loves me?"

Puzzled, Ben glanced down at her. "Love you? Why, I never saw a man love anybody so much!"

"What if you and me were both dying somehow—you know, drowning or something—and he could only save one of us."

Ben looked into Rachel's upturned face. It seemed almost luminescent in the pale light shining through the back window. "What in the world are you talking about?"

"If he chose you," Rachel continued, her eyes bright with emotion. "Saved you and let me drown. Would you think that he loved you?"

Ben was silent.

"That's what God did for you, Ben. He let His *only* child—His Son, Jesus—die for you. Do you think God loves *you*?"

Ben turned away, squatting by the grave.

"He even knows about this ol' mutt here," Rachel said quietly.

"How do you know that?" Ben asked, looking up.

Rachel knelt down beside Ben, her hand on his shoulder. "The Bible says that even a little sparrow doesn't fall to the ground without God being there."

Ben looked back at the grave. "I remember some of the Bible from when I used to go to Sunday school. Don't make much sense anymore. Just comes back to me in bits and pieces now."

Rachel was staring at the grave, her hand resting on Ben's shoulder, steadying her against the gusts of wind.

"You're a good friend, Rachel," Ben said, placing his left hand over hers. He noticed her hair shimmering in the pale light from the store window—felt its softness as it brushed against his cheek.

* * *

Ben lay on his cot in the still darkness, pulling his quilt around him for warmth—feeling the love his mother had placed in it with each stitch—feeling a part of her was there keeping the cold away. He knew he was in those hard hours after midnight—felt the blood sluggish in his veins—the empty hollow feeling that comes with too little sleep and too much thought. *The Hour of the Wolf. Is that what it's called?* Pete coughed in his sleep and turned over. Ben heard the back door open—a heavy tread on the porch—his bedroom door moved inward, creaking on its hinges.

"Son—? It's time to get up," Earl Logan said, gently placing his hand on Ben's shoulder.

Son? Ol' man's gettin' soft. What happened to "boy"? "I'm awake, Daddy."

"I got a fire in the stove," Logan said. "Time you get ready, I'll have coffee made."

Ben sat on the edge of the cot, his quilt wrapped around him for the last time, feeling the draft from the window he always raised an inch, except in the coldest weather. Dressing slowly, he felt the presence of his brothers in the tiny room they had shared since Micah was born. Pete coughed as Ben finished dressing and stood up. He placed the quilt on his sleeping brother, tucking it under the thin mattress. Kissing Micah on his tousled head, Ben stepped through the door of the tiny bedroom and walked down the path to the well. As he was finishing his Mason jar of water, Ben heard his father behind him.

"I seen you standing here so many times," Earl Logan said, "looking off in the distance, drinking from that ol' Mason jar. What crosses yore mind here, son?"

Ben thought of all his dreams, all the places his mind had taken him during the hundreds of times he had stood here, drinking from this same Mason jar. "Nothin'."

After coffee, Ben was walking across the yard toward the pulp-wood truck where his father sat behind the wheel, warming up the clattering, coughing engine. Above the roar of the machine, Ben heard his mother's voice. Turning, he saw her waving to him from the front porch. She came hurriedly down the steps in the dim light that spilled from the open door. Barefooted and wearing her flannel robe, she ran across the cold ground to him.

Earl Logan sat in the dark and the noise and the greasy smell of the truck, watching his wife lay her hands on the head of their son. Ben stood with his head bowed, arms hanging loosely at his side while his mother prayed for him. Earl saw his wife trembling slightly, lifting her left arm toward the heavens—saw her take Ben's face in her hands, kiss him on the cheek, and go back into the house.

When they got to town, Earl parked on a side street and they walked around the corner to the bus stop—two concrete-and-wood benches covered by a tin roof and walled halfway up on three sides. A small blue-and-white sign tacked to one of the supports carried a picture of a greyhound in full stride.

"I guess we ain't exactly been close these last few years, son," Earl Logan mumbled, glancing at his son.

Where'd that come to you—gettin' drunk at Shorty's or sneakin' around "Moon" Mullins' house in the middle of the night? Ben leaned back on the bench, arms folded across his chest, looking at a crescent moon that hung above the town.

"Anyhow, I reckon I ought to tell you about—you know, now that you're goin' in the service—about how . . ."

"I took biology, Daddy," Ben interrupted. "I know women are different from men."

Logan leaned forward, elbows resting on his knees. "Well, there's a little more to it than that. First of all—"

"I'll figure it out for myself," Ben said flatly. "Like I done everything else."

"I know I ain't been the daddy I shoulda been, son," Logan said, rubbing the back of his neck with his right hand. He made a bulky, awkward shape as he stared down at his worn boots. He was not a man of words, not the kind he wanted to use now, at least. Thoughts came to him of how he had felt the night this tall son of his had been born—how he had dreamed of a day when his son would grow up and make something of himself. He was ashamed of his occupation, though he would never admit it to a living soul. He was ashamed of his failures as a father and as a husband. "If I had been, you wouldn't of got in that mess and had to leave town."

"You didn't make me do it."

Logan continued as if Ben hadn't spoken. "Lord, I hate to see this happenin'! I messed up bad myself. Got kicked out of school. You see what kinda work I gotta do."

Ben looked at his father's scarred and calloused hands. He remembered as a child, the first time he noticed that the little finger of his father's left hand was missing. "What happened, Daddy?" he had asked. His father had picked him up, tossing him high in the air and catching him. "A bear bit it off."

"Did you know the head coach from Georgia Tech come down and talked to me my junior year in school?" Logan asked suddenly, staring at the sidewalk.

"You never told me that," Ben said, looking at his father in genuine surprise.

Logan looked squarely at his son. "It's a fact. Tole me if I done all right my senior year, he'd give me a full scholarship. Said I was one of the quickest high school halfbacks he ever seed."

"What happened?"

"Got to thinkin' I was a big shot," Logan answered, looking back at the sidewalk. "Next year I set a school record for yards gained in a single game—first game of the season. Went out and celebrated with some of the boys. Got drunk."

"Is that all?"

"Not quite," Logan said, taking out his tobacco and cigarette papers. "Coach called us in one by one the next Monday—me last. Didn't do me no worse than anybody else, but *I* got mad. Hit him with a lucky punch that broke his jaw."

Ben remained silent, as if a word from him would abruptly end his father's story.

Logan licked both ends of his cigarette, flicked a kitchen match with his thumbnail and lit his cigarette. "Well, that ended my football playin'. No more high school—no college."

"They put you out of school for good?"

"Yeah," Logan said bitterly, drawing deeply on his cigarette, its red tip glowing in the near dark.

Father and son sat on opposite ends of a bench at a bus stop in a little town in Georgia, immured by their separate thoughts—the father, gazing back on the sad clutter of his years—the son, running from an all-too-certain present toward a cloudy and foreboding future. The sound of a train whistle pierced the silence.

"Reckon I better git goin', son," Logan said, standing up. "The work's an hour's drive from here."

Ben stood up and faced his father. "Thanks for the lift," he said evenly.

"Take care of yoreself," Logan replied, his right hand rising slightly toward Ben—then dropping back to his side.

"You, too, Daddy."

Ben watched his father disappear around the corner—heard the roar of the truck engine starting—sat back on the bench, staring at the moon in its slide toward the earth.

Ten minutes later he saw Ring Clampett ambling along the sidewalk toward him, the headlights of the bus closing in on him from behind. Ben stood at the curb as the bus pulled over, its brakes hissing loudly on the quiet street. The door slammed open. Turning quickly and glaring at Clampett who was twenty feet away, Ben spat on the sidewalk and stepped aboard the bus.

Part 2

THE SAILOR

10

THE SUICIDE LESSON

*I*n the blue distance, the mountains rose like an impassable barrier, guarding the ends of the earth. Snow gleamed in the mid-morning sun along the shoulders of jagged rock, reaching upward to the peaks. Somewhere in this high lonesome world, the great iron gates of winter were slowly closing—the warm sleep of the cold time coming to an end—the earth below, stirring with new life.

Ben had gone to sleep in the early morning hours, the clacking rhythm of the rails acting like a narcotic on him. When he opened his eyes, there they were—bigger than the earth itself—higher than the moon—so beautiful it hurt to look at them!

Atlanta had been a honking blare of car horns and a rush of people in the station—the train ride, one town after another, tiresome in their unrelenting sameness. He sat on the tobacco-smelling cloth seats of the Pullman, watching the countryside roll by, seeing little, lost in thoughts of home—until he saw the mountains. Although he would see them again, they would never have that same heart-stopping, pristine beauty they held the first time he saw them.

As the train pulled into the station in San Diego, Ben still saw the mountains—couldn't get them out of his mind—was still in a daze of craggy peaks and sun-filled, alpine valleys when he stepped off the train with several other soon-to-be sailors.

"All right, you bunch of slime," the bull-necked, bullet-headed petty officer bellowed, pointing to them with a stubby, brown finger. "Get on that bus!"

The mountains disappeared. Ben looked toward the gray bus the man in the bell-bottomed jeans and light blue shirt was pointing at—stunned, like the others, at the sudden, overwhelming power of his presence and his voice.

"Move! Move! Move!" the man screamed, punctuating each word with a sweeping movement of his arm. "We ain't got all night to get you little girls tucked in! You're the last ten we need to fill out the company! The rest of 'em have been here for two days."

Ben and the other young men scrambled toward the bus, hurrying in the wake of the tirade from the simian creature wearing a man's heavy black brogans. When they were seated, he climbed aboard the bus, facing them in the aisle, his flat dark eyes scanning their faces.

"My name's Petty Officer Perez!" the man growled. "I'll take over where your mamas left off. Who's got the papers?"

The officer in Jackson, Mississippi had given all the recruits' paperwork to Bobby Lee Brannon to safeguard throughout the cross-country trip. Two years older than Ben, he was of medium height, broad-shouldered, with a ruddy complexion. He had green eyes, a quick smile, and hair so blond it was almost white.

Brannon rose from his aisle seat next to Ben, the thick manila folder raised in his right hand. "I do," he said, taking one step toward the front of the bus.

"I tell you to move, Maggot?" The words exploded from Perez's lips like buckshot. Before Brannon could answer, Perez took two quick steps and snatched the folder from his hand.

Brannon stood before him, dumbfounded.

"Let's get one thing straight," Perez growled. "You worms are lower than whale dung—and that's on the bottom of the ocean. You don't *move, talk,* or *think*—unless *I* tell you to. *And*—the first word out of your mouths at all times will be *Sir!*"

Ten pairs of eyes were turned in speechless disbelief toward this walking nightmare.

Perez leaned forward, his dark face two inches from Brannon's. "You understand that, Maggot?"

"Yes—"

"*Sir,* Maggot!" Perez screamed into Brannon's teeth. "The first word out of your maggot mouth is *always Sir!*"

Brannon's eyes were wide with fear as he tried to form words that wouldn't come.

"Sit down, Maggot!" Perez bellowed, hooking his left foot behind Brannon's ankles and jerking it forward, while slapping his right shoulder with an open left hand.

Before Brannon quit bouncing on the seat, Perez was starting the engine of the bus. The trip to the San Diego Naval Base was made in utter silence through the darkened town. Each of the young men felt the quasi-human driving the bus could be taking them to a place of incessant punishment for crimes they had yet to commit.

"Out! Out! Out!" Perez was screaming before the bus had come to a complete stop.

Twenty feet thundered down the aisle and onto the macadam outside a huge warehouse with a curved metal roof and gray wooden walls. They ambled about uneasily, like cattle before a storm strikes, looking around at the murky expanse of the naval base.

"Let's see if you can make two straight lines, girls," Perez said deliberately, stepping off the bus.

They couldn't.

"Too hard for you, huh?" Perez said, almost politely. "I can see you ladies ain't gonna make it." He stepped in front of Ben, their noses almost touching. "Where you from, Maggot?"

"I'm from . . ."

Perez clamped his hand over Ben's mouth. "What's wrong with your ears?" he asked, looking at the others in their two ragged lines, afraid to speak. He turned back to Ben, moved the hand from his mouth and bellowed *"Sir"* with the force of a small tornado. Then in a soft almost musical voice, Perez continued. "Sir is the *first*—I repeat, the *first* word out of your mouth. Now—let's try it again. Everyone ready? Where you from, Maggot?"

"Sir, Georgia," Ben said shakily.

"Don't sound right," Perez mused, placing the tips of his fingers against his chin. "I've got a *capital* idea," he continued. "Why don't we make *Sir* the last word out of your mouth too. Let's see how it sounds. Where you from, Maggot?"

"Sir, Georgia, sir," Ben said more clearly.

"Excellent. That where you got the peach fuzz?" Perez continued, rubbing Ben's chin with his big-knuckled hand.

Perez sidestepped in front of Brannon. "You have any idea where you come from, girlie?"

"Sir, Mississippi, sir!" Brannon said levelly, his green eyes holding Perez's onyx ones with a steady gaze.

"Mississippi! Well that pretty well says it all, don't it?" Perez sneered. "Be sure you got two buddies to witness your mark when you sign the payroll, Whitey."

"You got a name, Pock Face?" Perez rumbled, standing before a short, dark man with black curly hair.

"'Sir, Joe Tondi—New Jersey, sir," he barked quickly.

Perez placed his heavy-soled brogan on top of Tondi's foot, grinding slowly as he talked. "Anybody hear me ask Pock Face where he's from?"

Tondi's face was a mask of pain, his jaws tight as he struggled not to cry out.

Perez continued his grinding. "No one, eh? Well, Pock Face, I guess I didn't ask you where you was from."

Tondi looked directly at Perez, jaws clenched.

Easing his foot off Tondi's, Perez continued. "Now! Where you from, Pock Face."

"Sir, New Jersey, sir!"

"New Jersey? You and that other wormy little punk, Sinatra. You make the little girls scream and cry like he does?"

"Sir, no sir!"

"Where you from, Four-eyes?" Perez asked Joshua Davis, who was only two inches taller than Tondi, but heavily muscled. His brown eyes, a shade lighter than his hair, gazed placidly at Perez as though they were old friends having coffee together. He had gotten on the train in Shreveport, sitting next to Ben for part of the journey west. Ben soon learned he was not afraid to speak the name of Jesus, and he changed seats at the first opportunity.

"Sir, Louisiana, sir!"

"You shoot Huey Long?"

"Sir, no sir!"

"You look like the type. I think they made a mistake about that doctor shooting him," Perez said menacingly. "I got a gut feeling you shot him. I'm gonna be watching you close, Four-eyes. You ain't gonna murder nobody else."

Perez walked up and down in front of the two crooked lines of men, hands behind his back, shaking his head slowly. "We're gonna give each of you a field jacket—that is if you can find that warehouse behind you. It's a hundred feet long and thirty feet high, so you just may stumble onto it if I give you a day or two. Then we're gonna feed you and take you to the barracks 'til four-thirty—that's A.M. We don't want nobody gettin' bed sores in the Navy."

A tall, skinny boy with a hooked nose and wild, dark eyes raised his hand.

"Well, look at this," Perez said gleefully. "We've got our first volunteer."

"Sir, I . . ."

"Stop," Perez said firmly, but pleasantly, walking toward the boy. "I know what you want."

A nervous smile appeared on the boy's thin face as he looked down the lines at the others.

"You want to show your friends how you can do a hundred push-ups," Perez continued, his white teeth gleaming in his dark face. "I think that's splendid."

The volunteer's expression changed from nervous relief to one of bewilderment.

Perez was a foot from the boy's face when he screamed, "Hit the deck, Maggot!"

The boy tumbled onto the pavement, his long frizzy hair waving wildly as he began struggling with the first push-up.

"The rest of you stroll on over to that warehouse and get your field jackets—and bring one for the volunteer."

Ben was feeling uneasy about the way they were casually ambling along toward the warehouse, when a shout rang out in the night.

"Where do you *civilians* think you are? At a Sunday school picnic?" A man walked up, his face tense with anger. He made the word *civilian* sound like some kind of subspecies. Wearing his white cap at a rakish angle, the man made Perez look like a child. His eyes burned in the dim light, and he was striding toward them like a runaway truck. "This is Navy Boot Camp! You *double-time* everywhere you go!"

All nine men immediately froze in their tracks. With their sad, disheveled appearance, they reminded Ben of street urchins from a Dicken's novel. He glanced in Perez's direction and caught the sly smile on his face.

"Can't you do anything with this scum, Perez?" the man boomed across the street.

Perez assumed a humble posture. "They just won't listen to me, Chief. None of 'em. They think they're a tough bunch. Four-eyes there shot Huey Long—I'm pretty sure of that."

"Huey was a good man. Not like most of them big shots. He believed in the workin' man," the chief declared fervently, glaring at Davis. "I really liked ol' Huey."

Davis looked serenely back at the chief, his eyeglasses glinting in the pale street lights.

"Hit the deck!" the chief bellowed, parading in front of the men like Goliath before the Israelites.

All nine men stared at the huge man with the crooked teeth, shocked into incomprehension.

He grabbed Davis by his neck and the seat of his pants, slamming him to the pavement. "I said, HIT THE DECK!"

The rest of them fell face down in a tumbled mass, grunting as they hit the street.

"Now—give me a hundred push-ups!" the giant growled.

Grunts and groans and heavy breathing filled the damp air for two minutes as one by one the men reached their limit and collapsed gasping onto the pavement—except for Ben, Bobby Lee Brannon, and Joshua Davis. Ben gave up at eighty-three, Brannon at eighty-six, while Davis finished the course.

"Looks like this bunch is ready for the old ladies' home, Perez," the tall chief called out as he strode away down the dimly lit street.

The nine men, joined by the volunteer, formed two ragged lines and double-timed over to the warehouse. It was the biggest building Ben had ever seen, filled with aisle after aisle of twelve-foot high shelving that was stacked with coats, pants, shirts, shoes, and every other imaginable kind of military clothing and paraphernalia. Hundred-watt bulbs hanging from long cords lent a twilight look to the place with its dim recesses and wavering shadows.

Behind a linoleum-topped counter, a man about Tondi's size

sat on a high wooden stool smoking the stub of a cigar. His legs were crossed and his arms were crossed, elbows resting on his knee. He was pale to the point of whiteness, and his rheumy eyes spoke of sitting on other stools, his hand wrapped around a glass or a bottle.

The men nervously lined up in front of the counter, some still gasping for breath, all of them dreading the Navy's next surprise. They looked around furtively, half-expecting to be attacked out of the vast, towering corridors of the warehouse by a screaming horde of petty officers. Out of the corner of his eye, Ben saw Perez leaning against the main door, hairy forearms folded across his chest, observing the scene like a buyer at a livestock auction.

"Evenin', boys," the man on the stool said pleasantly. "Or is it mornin'? Hard to tell sometimes in this place. The Navy treatin' ya'll all right so far?"

You could see them relaxing—especially the men from the South. They smiled, looking at each other and back to the man on the stool.

"I'm Petty Officer Flowers," he continued, the corners of his eyes crinkling deeply as he smiled. "Promoted to chief five times— busted every single one of 'em. Mostly for bein' drunk—that and addin' to my collection of officer's teeth," he announced, holding up a small, knotty fist and inspecting it like a rare jewel. "Never cared much for officers. Reckon I still don't."

Laughter ran along the line of men like a stream of water, refreshing their spirits after the scalding words of Perez and the "Chief."

Flowers slid deftly off the stool, standing on the smooth concrete floor next to a pile of green jackets. "Everybody gets a field jacket. Don't want none of our fightin' men gettin' the sniffles."

A few chuckles among the men.

"We got two sizes," Flowers said, the harsh light glinting off his bald head. "Too big and too little—thirty-sixes and forty-eights. Have to do you 'til we get the next shipment."

With that Flowers began tossing the jackets at random to the men. Catching them, they looked them over carefully—checking the pockets, the heavy buttons, and the sizes.

"Put 'em on, *dummies!*" Perez roared from behind. "You ain't no inspectors in a garment factory!"

The men quickly struggled into the jackets. The volunteer, who was at least six-foot-three, got a thirty-six, the sleeves striking him just below the elbows, although the shoulders weren't a bad fit. Ben got a forty-eight and felt like he was wearing a circus tent. Three of the men actually had jackets that fit them.

"Hang on, boys," Flowers drawled as the men were beginning to file out of the warehouse. "You don't wanna miss the most important part of boot camp—do you?"

The men all turned around, walking back to the counter in anticipation. When they were settled, most leaning on the counter and giving him their full attention, he began.

"Suicide!" Flowers said, savoring the word. "Like everything in the Navy, we want you to have the best of instruction—see that it's done right."

Smiles were leaving the faces of the men gathered in the dead of night at the counter amid the pressing gloom of the warehouse. A foghorn sounded out on the bay, moaning like some lost soul adrift on the mist-shrouded waters.

Flowers let his words sink in. "There's usually one or two in every company that try to commit suicide—and they just end up makin' a big mess, most of the time—blood everwhere for their shipmates to clean up. One feller went through the last two months of boot camp with a crooked neck when his hangin' didn't take. Didn't get him out of the Navy though. No sir, when you join—it's for the *duration!*"

Perez still leaned against the door with his arms crossed, enjoying the show.

"Now—let me tell you about a surefire way to do away with yourself—if you really mean business," Flowers said, producing a razor blade from his shirt pocket. "First you wait 'til about two o'clock in the morning when everbody's asleep. Then you go into the head and kneel down in front of the commode. Put your elbows like this," Flowers demonstrated, "on the sides and let yore head hang right over the middle—remember, neatness counts."

A thick silence was settling over the men, standing woodenly along the counter.

Flowers held up the razor blade. "Next—you slice through the carotid artery right here, then catch the one on the other side. All you got to do now is rest on yore elbows and watch yore life drain right down the toilet. Now if you don't like this way, I got two or three others. One of 'em is bound to catch yore fancy."

The discourse on suicide lasted another ten minutes while the exhausted, homesick men stared vacantly at the skinny little drunk who had wasted his life.

On the way to the barracks, Perez instructed them in the fine art of close-order drill. They were able to assimilate the "Column left—Huuuh" and the "Column right—Huuuh" in a mere thirty minutes. In another twenty, formed up in front of the barracks, they learned "Left—Huuuh," "Right—Huuuh," and "About—Huuuh."

"That's really great, girls," Perez sneered, stalking back and forth in front of them. "A few of you could leave this place with the IQ of a stomped-on toad frog—if you pay attention real close."

The men stood limply in front of him like they were hanging on meat hooks, their eyes glazed over in utter exhaustion. A few of them began nodding off on their feet.

"Dismissed!" Perez shouted suddenly.

The startled men straightened, did the required about-faces and stormed into the barracks.

* * *

The quiet, dark barracks was a welcome relief after Perez walked into his quarters at the front on the first floor, leaving the men alone. Like all the others in this area, it was a two-story structure with two rows of bunk beds running the length of an open bay. A foot-locker sat on the floor at each end of the bunks, and a small shelf with a hanging rod for each man was attached to the wall. Across the short hall from Perez's quarters was the head with four showers.

Ben lay in the first bunk on the bottom. Above him was Bobby Lee Brannon, who was already "Whitey" to everybody, and next to them were Joshua Davis and Joe Tondi. The volunteer, Abe Meyers of New York City, was in the third bunk. Adversity had begun binding them together as a group.

Meyers sat on Ben's bunk next to him, the hollows of his long face shadowed by dim light seeping through the windows from outside. "That was a nice touch—Flowers's little discourse on suicide. Seems like such a compassionate man, too—you know, someone you could really trust—like a second father."

Ben looked at him solemnly. "He does have a lot in common with *my* father—same warmth, same bloodshot eyes, same rotten, liquor-smelling breath."

"Mine's a banker," Myers said, leaning back on his elbows. "Wanted me to follow in his exceedingly large footsteps. I couldn't stand the thought of it."

Brannon looked at Meyers in astonishment. "I'd give my right eye for my daddy to be a banker. He's a sharecropper and ain't had two nickels to rub together since I was born. Why in the world would you turn down a job like that?"

"One number's just like another to me—can't add two and two. All I wanted to do was write," Meyers responded, combing back his wiry hair with long, thin fingers.

"Yore daddy own this bank?" Brannon continued in amazement, his white hair giving off light in the darkened barracks.

"Chairman of the board," Meyers answered.

"Same thing," Tondi chimed in from his prone position, staring at the bottom of the top bunk. "That's just bank talk for being the number-one man."

"How's the writing goin'?" Joshua Davis asked, sitting on the top bunk, legs hanging over the side.

"My old man said I'd never make a penny at it. So far he's been right," Meyers responded absently. "I think he really enjoys my failures. Maybe I'll get a dishonorable discharge. His birthday's coming up next month—might be a nice present for him."

"Ya'll heard anything about the town?" Brannon drawled, looking about the small group. "Like where's the best place to get a drink of whiskey?"

Tondi sat up in his bunk. "I had a cousin joined the Navy a few years back—came here for boot camp. He said there's always a line of cabs outside the front gate. Any of the drivers can show you where the action is—day or night."

"Hope we get liberty soon," Meyers chimed in. "I'm already behind on my dissipation schedule. Liver might go on strike if it doesn't get its daily alcohol allowance."

"Anybody decided where they'd like to be sent when we finish this little boot camp tea party?" Davis asked, changing the subject.

"Who cares?" Brannon answered, as if for them all. "Long as we can get on a ship and see some of this big, wide, wicked world—and the sooner the better."

"I'm for that," Tondi chirped.

Davis pushed his glasses up the bridge of his aquiline nose with his left hand. "Maybe we'll be seeing some action, the way Hitler's been kickin' around in Central Europe."

"Never happen," Meyers said knowingly. "That Senator Borah from Idaho was right. It is the 'phony war.' Hitler's a bully. He crushed Poland 'cause their weapons were outdated fifty years. But he'll never take on a modern power like France."

Ben saw the conversation was going nowhere, but he had nothing better to do. "What about Japan? They're giving the Chinese a pretty rough time."

"That's true," Meyers agreed. "But China's all they want. You ever look on a map and see how small they are? China's all those little Nips can handle. Besides, they're on the other side of the world."

"Makes sense to me," Brannon concluded. "We get out in March of '44 and for the next four years it'll be smooth sailin' for all of us. Yes sir—smooth sailin'!"

11

DEN OF INIQUITY

GET UP!"

Ben was making the slow pull up from sleep—the glare of the naked bulbs, the coarse sound of the words—trying to invade the territory of his dreams, trying to lift him to the white, harsh light of reality.

In the aftermath of the two words, the barracks was slowly coming to life. The men were stretching, yawning, rubbing their eyes as men who come awake in their homes everywhere—but this was not their home, this big open room with stacked beds and the sounds of strangers everywhere. This was unfamiliar, lonesome ground, and they were in bondage to the noisy Neanderthal who slept cloistered at the end of the barracks—emerging like some kind of moving, breathing plague to heap his dark misery upon them.

After showers and shaves, Perez taught them to make a bunk properly—complete with military tucks. He told them of the roughed-in schedule they would be following for the next three months. Then it was outside for a brief session of Right Face—, Left Face—, and all the other Huuuh's.

Perez stood in front of the fifty-seven men, bright-eyed, with a big smile on his face. He looked as though he had just returned from vacation, instead of staying up most of the night.

It was still dark with a damp, morning chill to the air. Over the distant rooftops, there was a faint lightening of the sky where the sun would come up to bring into bright focus the trials the men would face today. The field jackets had been left hanging uselessly on the hooks under the empty shelves. The men were bleary-eyed and groggy, wishing they were somewhere else—anywhere other than at the mercy of this grinning tyrant.

"Well, girls—we've got a fun day planned for you," Perez began with exuberance, walking around the group. "First, we're gonna feed you better than any of you deserve. Then you're gonna get a haircut—and I mean a real haircut!"

The men had heard about the haircuts, and they groaned in unison, some smoothing their hair down gently in a kind of abbreviated farewell ceremony.

"Next we'll fit you out with the best military uniforms your daddys' tax dollars can buy," Perez continued, delighted at the effect his words were having. "And, after we've finished this day of unadulterated bliss, you might—just might—begin to have some semblance of military appearance."

Amazingly, the food was palatable—steaming mounds of grits and eggs, cups of strong coffee, milk, bacon, and stacks of buttered toast.

"This is near 'bout good as Mama's," Brannon mumbled through a mouthful of grits. "Maybe this Navy business ain't gonna be so bad after all."

"What's that white mush you're eating, Whitey?" Tondi asked, an expression of distaste on his face.

"Grits," Meyers answered for Brannon, who was too engrossed in the food to reply. "It's the staple of the Southern diet. Southern as watermelon and mint juleps. Am I right, Logan?"

"Better'n them bagels and cream cheese ya'll eat in New York City, Meyers," Ben answered sharply. "I'd just as soon eat a petrified donut covered with snot."

"Ben, people are tryin' to eat here," Davis said in disgust, dropping his fork on his plate.

Brannon looked up, chewing a mouthful of food. "Well, nothin's gonna ruin this for me. The Navy finally give us a little time to enjoy something in peace and quiet."

"OUT! OUT! OUT!" Perez screamed, storming in among the tables. "This ain't no French restaurant! You got more important things to do than fill your maggot bellies with free food."

The men looked in agony at their plates—at the hot food they had just begun to eat.

"UP! UP! UP! OUT! OUT! OUT!" Perez bellowed, jerking chairs away from the tables, the men stumbling backward or falling with a grunt to the floor. "HAIRCUT TIME!"

Haircut time took place two miles away in a low building with wooden sides and a canvas top. Wide shutters were propped open with boards, the canvas flapping in the sea breeze. Six white barber's chairs with black upholstery sat on the concrete floor inside, backed by large mirrors running the length of the building. The line of men was moving in the near door and out the other end of the building at a steady pace—each spending about two minutes in the chairs.

Ben stared at his black locks of hair falling rapidly on the floor among the white ones of Brannon, who sat in the chair next to him. His head felt lighter, cooler. The barber tapped him on the shoulder, and he headed for the exit with the others, feeling naked as he stepped into the bright sunshine. They all—as they had seen the men before them do—began rubbing their heads, back and forth from forehead to the back of the neck, again and again. There was something almost addictive to the feel of the soft bristles against the hand—the tingling of the scalp as the hand passed over it.

Ben had never experienced anything like the changes in appearance wrought by the haircuts. The white scalps were in stark contrast to the tanned faces and necks. Baby-faced men looked older without their hair—older-looking ones seemed younger. Some ears stuck out like the doors on a Model T—some lay flat against the skull like a squirrel's. The men were laughing and kidding each other, finding a kind of release in their common misery.

"That's enough head-rubbin', Maggots!" Perez screamed, rounding the corner of the building. "You look like a tribe of baboons with a bad case of fleas."

The men immediately formed up in their columns of four at the sound of Perez's voice. Ben noticed that they were already beginning to act more in unison rather than as individuals—perhaps because of their common fear and dislike of Perez.

"Now, girls," Perez announced, pacing back and forth, hands clasped together in front of him, "we're gonna dress you all up in some nice new sailor suits. You'll look just like Shirley Temple on *The Good Ship Lollipop*—except for the curls, of course. By the way, your new haircuts look splendid. I see you all asked the barbers for the same style."

After another two-mile march—most of it double-timing, they arrived at the same warehouse they were at the night before. Today they entered through heavy, metal double doors at the opposite end of the building, finding themselves in a high-ceilinged room with a concrete floor and a counter with shelves behind it at one end.

"All right, ladies," Perez boomed, "get your clothes off—all of 'em—and make a neat pile in front of you."

The men began undressing without a thought, as if it were an ordinary occurrence. In a few minutes, they were all naked, shifting about uneasily—waiting for something awful to happen.

"Everybody squat down," Perez ordered.

After they had—fifty-seven naked men squatting before their piles of clothes on the cold concrete floor—two young seamen in the ubiquitous blue denim trousers and light blue shirts took their positions behind the counter.

"Anybody with a waist smaller than twenty-eight, stand up," Perez barked.

No one stood.

"Twenty-eight," Perez continued.

Meyers and two others stood. The men behind the counters threw them each a bundle of three pairs of white boxer shorts.

"Down!" Perez barked.

The men squatted quickly.

"Thirty," Perez shouted.

And so it continued until size thirty-eight when *almost* all the men had their shorts.

"Forty," Perez barked. "Forty-two."

A pale man with sandy hair and freckles stood. He was about five-foot-six and weighed well over two hundred pounds. He glanced nervously at Perez, trying to hold his stomach in.

"There you are, *Moby*," Perez sneered. "If I'd thought to bring my harpoon along, you'd be in *big* trouble." He looked the man up and down as though he were inspecting a side of beef. "Matter of fact, you still *are* in big trouble."

The man began to redden—starting at the base of his neck and rising to his face.

"Give him thirty-eights," Perez snapped.

The bundle of shorts whizzed across the room, bouncing off the man's chest. He quickly snatched them up and squatted down.

"Stand up, Maggot."

The man stood, turned away from Perez, looking down at the bundle of shorts in his hand.

"In two weeks those shorts will fit you perfectly," Perez bellowed, "Am I *right?*"

"Sir, yes sir!" the man said in a high-pitched voice that broke on the last *sir.*

"Get down, Maggot!" Perez barked.

The man quickly squatted.

"Get up! Get down! Get up! Get down! . . . ," Perez continued for a full minute.

The man was gasping for breath on the final "Get down!"

The same sizing procedure was followed for t-shirts, and finally everyone was thrown a green sea bag.

"Throw your civilian rags in the bottom of that sea bag and follow me," Perez spat over his shoulder, walking through an open doorway into the main body of the warehouse.

The men entered into the gloomy, musty smelling regions of the warehouse. They snaked through the aisles behind Perez like ducklings following their mother. At intervals, they stopped before other counters for the rest of their issue. First was footwear. Each man got a pair of brogans and a pair of low-quarters.

Perez stood to the side, watching as the seaman flung the shoes without warning at the men as soon as they called out their sizes. Some grunted as they were hit in the chest or stomach. Ben snatched the brogans out of the air with his left hand, sidestepping as the low-quarters—thrown at the same instant—whizzed by his chest and thumped into the man behind him. Brannon somehow caught both pairs at the same time.

Farther along, they got denim trousers, blue shirts, dress whites, belts, buckles, socks, and the other standard government issue. Everything went into the sea bag. They completed their journey through the maze of aisles at another large, concrete-floored room. Everyone stood around in a daze after the mass confusion of the uniform issue—the constant shouting of the warehouse men, punctuated by Perez's growls, and clothes and shoes flying through the air in every direction.

"Keep the dress whites folded," Perez ordered. "You won't be needing them for a while. Trousers, shirts, brogans—cotton socks first, wool socks over them. Get movin'!"

Back to the barracks—dump the gear—then to the chow hall. The five minutes allotted to eat proved to be enough for most of the men this time. Ben noticed that the man Perez had dubbed "Moby" stared at his plate, eating nothing. Then a quick trip to the base PX, where the men bought razors, blades, shaving soap, stationery, and other articles that were essential or made their new lives a bit more palatable.

All that afternoon, Perez instructed them in the fine arts of spit-shining shoes, polishing floors, cleaning the head, and arranging the footlockers, shelves, and hanging racks. After double-timing to and from supper and rounding out the day with some close-order drill, they came back to the barracks exhausted. They showered at night—saved the shaving for morning.

In the brightly lit head, all the men were inspecting their newly discovered scalps—scars, bumps, and irregularities of any kind were thrown under the human microscope.

"Hey, Tondi," Brannon called out, blubbering and splashing in the shower, "the back of yore head looks like somebody tap-danced on it—with some real heavy taps."

Tondi turned from the mirror, facing Brannon. "Things like that happen when you grow up in the big city, you Mississippi huckleberry. We got more to do than lie around the creek bank with a fishing pole stuck between our toes."

"You think Jersey's rough?" Meyers asked, rubbing himself briskly with a towel. "If you could get a passport to cross the state line, I'd invite you through that tunnel one Saturday night. We got neighborhoods the Mafia are afraid to go in."

Tondi strutted over to Meyers, hands on hips, looking like a banty rooster gazing up at a giraffe. "Toughest thing you ever saw was a bad day at the stock market, banker's boy!"

Lights out was nine o'clock. Muted conversations drifted about the darkened barracks. Some tried to read or write letters by the frail bits of light angling through the windows. Silence began to settle upon the room, crowded with strangers moving toward acquaintances with their neighbors—some toward friendships. The man everyone now called "Moby" cried softly into his pillow. The men near him turned away, blotting him from their minds as if his weakness were some kind of infectious disease that would gnaw away at the barriers they had all constructed to house their own private fears.

The conversations had fallen of their own weight into silence —all that lingered were a few muffled coughs and yawns. Ben lay on his cot, crowded with memories of home. Foremost among them was the face of Debbie Lambert—the soft yellow cloud of her hair as he sat behind her in class—the timeless sway of her hips as she moved across the school ground toward him—the touch of her lips against his as he stood at his locker in the bustling, noisy hallway.

He thought of the early morning breakfasts with his family— the journeys he made in his mind as he drank from the Mason jar at the well—the good days working in the bright, clean drugstore for Ollie—the wondrous blue ball that came down, down to him on that long-ago day at Three Corners.

Ben listened to Moby's muffled sobs across the aisle—saw Joshua Davis slip down from the top bunk, walk over and sit on the bed next to him. Davis talked very softly to him for two minutes, then returned to his own bunk. The sobbing had stopped.

Drifting down into the dusky cobwebs of sleep, Ben thought he felt the silky touch of Rachel's hair against his cheek as she clung to him at the graveside of the little terrier, in the howling wind.

* * *

"YOU!" Perez screamed from his position on the wooden platform in front of the rows of men. "Seventeenth row, ninth column. Get up here on the double!"

Perez's ability to spot the slightest movement never ceased to amaze and confound Ben. Three or four hundred men were doing PT (physical training) in a dusty, rock-strewn field, and every time they got to their feet after a session of push-ups, sit-ups, or some other torturous "ups," the natural inclination was to brush the dust off with your hands. This was not allowed until the order was given, but at least one man would always succumb to the urge— and Perez had yet to miss it when it happened.

The latest offender was a stocky redhead, covered in freckles, who stood looking up as if he were a convicted murderer awaiting the judge's decision.

Perez wasted no time in handing down his uncannily consistent sentence. "Get down!"

The redhead threw his legs out behind him and thumped heavily to the hard ground on his chest and stomach.

"Get up!" Perez bellowed before the sound of the man's grunt had died away.

The redhead scrambled to his feet just in time for another "Get down!" This lasted until he could no longer get up, lying in the rocks and dust gasping for breath.

"Get down!" Perez screamed, looking out over the men.

There was a slight tremor of the earth as the hundreds of bodies hit at the same time. Since there was no other command, they all assumed the "leaning rest" position—body held above the ground on hands and toes in preparation for push-ups. Held . . . held . . . held . . . until one by one the men began dropping to the dust, their burning muscles no longer able to stand the strain.

Ben found that he could gradually slip one elbow under the edge of his stomach and rest. He would alternate elbows very slowly, very carefully—but not carefully enough. Perez spotted him, and he wished that he had never discovered his clandestine resting position.

After the primary torture was over, the men began running in place, moving out by companies. They ran around the crude dirt track that encircled the PT field until they lost count of the number of times. Usually after one to two dozen of them had collapsed, lying by the side of the track in their own vomit, the laps would end—*usually*.

Today marked the beginning of their second month in boot camp. Today they would take the swimming test. It was a perfect day for it—or for anything else for that matter—except perhaps the PT they had endured. It was seventy degrees with a cheerful sun brightly tracking the clear blue sky toward its western joining with the sea.

The men had been allowed the unheard-of extravagance of an hour's rest in the barracks after lunch. The pool was a five-mile march away, but this seemed reasonable after a month's worth of PT under the ever-watchful Petty Officer Perez.

When they reached the pool, the men were amazed at its size, except for those like Meyers, who had grown up with the Olympic-sized pools of the big cities. They lined up by sixes for the swim to the far end. Ben and his group of four, plus Moby, who had lost so much weight he now fit easily into his size thirty-eights, comprised the first heat.

"I notice that none of you has any questions," Perez said matter-of-factly.

They had learned better by now.

"Well, you don't have to worry," he continued.

Even those who were excellent swimmers had grave concerns after this assurance from Perez.

"The Navy is prepared for any contingency—almost," Perez grinned. "You will note our 'lifeguard extraordinaire,' Seaman Jones, who can easily rescue any *one* of you who can't swim in each heat.

The burly man in the wool knit bathing trunks, which were duplicates of the ones all the men were wearing, took an exaggerated bow.

"You will note I emphasized the word *one*," Perez said, holding up one thick forefinger. "If there happens to be more than one per heat who can't swim—well, perhaps Seaman Jones could expedite the initial rescue and reach the second man in time."

Jones stood at the edge of the pool, arms folded across his hairy chest, shaking his head.

"I thought not," Perez said, looking back at the men. "Doesn't hurt to ask though. You agree? First heat, prepare to swim."

There was an excited murmuring among the ranks of men, ending with a few changing places with others in different heats.

At Perez's command, the first six dove into the water. Ben, who learned to swim in a stock pond when he was five, knew he could easily swim the distance and glanced around him at the others. Tondi and Moby were flailing in the water, but they would finish the course. Davis was moving along steadily, his muscular body low in the water. Amazingly, Meyers was pulling away like Johnny Weismueller rescuing Maureen O'Sullivan from a crocodile.

Ben had almost touched the far end when he realized Brannon was missing. Jones had noticed too and dove cleanly into the water, searching for him. The men in the ranks were shouting that Brannon never came up after he dove off the side. Ben, Meyers, and Davis submerged quickly, searching the bottom of the pool.

Ben came up gasping for breath and saw Brannon sitting on the edge of the pool in the far corner, feet splashing in the pool, grinning at the frantic men trying to find him.

"You nitwit!" Perez screamed, running to where Brannon sat

and hovering over him like a carrion bird. "Whatta you mean staying underwater that long?"

Brannon smiled benignly at the raving petty officer. "Sir, no one said I had to swim it on *top* of the water, sir."

Perez almost smiled as he whirled and walked back to the other end of the pool.

* * *

"'Den of Iniquity,' huh," Brannon said gleefully, sitting next to the taxi driver. "Now *that* sounds like my kind of place."

Meyers sat in the back between Ben and Tondi, his long legs poking up above the back of the seat. "I like the sheer honesty of it," he said expansively. "None of this 'Chez Paris' come-on. Just up-front, unadulterated sin."

"What's it like?" Ben asked the driver nervously.

He glanced around at Ben, his red nose glowing under the bill of his leather cap. "It's like a sailor's paradise, boy," he rumbled in his whiskey voice. "Wild, wicked, and wonderful."

Ben wished he had stayed on base and gone with Davis and Moby to see John Wayne in *Stagecoach*, but Brannon had been so persuasive about what a good time they would have, and he had been so adamantly opposed to the "goody-two-shoes" Davis, that he had relented.

As they rode through the darkening town, Ben was struck by the differences between San Diego and Liberty. The trees here seemed to be stunted, so unlike the live oaks with their limbs spreading bountifully outward from massive trunks, or the pines that seemed to reach upward into the clouds. Adobe was a common form of construction for the houses with their red-tiled roofs, striking against the white walls. Ben had never remembered noticing roofs before.

Georgia's sultry hot days of summer and the wet, arctic blasts in the dead of winter were almost forgotten in the cool nights and mild days here. *Can't argue with the climate,* Ben thought, gazing at the passing houses through the taxi window.

"Here we are, boys," the driver announced as though he were ushering them into the Taj Mahal. "That'll be ninety-five cents. Tipping, by the way, is allowed."

Brannon handed him a one, turning to leave the cab.

"All this for me? My wife'll be so excited. Now we can take that trip to the Riviera."

Ben noticed Meyers slip the driver a dollar bill as he stepped from the taxi.

The smoke inside the "Den of Iniquity" was so thick Ben's eyes began watering immediately. "In the Mood" boomed from the jukebox—Ben noticed it was exactly like the one in Ollie's, but the volume was three times as loud. Couples gyrated on the dance floor, packed so closely they continually bumped into each other. The girls in their bobbysox and saddle oxfords were whirling and being thrown high into the air by their partners, their skirts flying above their waists.

The four of them made their way across the dance floor and found stools at the bar. Ben saw that most of the girls looked a lot like those at Liberty High, but there was another group that sat at the far end of the bar and at tables near it with sailors and older men— they had not looked like high school girls for a very long time.

Ben saw one of those women look toward him, speak briefly with the two women who sat with her, and begin a high-heel clicking, hip-rolling walk toward him.

"Four bourbons neat with draughts on the side, Barkeep," Meyers told the man in the white shirt, black bow tie, and apron.

That bartender's getup is the only thing this place has in common with Ollie's, Ben thought.

"Hello, *men*," the woman said to Ben as she walked up to the bar. "Want some company?" She glanced at her two friends who remained seated at their table.

"Sorry, Sweetheart," Meyers answered, downing his shot glass of whiskey. "I'm afraid we can't afford your—ah, *expertise*. We'll have to stick with the amateurs tonight."

"What're you waiting on, Logan?" Meyers asked, watching the woman swivel her way back to her table. He took a big pull at the mug of beer. "Drink up."

Ben held the dark liquid before his face, the diluted light striking it with a malignant glint. As though unbidden, his hand lifted to his mouth and he knocked back the jigger of bourbon with one swallow as he had seen Meyers do. Liquid fire raced down his throat and into his stomach. Coughing, he downed half of the beer chaser before he realized it tasted almost as bad as the bourbon.

133

"Can't handle a man's drink, huh, Logan?" Brannon gibed, finishing his beer.

Ben coughed and sputtered. "Just a little out of practice," he lied.

Tondi had wasted no time in finding a partner and was out on the floor swinging his bobbysoxer to the Andrews Sisters' "Beat Me, Daddy, Eight to the Bar." Meyers held a second shot of bourbon in front of him, saluted Ben, and turned it up. Brannon was talking to a girl who had just entered the bar.

Ben leaned back on his stool, elbows on the bar, the bourbon coursing placidly along in his brain. A warmth had radiated outward from his stomach, and he felt a mild euphoria. The sharp corners of the world seemed to have been somehow rounded off and softened. He threw back the second jigger Meyers handed him, finishing his mug of beer. "You know, Abe," he grinned. "I'm glad I decided to come along. This is gonna be a lot of fun."

* * *

Ben held the sides of the commode with both arms. The bourbon, mixed with stomach bile and the remnants of the hamburger he had eaten, burned much worse coming up than it had going down. It came out his mouth and nose at the same time. His head felt as though someone had driven a railroad spike into it and was twisting it back and forth. The last thing he remembered was telling Meyers, "This is gonna be a lot of fun!"

* * *

The rest of boot camp lapsed into a monotonous routine of marching, PT, shoe shining, policing the barracks, and the hundred other menial chores all services use to mold fighting men into efficient cogs in the enormous military machinery. Ben moved through the bland days on the base and raucous nights in town with little thought of the future. Orders came through and all five of their little band were to get a thirty-day liberty and then be assigned to a ship bound for Sydney, Australia.

Graduation day was a blur of dress whites, gold braid, flags, and a Navy band—John Phillip Sousa marches thundering out across the parade ground under a mild blue sky—proud smiles on the faces of families who had been able to come watch their sons become defenders of the homeland.

Ben left the next day just after dawn. Sitting next to the window, listening to the steady clackety-clackety sound of the rails, he eagerly awaited the high, shining world of the mountains—but the train passed through them in the dark.

12

LIBERTY!

I'm worried about him, Rachel," Jewel Logan said, running her finger along the edge of the bowl and licking the cake batter from it. "Ben just doesn't sound like—well—*Ben* in his letters."

Rachel was placing the cake into the oven, her face beaded slightly with perspiration. "I think I know what you mean, Mrs. Logan. It's like he's trying real hard *not* to be Ben anymore. He writes a lot about the good times he's havin', but it seems like he's just runnin' away from things to me. Those three friends of his don't sound like they're a very good influence either."

"Lord, I hope he hasn't started drinkin'!" Jewel exclaimed, shaking her head slowly. "Surely he's got better sense than that after he's seen what it can do to a man."

"Well, I guess everything's about ready for his comin' home party," Rachel offered, noticing the faraway look in Jewel's eyes. "I bet you just can't wait to see him."

Jewel turned toward Rachel, her face softening. "He was always my favorite, Rachel. It's a shame for a mother to say it, but it's the truth."

Rachel looked out the kitchen window where the June sunshine, yellow as butter, was warming the world.

"Rachel?"

She turned toward Jewel.

"I know how you feel about Ben," Jewel said, a gentle light in her eyes. "I've seen it growing on you for years. And when he sees how much you've changed these last three months, he'll look at you in a different way. It's something you'll have to handle the right way."

Rachel blushed slightly. "Oh, Mrs. Logan, Ben and me are just friends. Besides, he won't have time for me now."

Jewel smiled, remembering how hard it was to be a girl suddenly living in a woman's body. "You'll find out pretty soon, I guess. His daddy's pickin' him up at the bus stop just about now. That sure is a pretty dress. Don't think I've ever seen you wear it before."

"Mama done some ironin' for Mrs. Spain," Rachel said, holding out her skirt and turning around. "Said it was out of style and I could have it."

At that moment, Earl Logan was sitting on a bench waiting for his son. He was eager to see him, but afraid things would go wrong between them as they had so many times in the past.

"Greetings and salutations to you, Earl, on this splendid summer morn," J. T. Dickerson extolled, shambling up to the bench.

Logan looked up at his longtime friend. "Why don't you give it a rest, J.T.? Everbody knows you went to Harvard. All them big words don't mean nothin'."

"Ah, but they do, Earl," Dickerson responded, sitting next to Logan. "That's the very essence of it—the words are an end in themselves."

"More riddles, J.T.?"

"Not a riddle, old friend," J.T. said, his greasy face glistening in the sunshine, "a *mystery*. One that I must safeguard. I have—as you may have guessed by now—squandered my life."

"I hadn't noticed."

Dickerson smiled sadly. "I've long realized that I have absolutely nothing of any merit to say—but I say it so eloquently. And that's the essence of my being—mystery and eloquence."

Logan looked at his friend with a tinge of sorrow. "J.T., you need to be in a home somewhere. When's the last time you had a meal—a bath?"

Dickerson turned his cocker spaniel eyes on Logan. "You got a snort in that truck, Earl?"

"J.T., I'm waitin' for my boy to come home from the Navy. Don't bother me now."

"Ben? Why I'd like to see that boy myself. Never could figure out how a nice-looking kid like that could spring from your loins, Earl. A genetic marvel."

The bus pulled in with a hiss of brake and the whoosh of the door opening. Ben stepped off quickly wearing his dress whites, a navy sea bag over his shoulder.

"Hey, son," Logan said, getting up and holding his hand out. "How you been?"

"Hey, Daddy," Ben replied, shaking his hand stiffly.

They stood three feet apart—looking across a vast distance at each other. Logan smiled awkwardly. "You shore filled out some. Guess the navy's feedin' pretty good these days."

"I need a drink, Daddy," Ben said sharply. "Let's go to Shorty's."

"I don't know, son," Logan mumbled, "yore mama's got a little get-together planned for you."

"I said I need a drink, Daddy!" Ben said evenly. "You oughta know *that* feelin'. Come on, I'll buy you and J.T. both one."

"The boy's defending our freedom, Earl," Dickerson chimed in, struggling up off the bench. "Be a serious breech of patriotism to turn him down."

Five minutes later, they rattled and bumped into the rut-filled parking lot at Shorty's, parking under the old cedar. Ben noticed the blade of "Moon" Mullins's knife still embedded in the center of the Pabst Blue Ribbon sign. Jimmy Rogers's plaintive wail poured from the jukebox.

"First time I ever saw the inside of this place," Ben observed, looking around. "You always kept me waitin' in the truck—'member, Daddy?"

"Uh, I guess so, son," Earl muttered. "Ben, why don't we just git us a R.C. and go on home? Yore mama's real anxious to see you."

"Whiskey, neat, and a beer chaser," Ben ordered, ignoring his father.

J.T. slipped onto the stool next to Ben. "You're mighty young to be drinking boilermakers, Ben," he cautioned. "Usually takes years to reach that stage."

Hearing the order, Shorty came over to them. In the way of some nicknames, he was well over six feet tall. His eyes were pale, making him look like those fish that have acclimated themselves to underground lakes, spending all their lives in the dark. "What's this *neat* business, Ben?"

"Just leave the jigger of whiskey on the bar, Shorty," J.T. interrupted. "The boy's trying to burn his liver out in three months' time."

Ben frowned at J.T. and gulped the whiskey.

"You got any money, J.T.?" Shorty asked with a hard look.

"I'm buyin'," Ben declared bluntly, slapping a five on the bar.

"I'll have what the admiral's having," J.T. grinned.

"R.C. for me, Shorty," Logan muttered toward the floor.

Shorty stepped next to Logan, reached across the bar, and placed his hand on his forehead. Then he reached into the box under the counter, pulled out a dripping bottle of R.C. Cola and opened it. "You feelin' poorly, Earl?" he asked, setting the bottle on the bar.

"Naw. Jewel's havin' a little homecomin' for Ben. Don't want to mess things up."

"Wouldn't be the first time he messed somethin' up," Ben nodded to J.T.

"Nothin' I can do about all them times, son," Logan said stonily. "Why don't you just finish that one, and we'll go to the house."

"Man's gotta be a man," Ben announced, saluting J.T. with his mug and draining it. "Hit me again, Shorty."

*　*　*

As the pulpwood truck bounced into the yard, Ben saw his mother run out the front door. She threw both arms around him just as he stepped down from the cab. "Oh, Baby, it's so good to see you!" She hugged him tightly, then stepped back. "Let me have a look at you! I like that short haircut and goodness you must have put on ten pounds! Look at that fine lookin' uniform! I do believe it's the purtiest suit of clothes I ever seen!" She hugged him tightly again.

"Slow down, Jewel," Logan laughed. "Give the boy a chance to catch his breath."

Micah and Pete came running around the corner of the house.

"Boy, look at Ben!" Micah shouted. "He's a real soldier."

"Where's yore gun?" Pete called out.

Ben put his arms around both of them as they crashed into him. "Settle down now. First of all, I'm a sailor—not a soldier. And second, the guns we shoot in the navy are too big to carry around."

In the commotion, Ben saw Dinah on the porch waving to him. He fought his way through the boys and hugged her. "How you been, little sister? I bet Daddy's beatin' the boys off you with a stick, ain't he?"

"Oh, hush, you bad thing! They don't even look at me," she objected. "Ben, that's such a cute outfit!"

"Ol' Perez'd just love to hear you say that," Ben laughed.

"Who?"

"Nobody. Presents for everyone in my bag," Ben shouted to his father, who was carrying the sea bag toward the house.

The boys and Dinah ran toward their father with shouts for him to open Ben's bag. Jewel was trying to calm them down.

Ben walked through the house toward the kitchen—everything so painfully familiar, even the same smells. As he stepped into the kitchen, Rachel turned from the counter where she had just set the cake down. Ben stood open-mouthed, his eyes taking in every inch of the girl he hardly recognized. Her hair was longer and pulled back from her face, held behind with a silver comb. The lashes over her clear, hazel eyes seemed longer and her lips looked as if they were touched with lipstick, although he knew she never wore any. A lilac dress hung in folds over the soft curves, contouring the perfect, elegant symmetry of her body.

"Hello, Ben," she said.

Ben shook his head slightly. "Rachel?"

She blushed, looking back toward the cake and sliding it two inches farther away from the edge of the counter.

"Have I been gone just three months? You look two years older."

"You look different too, Ben," Rachel smiled, the blush gradually fading from her cheeks.

Ben felt embarrassed by his reaction to this girl—this silly kid. "Yeah? Well—the Navy's no place for boys."

Micah stormed into the kitchen. "Rachel, look at this pocketknife Ben brought me! Is this the kind soldiers use, Ben?"

Dinah was next. "Ben, this scarf's just beautiful! Look, Rachel, it's real silk."

Then the whole family was crowded into the small kitchen. Jewel looked at her family gathered around the returned son. There was a heavy tinge of sadness in her gray eyes. She had smelled the liquor on Ben's breath, but what worried her most was the change she had seen in him—the glint of hardness in his eyes, the almost tangible smell of evil that his surroundings had left on him. *Oh, God! Let him not be taken! I pray the precious blood of Your only Son will cover him—protect him—save him! In the mighty name of Jesus!*

* * *

The last week of school, Ben thought, walking down the bustling hallway in his dress whites. *Boy, I remember how good that felt when I was a kid.* A few of his friends greeted him on their way to the lunchroom. Looking in the glass door of his old English class, he saw Leslie Gifford sitting at his desk reading and eating an apple.

"Hi, Mr. Gifford," Ben called, opening the door slightly.

Gifford glanced at the door, then sat upright in his chair. "Ben? Ben Logan! Come on in. I'm glad to see you."

Ben walked over to the desk and shook Gifford's hand, then sat in a chair, legs crossed, hat resting on one knee.

"Looks like the Navy's treating you well," Gifford smiled. "I like that haircut. Learning anything interesting?"

"Oh, yeah. Real important stuff," Ben laughed. "How to mop a floor, do KP, salute—now that's real crucial to the defense of the nation—making sure your hand's at the proper angle with your eyebrow."

Gifford laughed warmly, and, for the first time, Ben could see the kindness in his eyes. "Well, Ben, we can't all be kings and princes. Besides, we commoners are the real salt of the earth."

Ben enjoyed the brief visit, realizing how much he had lost when he left Leslie Gifford's class. "Well, I guess I better go, Mr. Gifford. I want you to know though—you're the best teacher I ever had."

Gifford looked at the floor. "Ben, you've got a lot of ability. I hope you'll continue your education. I'd still like to see you teaching at this school. Preferably English literature."

After they shook hands, Ben paused briefly at the door as he was leaving. Gifford had returned to his book, his bad leg propped at that bad angle on the desk. *He's more of a man than anybody I ever met*, Ben thought as he left the room.

Ben was leaving the school ground when he saw Debbie Lambert sitting underneath a live oak, surrounded, as usual, by a bevy of admirers. "Hi, Debbie," he said, walking up to her.

The blue eyes widened, her hand went to her breast. "Why, as I live and breathe—if it isn't Ben Logan."

"That's a snappy outfit, Ben," Doak Myles remarked, standing up to shake hands with Ben.

Keith Demerie and Taylor Spain remained seated on the ground to Debbie's right.

"Thanks, Doak," Ben replied and turned to Debbie. "How 'bout a movie tonight, Debbie?"

Debbie looked at Demerie and Spain with a deliberate smile. "I'm afraid I can't," she said, turning back to Ben. "Daddy wouldn't allow it."

"I've known you to do things your daddy didn't allow," Ben suggested firmly. "How 'bout it?"

Demerie stood up, taking a step toward Ben. "What she's saying, sailor boy, is she's not interested in going anywhere with a loser."

Ben's gray eyes narrowed, his lips going white, but he ignored Demerie. "C'mon, Debbie," he insisted, "one little movie can't hurt anything."

Debbie looked up at Demerie. "Keith," she pleaded.

"Logan," Demerie said, glaring at Ben, "you couldn't cut it in the 'real world,' so you had to tuck your tail between your legs and run into the Navy. You think any girl wants somebody like that?"

Ben looked directly at Demerie. "I'm 'bout out of patience with you, you overgrown ape. If you didn't learn your lesson last time, I'm still in the teachin' business."

Demerie's face went red. With a roar he was on Ben, grabbing him in a bear hug, using his forty-pound weight advantage to man-handle him. But Ben had lifted his arms just as Demerie grabbed him so they wouldn't be pinned at his sides. He cupped his hands and slammed them viciously onto Demerie's ears.

Demerie screamed in pain, his head roaring like hurricane winds—one eardrum broken, the other damaged—he was by no means finished. Blood running from his left ear, he charged like a runaway truck. Ben hit him squarely on the chin with a straight right, but Demerie's momentum carried him into Ben, knocking him to the ground. Dazed from the punch, Demerie hung on as Ben scrambled to free himself.

Demerie knew if Ben gained his feet he would be no match for his quickness—desperation gave him strength. He pulled Ben toward him, felt two hard blows on the side of his head, but got his huge hands around Ben's throat and tried in a blind rage to crush it.

Ben's world turned black, and he seemed to be sinking into a deep pit with no bottom—falling, falling, falling—

He might have been in the darkness for as long as it took to build the pyramids—or only for a few seconds, he was not able to tell—but finally a cool wind seemed to blow the suffocating darkness away. He coughed, gasped and felt a rush of air into his lungs. He coughed again, taking a deep breath through the searing pain in his throat. The blinking light before his eyes settled into a steady brightness, and he struggled to get up.

"Take it easy," Doak Myles said, holding Ben by his shoulders. "Just sit there a minute."

As his vision cleared, Ben saw Keith Demerie walking slowly away across the school ground, supported on either side by Debbie and Taylor Spain.

"I think you'd better leave, Ben," Doak said, helping him up. "Nobody called the law 'cause Keith hit you first, but his daddy owns Ring Clampett."

"You're right," Ben said hoarsely. "Thanks for your help, Doak. You've always been a good friend."

Ben walked aimlessly through the town, talking with a few people he knew, the early afternoon sun causing him to sweat through his dress whites, stained from the scuffle with Demerie. Passing the courthouse, he saw Ring Clampett ambling toward him, twirling his Louisville Slugger. Ben stood glaring at Clampett as he approached. When Clampett was ten feet from him, Ben spat on the sidewalk. Clampett smiled broadly, showing his yellow teeth and walked on by.

Finding himself in front of Ollie's, Ben went in and sat at the counter. "Hey! What's a man gotta do to get some service around here?" he called out.

Ollie's head appeared around the door leading into the

prescription and stock rooms. "Ben! My goodness! How in the world have you been?" Ollie exclaimed, wiping his hands on his apron. He shook Ben's hand, clapped him on the shoulder, and immediately grabbed a sundae dish.

"I'm just great, Ollie," Ben answered, happy to be back in the drugstore. "How 'bout you?"

"Can't get any help good as you were," Ollie said, dipping chocolate ice cream into the dish. "Doin' fine other than that."

Ollie set the sundae before him and they chatted about the Navy and the town for a while. "Well, I've got to get some prescriptions out," Ollie said, clapping Ben on the back again. "Gotta have 'em ready early. Jack Clampett took your place and that boy's as slow as molasses in winter."

As Ollie disappeared into the back, Ben caught a movement in the last booth near the jukebox. Angela Spain slid her hips around on the leather seat, her black dress sliding up her thighs almost to the tops of her silk stockings. She glanced at Ben from underneath incredibly long lashes, her violet eyes catching the light from the front window. Standing, smoothing her dress down over her hips, she turned to the jukebox.

Leaning on the jukebox with both hands for a full minute, she dropped a nickel in and punched a button. Turning slowly, she leaned back against the jukebox, her pale hands draped gracefully on its sides. She gazed directly into Ben's eyes, her red lips parted slightly. The strains of "Stardust" filled the air, drawing Ben inexorably back to that rainy night and the sounds and the scent of Angela Spain's wine-dark room.

* * *

At two o'clock that morning, a black La Salle wheeled into the parking lot in front of Three Corners, spraying gravel onto the Texaco pump. The sultry night air hit Ben as he opened the door. Angela Spain's warm hand caressed the back of his neck as he turned to her. She leaned forward, her mouth slightly open, pressing her lips against his.

Pulling away, Angela whispered, "Tomorrow, Ben?"

Ben looked at her pale, drowsy face, lost in the cloud of dark hair. "Why not?"

Ben felt better after the walk home, the scotch working its way through his system. He stood at the well, the Mason jar of water in his hand—but the places he had traveled to so often in his mind would not come. He felt himself in a swirling darkness, falling through a bottomless void—and in the darkness was the pale, shimmering form of Angela Spain.

* * *

"Ben, Dinah just told me Hartley Lambert sent word that he'd have Ring jail you if you tried to see Debbie again," Jewel Logan said, still holding a partially peeled potato and a paring knife.

Ben looked up from packing the last of his clothes into the sea bag. "I told her not to worry you with that. Where is she?"

"Went into town. Is it true, Ben?" Jewel asked, her brow furrowed with concern.

"Mama, you know how rich people are," he replied, throwing the sea bag over his shoulder. "Any little thing happens they don't like—they start handin' out orders. I get enough of that in the Navy."

Jewel followed Ben through the house to the front porch. "I'm worried about you, Ben," she sighed.

"That's your job," he laughed, kissing her cheek. "You're my mama."

She gave him a brief smile. "You've been here a month and we've hardly seen you. Out all night—sleeping most of the day."

"I can take care of myself, Mama," Ben assured her. "I'm a grown man now."

Pete and Micah were playing mumbletypeg under the walnut tree. Seeing Ben, they ran over to tell him good-bye. He gave Micah a big hug and shook Pete's hand.

"C'mon, Pete," Micah urged, tugging on his hand. "I'm gonna beat you this time."

"Well, I'm off to the sea, Mama," Ben said, putting his arms around her. "And don't you worry—I'll be fine."

Ben made no protest as his mother lay her hands on his head. He stood there in the July heat, feeling the rivulets of sweat rolling down his sides beneath the dress whites, listening to his mother talk to God.

Approaching the giant oak where Rachel always waited, Ben saw her standing in her usual place, as she had done on hundreds of school days. She had on the same lilac dress and held a package in her hand.

"Hi, Ben," she said cheerfully. "I've got a little goin' away present for you."

Ben felt embarrassed as he had not tried to see her since the day of his homecoming party. "You shouldn't have done that, Rachel," he admonished. "Where would you get money for a present?"

"Ben Logan, you ungrateful—man!" she scolded. "That's none of your business. When a person gives you a present—you say, 'Thank you—That's mighty nice of you.'"

Ben smiled at the sudden outburst of temper, a side of Rachel he had never seen before. "Thank you, Miss. That's very nice of you," he said, accepting the present.

"Well, aren't you going to open it?" Rachel asked as Ben hefted the present, turning it over in his hands.

Ben ripped the paper off and opened the box. The smile left his face. "Rachel," he said, lifting the black, leather-bound Bible from the box. "I can't accept this. It's too expensive."

"You will too accept it, Ben Logan," she snapped, anger smoldering in her brown eyes.

Ben thought of the things he had done during his thirty-day liberty—the bars and brawls and binges of boot camp. He remembered the bitterness that festered in him when he lost the part in the play—when Debbie went to the party with Demerie instead of him. He glanced down the road and saw a long black snake slither across, through a ditch, and into a fence row. "Rachel, you're a nice girl. But—there's no room in my life for a nice girl."

"You're just actin' tough, Ben," Rachel persisted. "You can't fool me. I've known you too long."

Without a word, Ben dropped the Bible on the ground, grabbed Rachel, pinning her arms to her sides, and kissed her roughly on the mouth. As he released her, he felt a sudden stinging as she cracked him sharply across the face with her open hand.

"You think that's being a *real man*, don't you?" Rachel said hotly. "You're a spoiled *brat*—a *baby*."

Ben watched the flush rising in Rachel's cheeks, saw the cold fire in her eyes.

"A *man* doesn't need to force a woman," Rachel continued, her fists clenched at her sides. "And a *man* would care enough for his family to spend some time with them, instead of—whatever it is you were doing the whole time you were home. Maybe I was wrong about you, Ben Logan. Maybe this blustering little boy is all there is to you!" Rachel whirled and walked briskly down the road toward her home.

Ben was stunned at Rachel's outburst—the fury of her words piercing him like arrows. He hurried to catch up with her. "Rachel! Rachel wait!" He caught her and reached out for her—but quickly drew his arms back.

"What do you want now?" Rachel blurted out, stopping so quickly he almost ran into her.

Ben looked back at his sea bag and the Bible lying on the ground under the oak. "I'm—I'm sorry, Rachel. I really am."

Rachel stared at him, fists still clenched, breathing deeply.

"Forgive me, Rachel. You're right. I didn't treat you or my family right."

Rachel's breathing slowed—she rubbed her eyes with the tips of her fingers. "I forgive you, Ben," she said softly, taking a deep breath. "But there's more to it than just you and me."

"What're you talkin' about?" Ben frowned.

Rachel took another deep breath. "God told me I'm going to be your wife!"

Ben was double-stunned this time. He stood there with his eyes wide, unable to speak.

Rachel took his face in both her hands, kissed him firmly on the lips, and ran down the road toward home.

"Are you crazy?" Ben yelled after her. "You believe in the Easter Bunny, too, you fanatic?"

Rachel was walking briskly now, never looking back.

Ben cupped his hands to his mouth, shouting, "I'd never marry you in a hundred years!"

Part 3

PEARL HARBOR

13

THE GAUNTLET

*T*he USS *Dobbin!*" Brannon announced, pointing across the slate-gray water toward the ship. "What do you think of her, boy? That's gonna be our home for the next year, maybe more."

Ben sat next to Brannon at the gunwale of the navy launch, cutting a white wake across the smooth surface of San Francisco Bay toward Treasure Island Naval Station. "I never saw anything so big," Ben shouted into the wind.

They had come in on the same train that morning, had taken Stockton Street into Chinatown for a sumptuous lunch, had ridden the cable cars, and had reported to the navy launch that afternoon. Like the others in his small group, Ben was eager for sea duty and requested assignment to a ship rather than a school.

Aboard the ship, Ben and Brannon stood at the four-foot-tall, solid-iron railing that ran the length of the ship. It was actually an iron wall, and Ben felt a security behind its solid bulk in the awesome presence of the sea. The Golden Gate Bridge, burnished by the afternoon sun, spanned the gateway to the Pacific Ocean. Alcatraz Island, with its hopeless population, loomed on their right like a granite nightmare. Ben wondered if any of their haunted number had memories of Ellis Island in that other harbor on the eastern coast of "the land of the free."

"Ben and Whitey—the South's hope for redemption," Meyers said, strolling toward them.

"Redemption from what, carpetbagger?" Brannon snapped.

"Why, from losing the war. What else?" Meyers replied, leaning on the rail next to them. "Maybe you'll get to fight on the winning side for a change."

"We ain't at war that I know of," Brannon declared bluntly.

"That could change, my friend," Meyers said, the smile leaving his face. "Hitler's got Europe, except for England, and now he's bombing her. Cunningham whipped the Italian navy at Calabria, but that's a hollow victory for the British—Hitler's their problem."

"What did you do on liberty," Ben grinned, "tour the Western Front?"

"By way of the *New York Times*," Meyers answered. "And I also visited my little yellow brothers in the east. They're playing soldier in earnest too."

Ben turned from his view of the bridge. "Weren't you the one who called it the 'phony war,' Meyers?"

"Good point. But that was four months ago."

"You seen Davis and Tondi?" Brannon asked, his hair shining bone-white in the afternoon sun.

"Yeah, they're both on board," Meyers answered, his hooked nose in profile giving him the appearance of a gangling, earthbound eagle. Tondi's assigned to the galley, and Davis is a 'wood termite'—which sounds redundant to me, but who am I to question the Navy's technical terms?"

"What's a 'wood termite'?" Ben asked, watching the ship cutting through the hammered-iron surface of the bay.

"Carpenter shop," Meyers answered shortly. "I'm in Admin, by the way, as befits my several talents."

"You're there 'cause a pencil's the only thing you're strong enough to pick up," Brannon jibed.

Meyers grinned at him. "You're the only one in the company could outswim me."

Brannon frowned. "Water don't count. You're 'bout as coordinated as a drunk paraplegic."

"'Water don't count,'" Meyers repeated. "Where'd you learn that logic, Brannon, the philosophy department at Redneck U? We happen to be in the *Navy*. Water *does* count. I want you to go to your bunk and write 'Water does count' a hundred times."

"Oh, yeah!" Brannon shot back adroitly.

"What kind of jobs do you think we'll get?" Ben asked.

"I *know* what you'll get," Meyers answered quickly. "Backbone of the Navy—the ordinary seaman."

Not long after they passed through the Golden Gate, the smooth water of the bay gave way to the long, rolling swells of the open Pacific. Ben felt a queasy feeling in his stomach and soon found himself below, hanging over the toilet.

"This is worse than comin' off a drunk," he said to Brannon, who had the one next to him.

"Yeah," Brannon agreed, "and you don't even have a good time before it happens."

Every man had been issued a cot, a mattress, and a hammock. The latecomers, which included Ben and Brannon, soon found out what the hammocks were for. The *Dobbin* had been built in 1916 when the sleeping quarters were designed for hammocks—hooks built into the walls for three levels. It was found that hammocks were damaging to the kidneys, but this medical discovery didn't increase the space that was needed for cots in the sleeping quarters. The latecomers discovered that all available cot space had been taken—cots were set up on all decks, including topside, every night, and folded away each morning. Ben found the hammock comparable to trying to sleep while hanging from a meat hook.

Joshua Davis was assigned to the same sleeping quarters as Ben, and after he had given his cot space to a man with a bad back, they hung their hammocks side by side.

"What part of Louisiana are you from?" Ben asked, as they hung their hammocks amid the hundred other sailors who were settling down for the night.

"Galvez," Davis replied, balancing himself in the hammock. "Between New Orleans and Baton Rouge."

"That sounds Spanish. I thought the French settled that area."

"Mostly there's French influence, but the Spanish got there first," Davis said, folding his hands behind his head. "Then a couple hundred years later came the great Redneck Migration. That's how my folks got to the area."

"I got a little redneck blood in me, too," Ben laughed.

"Ben, let me ask you something," Davis said in a sober tone.

"Sure."

"Why do you run around with that same bunch—do the things they do? I've talked to you enough to know you spent some time in church—know something about the Bible."

Ben was silent for a few seconds. "I'd just as soon not talk about it."

"You know that part of the country I come from is famous for drinkin' and carousin'. Did some of it myself," Davis confessed. "But it's an empty life."

"Now you're gonna tell me everything is all shiny bright since you got to be a Christian—right?"

Davis laughed. "Life's still life, Ben, but somehow the things that bothered me so much—don't anymore. It's like the hurts don't hurt as much—the problems aren't nearly as big. Guess it's hard to explain."

"You know for a fact Jesus did all that for you?" Ben said, on the verge of anger.

"I know as much as the blind man did—the one that Jesus healed."

Ben didn't respond.

"The Pharisees told the blind man Jesus didn't heal him because Jesus was a sinner," Davis said and waited.

In half a minute, Ben asked, "Well, what *did* the blind man tell them?"

Davis smiled. "He said, 'Whether he be a sinner or no, I know not: one thing I know, that, whereas I was blind, now I see.'"

"Davis, you're a nice fellow, but if there's one thing I don't need in my life right now it's another sermon," Ben snapped, ending the night's conversation.

The next morning, right after chow, Ben found out something about the "backbone of the Navy." He, Brannon, and several other seamen were given buckets of sand, buckets of water, and scrub brushes with four-foot-long handles. They were taken to the forecastle, which was constructed of four-by-four wooden decking.

The petty officer in charge reminded Ben of Perez. He was bare chested and had more hair on his back than he did on his head. "Throw the sand out by hand, then the water, and scrub 'til I can eat off this deck," he growled. "You men are the youngest, greenest, and lowest on the ship. You get the details nobody else wants."

And they did. Their detail included scraping every conceivable part of the ship, painting, mopping, and starting every day with the sand-and-water scrubbing of the forecastle deck. Ben would have eaten off it himself when they finished.

The days settled down into a mindless routine of hard work, meals, showers, and sleep. Ben, Davis, and the three others from boot camp managed to find cot space on the main deck. The nights were cool, with a breeze most of the time. They would lie under the open sky, the stars so close they felt they could pick them like shining, silver apples. When the weather turned, it was back to the hammocks, but sleeping topside was pleasant. Awakenings in the Navy, however, were not so pleasant.

The days became increasingly warm until they were blistering hot. The *Dobbin* crossed the equator and to commemorate this event for the first-timers, the old salts arranged a time-honored ceremony—a seafaring rite of passage—the gauntlet!

"All right, girls!" the old chief bellowed, after all forty of the young seaman stood at attention on the fantail. "We've crossed the equator. It's time to make 'salty sailors' out of you. You'll notice some of our petty officers have generously given of their time to help you in this important stage of your naval careers."

The "generous helpers," all twenty of them, had formed two ranks of ten, facing each other six feet apart. Each of them held a cudgel—a canvas tube three inches in diameter and thirty inches long, filled with sand. They sneered at the young sailors, pounding the cudgels into the palms of their hands, reminding Ben of Ring Clampett and his Louisville Slugger.

"This looks like a death squad!" Tondi said, his voice tremulous.

"They do seem to enjoy their work though," Davis added. "That's admirable."

"You've been at sea too long, Davis," Meyers murmured.

"Maybe he's just crazy with the heat," Brannon added.

The chief stood next to the first seaman in the first rank. "Let the games begin," he barked, slapping him on the shoulder.

Ben heard the dull thuds of the cudgels striking flesh and bone—the groans and screams as each man received his slap on the shoulder and ran the short alley of pain. The chief's hand struck Ben's shoulder like a thrown brick. He took a deep breath and sprinted toward the gauntlet. Staying low, he protected his face with both arms. The first sledgehammer blow caught him at the base of the skull—he saw stars spiraling through a black universe but kept his feet. Time became a snail, crawling across a trackless, burning desert. Ben felt a heavy thud on his left shoulder, pain searing across his back. The last man swung his cudgel upward, catching him in the stomach, the air rushing from his lungs.

The young men hung on the rail, knelt doubled over clutching their stomachs or sprawled half-conscious on the deck—moaning, crying, vomiting.

"Well, you're all 'salty sailors' now!" the old chief said, walking away with the laughing group of "helpers."

* * *

After twenty-six days of zig-zagging across the Pacific, the *Dobbin* finally made port. Sailing into Sydney harbor, Ben was reminded somewhat of San Francisco as he gazed at the hills that rose from the waterfront. What struck him most, however, were the roofs of the houses, scattered across the hillsides like hundreds of bright red coals, glowing in the morning sunshine. It seemed that every house in Sydney had a red-tile roof.

The *Dobbin* tied up at a wharf that backed up to a huge warehouse along its entire length. At one end of the wharf was the open harbor—at the other end was a locked gate manned by the Shore Patrol to keep the sailors in—and the women out! Fraternization was allowed while on shore leave only.

Ben and his four buddies leaned on the rail watching the *Dobbin* being secured to the wharf. When the men handling the task began welding the two-inch-thick steel cables around the heavy stanchions, a moan went up from four of the five in Ben's group.

"Well, that means we're stuck in this stinkin' hole," Tondi said dejectedly. "No sailing to exotic ports of call."

Meyers had a mischievous grin on his face.

"What are you grinnin' like a possum for?" Brannon asked him.

"Because Australia is part of the British Empire, that's why," Meyers laughed.

Brannon looked puzzled. "You read that in the *New York Times*, Meyers?"

"Maybe it's our political science lesson for today," Davis interjected, pushing his glasses up the bridge of his nose.

"Neither," Meyers responded. "What I did read in the *New York Times* is that the British are going toe to toe with the Germans and Italians in North Africa."

"And the Aussies are sending troops to fight with the British—right?" Ben blurted out.

"Bingo!" Meyers said. "Leaving all their lovely girlfriends lonely and forlorn—pining away down here with no one to comfort them."

Brannon picked up on the last line. "Except for the American sailor, ever ready to step into the breach," he grinned licentiously.

The days quickly assumed a comfortable, steady monotony. Work details every morning and some afternoons. If a destroyer came in to be repaired and resupplied, it would mean several days of hard work—but this was exceptional as the Pacific truly was as "peaceful" as it must have been when Balboa christened it.

Shore leave became the men's alpha and omega—first and last in their imaginations and machinations. One quarter of the crew started shore leave at 1:00 P.M. and half started at 5:00 P.M., leaving at least one-quarter on the ship at all times. The first afternoon there were perhaps a dozen young Australian lassies waiting beyond the gate at the end of the wharf. In a month's time there were between 100 and 150 each afternoon. Half of them had dates—half were up for grabs.

Each afternoon or night the men would go to the taverns, drink gin slings, and play the jukebox. Every place they went was packed with people—restaurants, movies, taverns. An air of desperate excitement hung over the city, fanned by news of fighting in the north. It was as though some unseen malevolence were drawing them inexorably into the gaping maw of war.

As the months wore on, the nightlife became more exacting and tiresome for Ben than his duties in the Navy.

"Cheer up, Ben," Brannon called out, pulling his date-for-the-night onto the dance floor. "We've got two hours to get back to the ship."

"He's right, honey," the half-drunk girl sitting next to him trilled. "Aren't you having fun?"

She had red, curly hair and reminded Ben of Peggy Jackson, Debbie's close friend and classmate at Liberty High. "Just tired, I guess," Ben answered. *Tired of you and these loud, smoky taverns and this skull-busting rotgut and* . . .

Jimmy Dorsey's recording of "I'll Never Smile Again" was playing on the jukebox. As Ben listened to Bob Eberle sing the bittersweet lyrics, Rachel's face suddenly appeared before him. He saw the tiny flecks of green in her clear brown eyes—the light dusting of freckles across her face—felt the silky touch of her hair as it blew against his cheek. Pouring a shot glass full of gin, he downed it in one gulp. The image never wavered—never changed.

"C'mon, sailor boy, lets dance," the redhead urged in a gin-slurred voice, pulling Ben by the arm.

Ben jerked his arm free, turned the bottle of gin up, drained it, and walked unsteadily out of the tavern into the warm February night. He strolled aimlessly through the darkened streets in the general direction of the ship. In a small park lit by gas lamps, he sat on a bench, watching the pale yellow lights mirrored in pools of rainwater under the trees.

Feeling something against his leg, Ben saw a small black-and-gray dog with hair hanging over his eyes. He reached down, scratching him behind the ears, and the dog suddenly leaped onto the bench and stretched out, his head in Ben's lap. As he petted the dog, Ben thought of the black-and-white terrier that had trotted around the streets of Liberty—and of standing next to a freshly dug grave behind Three Corners Grocery in a howling wind. He shivered as though that same wind had found him in a warmer climate, in another hemisphere. The little dog followed Ben all the way back to the ship, where he stood waiting outside the gates.

Ben awakened with a splitting headache, his mouth dry as a bushel of shucks.

"Here—drink some of this," Joshua Davis said, handing Ben a heavy white mug of steaming coffee. "It might get your heart to pumping—put a little oxygen in your brain."

Ben sat up slowly in his cot, put his right hand on his forehead, and eased his legs over the side. He took the proffered mug in both hands, sitting with his head down, steam rising into his face.

After he had drunk half the coffee, Davis spoke. "Ben, Meyers saw a cable from your mother. I told him I'd bring you the news."

Ben turned his head toward Davis, his gray eyes tinged with blood—his tanned face carried a grayish tint.

"Your brother's real sick, Ben," Davis said gently. "I'm sorry.

Meyers is working on the military flight schedule to get you back as soon as possible."

Dropping his head toward the floor, Ben gripped the mug until his knuckles almost matched its color. He shivered, saw a tear dimple the surface of the black coffee, felt an ache so deep he feared it would stop his breath.

Davis stayed with him, head bowed, praying for his friend.

* * *

"He's been wantin' to see his big brother," Jewel Logan said, her eyes puffy and red as she greeted Ben on the front porch. Behind her was his father, with Dinah and Micah.

Pete was in the living room on his cot, wrapped in Ben's quilt. Ben sat next to him in a kitchen chair, listening to the shallow, labored breathing. The skin on his brother's face had a weak purple tint to it, his eyelids thin as tissue paper. His left hand lay limply on his chest. On his forefinger he wore the Jack Armstrong secret decoder/whistle ring that Ben had given him years before.

The room darkened as the rose-colored western sky faded into a deep blue. Ben stayed with his brother, remembering how they used to sit on the floor in front of the radio listening to "Jack Armstrong! The All-American Boy!" And the male chorus would sing the Hudson High Fight Song. In the last episode they listened to together, an old Tibetan Monk was speaking to Jack: "Tell the boys and girls of the United States if they have hearts of gold, a glorious new golden age awaits us. If they are honest . . . If they are kind . . ."

Hearts of gold, honesty, kindness—maybe these things don't amount to nothin' more than a stupid radio program. Look at my little brother. He's honest and kind. What golden age awaits him?

Hearing the sounds of Dinah and his mother preparing supper in the kitchen, Ben slipped back into the present. Time had lost meaning for him.

"You want to eat now, Baby?" his mother called from the kitchen door. "It's 'bout ready."

"No ma'am. I'm just gonna sit here for a while."

As Ben heard his mother praying before the meal, Pete suddenly opened his eyes.

"Ben—is that you?" Pete asked, his voice so weak Ben could barely hear him.

"It's me, Pete. I come a mighty long way to see you," Ben said softly.

"I done what you told me to with the money," Pete smiled.

Ben smiled back. "I knew I could depend on you."

"Gimme a hug," Pete whispered, trying to lift his arms.

Ben pulled the chair closer, taking his brother in his arms. He held him like that for a long while, feeling the faint beating of his heart, listening to the sounds of his family in the kitchen.

"He's so beautiful!"

"What? What did you say, Pete?" Ben asked, sitting up slightly and taking both his brother's icy hands in his.

"So beautiful." Pete whispered, his dark eyes looking beyond Ben at something only he could see.

"Pete? Are you all right?"

Pete turned his face toward Ben. "I love you, Ben." His breath came out in a long, soft whisper, his face relaxed and serene.

Ben held his brother's pale hands, smoothed his hair back from his forehead. The last of the light faded outside the window as the cold, hard night began.

* * *

February rain fell like leaden drops of sorrow on the grave of Pete Logan. Ben sat with his family under borrowed umbrellas in the five folding chairs the funeral director had lined up next to the grave. Across Pete's grave from them were other family members and the friends who loved and would miss him.

Rachel was gazing at Ben, the grief on his face pulling at her like an undertow. Noticing her, Ben gave her a weak smile, but smiles were for the living, and he felt as dead and cold inside as the February day.

Samuel Shaw stood at the head of the grave, his blond hair bright against the dark day and the long dark coat he wore. He opened his large black Bible and began to read. "Let not your heart be troubled: ye believe in God, believe also in me. In my Father's house are many mansions: if it were not so, I would have told you. I go to prepare a place for you. And if I go and prepare a place for you, I will come again, and receive you unto myself; that where I am, there ye may be also."

"Funerals are for the *living*," Shaw continued, his voice calm and strong in the sound of the rain beating on the umbrellas. "The dead are beyond *our* means to help them. They decide *themselves* what happens to them beyond this fleeting shadow we call life."

Ben heard the preacher's voice as if from a great distance, understanding little, remembering the sound of his brother's voice as he said, "I love you, Ben." But Shaw's words were lodging themselves in his heart.

As Shaw came to the end of the service, a strong gust blew a cold spray of raindrops across him, wetting the pages of his Bible. He closed it, looking at the family, his face full of promise. "Last November, on the night before Thanksgiving, in a little brush arbor meeting, Pete Logan decided to give his life to Jesus Christ. He is in the arms of Jesus now and there is, my dear brothers and sisters, no better place to be."

14

"I HAVE CALLED YOU FRIENDS"

You been mopin' around four months, Logan," Brannon pronounced, combing his silvery pompadour in the metal mirror of the ship's head. "It ain't helping you one bit—this goin' off by yoreself all the time. You come on out with us and have some fun."

"Maybe you're right. I hear we might be leavin' this place in two or three months. Might as well give the Aussie gals a few more thrills," Ben said cockily, watching Tondi set up his favorite prank.

A low wooden wall separated the showers from the toilets, which were nothing more than open seats individually partitioned off with a trough of running water beneath them to carry off the waste.

Tondi squatted next to the spigot where the water flowed into the trough, wadding up a piece of newsprint. He struck a kitchen match, set fire to the paper and dropped it into the stream of water. As the floating fire passed beneath the sitting men, heads began popping up above the partitions accompanied by screams of pain.

"Doesn't he ever get tired of doin' that?" Ben asked Brannon, glancing at the spot where Tondi had disappeared.

"When the Good Lord was handing out brains, Tondi thought he said rain, and he run off to find a shed," Brannon replied. "Now get ready, boy. Them little gals are pinin' away for you."

"OK, buddy, whatever you say." Ben smiled, wrapping the towel around his waist. "Wine, women, and song."

But if anything, the tavern life was worse than before. In the smoke and noise and people-filled building—in the midst of music and laughter—Ben had never felt such loneliness and isolation.

"Don't be so gloomy, Logan." Meyers was tapping on the rim of his glass with a swizzle stick, keeping time to Orrin Tucker's recording of "Oh Johnny," with Wee Bonnie Baker's kittenish vocal.

Brannon turned from his radar-like scanning of the tavern, toward Meyers. "I think he misses ol' Perez tuckin' him in at night. Been a year now since boot camp."

"Well, I got some news to cheer him up," Meyers said. "The Limeys sunk the *Bismarck*. That's one for the home team, ain't it, now? The biggest and best the German's could build—she had eight 380 millimeter guns and nineteen 152's—and they got her on her first mission!"

"How'd you find that out?" Ben asked, amazed at the information Meyers always seemed to come up with.

The song ended and Meyers dropped his stick into the glass. "Admin, my boy. We keep our fingers on the pulse of the war." Meyers took a long pull from the glass of whiskey and soda, his face clouding over. "The Krauts blew the *Hood* out of the water though. One shell into the stern magazine. Went down like a rock. More than fourteen hundred men on her and three survived."

Ben noticed the dark circles under Meyer's eyes and wondered what else he was learning in his proximity to privileged communication.

"Well, that's the news for tonight, gentlemen," Meyers concluded. "I see some strays over yonder, partners. What say we mosey on over and have ourselves a roundup?"

Ben stayed at the table while Brannon and Meyers walked over to a group of five women. They talked for a few seconds and then motioned for Ben to join them. He waved them off. All five of the women were attractive, but to Ben they looked like mannequins in the display window of Hightower's—their laughter sounded like breaking glass.

There's nothing wrong with them, he thought sourly. *The problem's with me—and I don't even know what it is!* Ben watched Meyers walk over to the jukebox and drop a nickel in. He and Brannon walked their partners onto the dance floor, held them tightly around their waists, and began swaying slowly to the music.

Ben recognized "I'll Be Seeing You" from the very first note. Images of Liberty drifted slowly across his mind in time with the music. He drank a jigger of whiskey—then another and a third. His vision began to blur, but the pictures in his mind seemed to leap into sharper focus.

Even though the tavern was dimly lit, Ben felt as if he were impaled under a spotlight. He dropped two one-dollar bills on the table and walked out into the knife-edged uncertainties of the night. Street lamps burned the darkness like yellow blossoms—a ship's horn sounded out in the bay. As he once again shambled down the deserted streets, the damp air became crowded with silent reproaches.

The next afternoon, after he had scraped and painted all day, Ben returned to the cot he had set up against a bulkhead on the fantail. He waved off the usual invitations from Meyers and Brannon, watching them swagger down the dock toward the gathering of young women behind the gates. A sea wind wrinkled the smooth surface of the harbor under a sky the color of ashes.

Ben probed the depths of his sea bag for a small volume of A. E. Housman poems Leslie Gifford had given him almost two years ago. His hand touched smooth, supple leather, and he grasped the Bible Rachel had bought for him. Throwing his sea bag behind him against the bulkhead, Ben leaned back and opened the Bible. He thought back to the last time he was in church, the brush arbor service that cold Thanksgiving eve when Pete went to the altar. *The third chapter of John—that's what Rachel's daddy read from.*

Turning to the third chapter, Ben read until he got to the third verse, "Verily, verily I say unto thee, Except a man be born again, he cannot see the kingdom of God." *Now that don't make a lick of sense to me.* He continued, stopping at the sixteenth verse. "For God so loved the world, that he gave his only begotten Son, that whosoever believeth in him should not perish, but have everlasting life." *I believe in Jesus. Heard about Him all my life. But Jesus is God—way up in heaven somewhere! What am I to Him?*

Ben continued to read in the Book of John, skimming over some verses, stopping when something caught his attention. Night fell, and still he sat there, engrossed in the Scripture, reading by the dock lights.

Time seemed to cease, and finally he was startled to notice a thin line of light in the east, the harbinger of dawn. Still he read on. In the sixth chapter he read, "him that cometh to me I will in no wise cast out." *That's simple enough—if I can just figure out how to get there.*

In chapter nine Ben saw, "whereas I was blind, now I see." *So that's where Davis got that story about the blind man. That's where that line in "Amazing Grace" came from, too.* He read "Jesus wept" in the story of Martha and Mary's brother, Lazarus, who died and was raised from the dead by Jesus, when even the people who didn't believe in Jesus said, "Behold how he loved him!"

Ben glanced over toward the gate where the sailors and Sydney girls were pairing off for the night. *Lazarus and Jesus were friends. If I lived way back then He might have been my friend. Maybe things would have been different.*

The first three verses of chapter fourteen took Ben back to his brother's grave and the sound of Samuel Shaw's voice that cold, rainy February day. "He's in the arms of Jesus now . . ." Ben felt the same pain, the same hopeless sense of loss he had felt at the graveside. He looked out across the bay, glistening and blurry through the tears that had sprung up into his eyes. *Jesus, help me!*

A quick breeze stirred the air, turning a page in the Bible. He glanced down and the words seemed to come to life. "Greater love hath no man than this, that a man lay down his life for his friends." Several lines below, he read, "I have called you friends."

Somehow Ben felt the terrible pain of Pete's death draining away. The heavy, leaden weight and fear of death that had burdened him for so long slowly faded. He knew with an absolute, inexplicable certainty that he would someday see Pete again. It was as if he would go on liberty again and see his brother, healthy and smiling this time—though it might be a long while off.

You died for me, Jesus—I know now that You are my friend. I've messed up bad, but right now I give my life to You, Lord Jesus. Clean me up and help me to be the man You want me to be.

Ben closed the Bible slowly, holding it against his chest with both hands. In the eastern sky, the cloud cover was rising from the earth like a curtain going up. A lamb-white gull lifted from a piling, riding the wind, the first rays of the sun gleaming like cold fire on its wings. Watching the flight of the bird as it sailed over the water, Ben felt tears running down his cheeks, and he had a smile on his face so big he thought his mouth would split open at the corners.

The next morning Ben was up at dawn, weaving his way through the tangle of cots that dotted every available flat space on the deck of the ship. Making his way to the mailroom, he dropped the letter he had written to his mother into the slot. It began, "Dear Mama, Today I got saved!"

An hour later, Ben blurted out in the middle of breakfast. "Boy, it's a beautiful day, ain't it?" He looked about the mess area as if it were the banquet hall of a castle, then resumed wolfing down his scrambled eggs and toast without another word.

Joshua Davis looked up from his meal and, seeing the unmistakable light in Ben's eyes, gave a silent prayer of thanksgiving.

Meyers and Brannon looked at each other, puzzled expressions on their puffy faces. Brannon made a fist, his knuckles pointing toward Meyers, the thumb lifted as if it were the neck of a bottle. He pointed to Ben and raised his thumb to his mouth. Meyers nodded in agreement and sipped his black coffee, his eyes so bloodshot the irises were discolored.

Brannon leaned close to Ben, whispering out of the side of his mouth. "You better lay off the sauce, Ben. Drinkin' on duty is a one-way ticket to the brig."

"I ain't touched a drop, Whitey," Ben beamed. "I got saved!"

Brannon stared at Ben, astonishment etched on his face.

"What'd he say?" Meyers asked, sitting on the other side of Brannon, his face turned toward him.

Brannon turned slowly toward Meyers, shaking his head sadly. "He's lost his mind. I knew it would happen when he quit chasin' women."

*   *   *

The whole world changed in the next three weeks, or so it seemed to Ben. No longer did he seek refuge in a bottle from those shapes and shadows of memories in the night. No longer did he writhe in the depths of sleep, awaking in a cold sweat, or face in his daydreams the intolerable bitterness of the past.

Each morning was full of bright promise, and he savored the simple pleasures of food and work and friendship. He understood little of what had happened to him but accepted it as a gift—as he had the wondrous blue ball that long-ago day as a child, when it was handed down to him from so high up.

"I haven't felt this good since I was a kid," Ben said, leaning back on his cot.

Josh Davis sat next to him. "It's a whole new life, Ben. Same old world, but a new life. You're startin' out right, too—readin' your Bible every day."

Ben stared at the white moon just above the eastern horizon, facing the orange afterglow in the west. "Yeah. I finished the New Testament yesterday. You've been a big help to me, Josh. The Bible's startin' to make sense to me now."

"Have you told anybody else about Jesus?" Davis asked, watching the sky grow dark around the rising moon.

"You know—I guess I haven't," Ben mused. "I've been so happy and so busy—I just haven't."

"Well, you've just been touchin' the ground now and then," Davis laughed. "Doesn't affect everyone that way. But it's just as real no matter how we react to it."

"I know what!" Ben exclaimed. "Why don't we ask Whitey and Meyers and some of the others to join us after work? We'll read the Bible and study and talk about it—you know, like you and me have been doin'."

"I'm ashamed I didn't think of that myself," Davis confessed. "Out of the mouths of babes . . ."

At that moment, Brannon walked across the deck to his cot just down from Ben's and sat down. He opened his sea bag, digging in it until he came out with several bills. Putting them in his wallet, he turned to Ben. "You'bout over your nervous breakdown, boy?"

Brannon had been especially rough on Ben the last few weeks, goading him at every opportunity. "Don't know what you mean," Ben answered.

"What I mean, Jesus Boy, is—are you ready to go out with us and have some fun?"

"I'm having fun right now," Ben smiled.

Walking over and standing in front of him, Brannon sneered, "You think you're better'n me now, don't you? Readin' that Bible all the time, quit drinkin', big smile on yore face like you know something nobody else does."

"It's not like that, Whitey. I just told Josh we should ask you and some of the other boys to study the Bible with us."

"Don't need to study it," Brannon shot back sarcastically.

Ben looked up at him, puzzled. "I don't—"

"It says turn the other cheek," Brannon snapped, his right arm a blur as he hit Ben across the mouth with the back of his hand. There was a sickening thud of bone against flesh, blood spattering onto Ben's Bible that lay on the cot beside him.

Ben was stunned by the sudden violence of the blow. His right arm tightened, the fist knotted, his legs going under him to propel him off the cot. Suddenly the whole thing was ludicrous. In the person of Bobby Lee Brannon, bowed up like a bulldog, Ben saw all the petty bickering, envy, and bitterness that had defeated him for years. The heat of his anger somehow vanished—blown away like a mist on the water. He began laughing. "That the best you can do, Whitey?" The laughter grew. "Better lay off the booze," he gasped, tears rolling down his cheeks. "It's makin' an old man out of you."

Brannon stared at Ben dumbfounded, his mouth open. "You really *are* nuts!" He spun around, striding briskly around the corner of the bulkhead.

In the first week of August, Ben sat against the rail of the ship writing a letter by the dock lights, blurred by a mist that had crept in from the sea.

Dear Rachel,

It's cold as I sit here on deck writing you—like February is in Liberty. Can't get used to cold days in August. We still sleep outside though. It's either that or the hammocks.

I'm finding that it's not always fun to be a Christian. A lot of my friends have quit having anything to do with me. Some of them just make fun of me. I know how it feels to be called a fanatic. But I wouldn't trade the peace I've found in Jesus for anything in the world. To quote a good book I've been reading, "I am not ashamed of the gospel of Jesus Christ." When things get rough, it seems like He comes and gets me through the hard times. I don't mean I really see Him or hear Him—He's just there.

The Bible study's coming along all right. Josh leads it, and I do a little now and then. Meyers came once. He said as a "Wandering Jew," he just happened to wander in. Whitey won't come at all or even talk to me any more.

And now for the good news. Tondi got saved! Praise the Lord! He'd never read one word in the Bible before and said he'd only been to church a couple of times. It's all so new to him he walks around in a daze. He stole money from some of the men, and he's already given it all back.

Guess I'll close for now and get some sleep. Tell your family and everybody hello for me.

> Your friend,
> Ben

Chewing on his pencil, Ben thought of all the times Rachel had waited for him under the oak tree on those long ago school mornings and how he had always taken for granted the bright smile she always greeted him with.

P.S. I think about you a lot.

*   *   *

"All right, sailor," the old chief growled, chewing on a stub of a cigar. He had washed-out blue eyes, a belly that looked like it had been pumped up with a bicycle tire, and skin the color of a fresh sunburn. "Your D.I. at boot camp said you had the eyesight and timing for it. Here's your chance to be a star."

The *Dobbin* was in the open sea outside Sydney harbor, steaming north along the eastern shore of Australia. It was a bright August morning with a glaze of sunlight on the blue-green surface of the sea. A single dolphin swam directly in front of the bow of the ship as if he were towing it with an invisible cable.

Ben walked up to the twenty millimeter cannon, fitted his shoulders into the padded rests, and gripped the trigger mechanism. When the chief strapped him in, he knew it was going to be quite a ride. "I can't see to shoot with that thing on the end of the barrel."

"What thing?" the Chief asked, scratching the back of his grizzled head.

"Them circles."

The Chief looked at the concentric circle sight on the end of the barrel—took a deep breath, letting in out between his lips like a horse neighing. He unstrapped Ben, motioning for him to sit on a metal ammo case. "That *thing* is a sight—it's how you aim that cannon so you can spray a bunch of them twenty millimeter shells into an enemy airplane and make it go BOOM! You understand?"

"These planes are gonna be moving pretty fast, ain't they?"

"Unless the good Lord hangs one on a rope out there for you," the Chief said, shaking his head slowly.

"Chief, if I'm gonna be tryin' to hit a movin' target, I got to look at the *target*—not the end of the gun barrel," Ben said earnestly. "Just like when I played baseball, I had to look at the *ball*—not the bat."

"You had a lot of experience with cannons, have you?"

"No, but I shot a lot of squirrels with a .22 my Granpaw gave me. Same thing."

"A squirrel's the same as an enemy fighter—a .22 caliber rifle's the same as a twenty millimeter cannon," the Chief mumbled. "There may be a tad bit of difference here, son."

Ben continued undeterred. "When Granpaw gave me that rifle for Christmas, the first thing he done was to file the bead sight off and polish the end of the barrel real smooth. 'So there won't be no distractions,' he said."

"Is this gonna take all day?"

"No sir. Then he told me, 'Ben, you just pretend that this ol' gun barrel here is a part of yore arm. Keep yore eyes on the squirrel as he skitters through them trees and pretend you're pointin' at him with the barrel of this .22 like it was yore finger. It'll take a while to get the hang of it, but when you do, you'll be deadly on movin' targets."

"How'd it work?"

"Well, I always got more squirrels with my .22 than anybody else did with their shotguns."

"That's a real interesting story, son," the Chief growled around his wet stub of a cigar, shifting it to the side of his mouth with his tongue. "Two things you need to know. First of all, *I* ain't your grandpa. Second, this is the *Navy*, and you'll do things the *Navy* way."

"Yes sir."

"Now in about ten minutes a plane's gonna tow a drone by for you to fire a few rounds at. You'll line the center of that sight up with the drone and try to put some holes in it with this squirrel gun here. That clear enough for you?"

"Yes sir," Ben replied as the Chief strapped him to the cannon, tighter than he had the first time.

Ben tried to line the sight up with the drone as the tow plane pulled it by in front of a bank of clouds rolling up the horizon. He squeezed the trigger, feeling the jackhammer kick of the big gun, but as he watched the sight he kept losing the drone, and when he looked at the drone the curved maze of the sight only confused his aim.

After two passes with no bursts coming near the drone, the Chief began to unstrap Ben from the cannon.

"Not yet," he barked. "Give me another chance, Chief."

The Chief stepped back, arms folded across his chest like carved fenceposts.

As the drone sailed along silently behind the tow plane, Ben kept his eyes on it, throwing the sight out of focus, trying to imagine that it no longer existed. He remembered the feel of the .22 against his shoulder and translated that feeling to the twin padded stocks of the cannon. He squeezed off a few short bursts, riddling the drone. In three more passes he did the same thing.

"Now that's the Navy way to shoot that thing, son," the Chief grinned, unstrapping Ben from the cannon.

"That's fun," Ben said excitedly. "When can I practice with this squirrel rifle again?"

"Maybe when we get to Hawaii."

"Hawaii?"

"That's right, son," the Chief rasped, taking the last of the mangled cigar out of his mouth. "We're headin' for Pearl."

* * *

The *Dobbin* swung to a buoy on the incoming tide in Pearl Harbor. The air was as warm and as soft as the slow tropic sun that lifted from the sea, lending a rosy hue to the ship and the surface of the harbor. Above the turrets and masts of the warships, above the docks and warehouses, the hills rolled upward, lush and green against the lightening sky. It was September 7.

That afternoon, Meyers strolled onto the fantail, a sheaf of papers in his hand. "How'd you like to be assigned to a *real* ship, Logan?" he asked, plopping down on his cot which was two over from Ben's.

Ben looked up from his Bible, the sea breeze ruffling his black hair. "What's this we're on—a ground slide?"

"Not familiar with the term. I assume it's some kind of farm implement though. You Southern Sons of the Soil are always enamored of earthy colloquialisms."

"You know, Abe—you remind me of a man from Liberty," Ben observed, closing his Bible. "He talks a lot like you." Ben seemed to look at something far out on the bay. "I need to go have a little visit with him next liberty I get. Abe, why don't you come back to our Bible study sometime? You acted like you enjoyed yourself in Sydney when you came."

"I'm a Jew, Ben."

"So was Jesus."

"Well, that's enough of a stroll down 'Memory Lane,'" Meyers remarked, sifting through the papers. "In the next couple of months, there'll be some reassignments taking place. Some good—some not so good."

Ben stepped over to Meyer's bunk and sat beside him, staring at the form on top of the small stack.

"I am, of course, indispensable to the captain and will remain. Tondi's culinary abilities have gained him the same dubious honor. You, Davis, and Brannon will be leaving us in the next month or two."

"Any idea where?"

"Hopefully not the North Atlantic or one of the other not-so-good assignments," Meyers said encouragingly. "I think I've managed to thwart that."

"Well, where are we goin'?"

Meyers stood and walked toward the railing, the sun casting his profile in deep shadow. His silhouette looked like it had been cut out with tin snips. Ben walked toward him as he stood gazing out over the bay.

"I've become fond of our little group," Meyers mused, as if he were standing there alone. "There's a distinct possibility that I can keep all five of us in close geographical proximity."

"How close?" Ben asked, eager to have Meyer's little guessing game over with.

"That close," Meyers answered quickly, pointing beyond the far corner of Ford Island.

Ben walked to the rail, looking out across the wind-rippled water. "That's 'Battleship Row.'"

"Give the man a cigar."

"All three of us gonna be on the same ship?"

"That's right."

"Which one."

"The *Arizona*."

15

BLOOD AND FIRE AND PILLARS OF SMOKE

Rachel Shaw stood in her father's newly constructed church singing "Just As I Am" along with the congregation. When they sang, "Oh, Lamb of God, I come, I come"—a boy, who looked so much like Pete Logan that it startled Rachel, walked slowly down the aisle. As he stood at the altar with his head bowed, Rachel slipped quietly from her pew. Placing her hand on his shoulder, she prayed for him as she had for Pete the night he walked the sawdust aisle of the brush arbor.

* * *

By dawn of the same day, the Japanese fleet had positioned itself 250 miles north of Pearl Harbor and the airfields of Hawaii. The force was comprised of six aircraft carriers (with a total of 392 aircraft), two battleships, two heavy cruisers, a light cruiser, nine destroyers, three submarines, and eight support ships. At 6:00 A.M. the first wave of attack planes lifted from the decks of the carriers. Forty-nine high-level bombers, fifty-one dive bombers, and forty torpedo aircraft reached altitude and headed south, escorted by forty-three Zero fighters.

The fleet had stolen out of Hikotappu Bay, at Iturup in the southern Kuriles, on November 26, heading for Pearl on the northern route, which was little traveled because of frequent and severe storms.

Lieutenant Sesu Kasumi felt an adrenal rush of excitement as he brought his Zero into escort position, the powerful Mitsubishi engine running smoothly. Exultation filled him as he thought of the glory the mission would bring to the Emperor and to the Empire of the Rising Sun. He pictured his wife and three-year-old son in their apartment in Hiroshima, savoring the moment he would return to the homeland—the pride he would see reflected in their faces.

This was the real thing! This was what all the months of preparation was for—the interminable briefings, hours and hours poring over maps and charts, all the touch-and-go's on the tilting, swaying flight deck.

*　*　*

On a hilltop overlooking Pearl Harbor, two soldiers manning one of five Army radar systems had volunteered to stay overtime for further training in the new system. They picked up several blips on the radar screen and reported them. The warning was not heeded. One of the officers who received the report said, "Hell, it's probably just a pigeon with a metal band around its leg."

The Army, which had the responsibility for defending the base, had put itself on the Number One or anti-sabotage alert. This meant that all the aircraft at Hickman Field, Wheeler Field, and the air base at Ewa were lined up in clusters along the runways. They were easier to protect against sabotage, but they would be sitting ducks for attacking aircraft. It also meant that the anti-aircraft guns were retained in parks, the ammunition stored in magazines, so that it would take from one to four hours to bring the guns into action.

The Navy had also put itself on Condition Three—its loosest alert, which called for 25 percent of its anti-aircraft guns to be manned. No reconnaissance planes were flying, no barrage balloons were up, and there were no torpedo nets. Most of the fleet had been brought into Pearl and were moored side by side.

Meyers and Tondi slept in their cots on the fantail of the *Dobbin*, shaded by the rear bulkhead. Forty-five minutes later, Tondi boarded the Liberty Boat for Honolulu, where later in the day he was to meet Ben Logan and Josh Davis for church. He had asked Meyers to go with him. Meyers, who had stayed up until 3:00 A.M. working on a short story, grunted, rolled over, and went back to sleep.

As Meyers slept peacefully on the fantail, a white mist as fine and soft as smoke drifted over the waters of Pearl Harbor. The palm trees along the shoreline, touched by an ocean breeze, lifted their fronds slowly, as a young girl might lift her skirt when walking through a puddle of water.

In the light-rimmed east, the tip of an orange sun, shimmering in the layered air, slipped between the seam where the sky met the sea. It pushed itself free and began its slow diurnal journey up one side of the sky and down the other.

Ben sat at breakfast with Josh Davis, talking about the church service they were going to in Honolulu. "Hey, Whitey," Davis called out, as Brannon entered the enlisted mess. "Why don't you go to church with us today? We're catchin' the Liberty Boat at ten o'clock."

Brannon walked toward them, his dress whites wrinkled, with a beer stain on the front of them the approximate shape and size of Texas. His right shoe had all the color scuffed off the toe, the raw leather looking like an open wound. He set his tray down across from them, dropping into the chair with a thud. "Church, huh? Well, I just had an all-night service, boys. I'm about, uh, churched out."

"C'mon, Whitey," Ben joined in, with a smile that had become a constant companion. "You might enjoy it."

"Yeah," Davis added, stirring two spoons of sugar into his coffee. "You can catch three hours' sleep and still make it. It's worth a trip over just to hear the music."

Brannon sipped his coffee loudly, smacking his lips as he set the cup on the table. He looked at Ben, then at Davis, a lascivious grin on his face. "Let me tell ya'll about some music me and this little hula dancer was makin' last night. I picked her up at two o'clock when she got off work, and by three-thirty this mornin' she was singin' notes ol' Mozart never heard of."

"Why don't you bring her with you, Whitey?" Davis pushed his glasses up the bridge of his nose with his left hand, unfazed by Brannon's verbal javelins. "Sounds like she'd make a fine addition to the church choir."

Brannon's face flushed, his hand tightening on the cup. He slammed it onto his tray and stalked out of the mess.

"He'll sleep like a dead man all day. Probably take a hurricane to wake him up," Ben offered, turning to Davis. "How 'bout another cup of coffee?"

Davis picked up his tray. "No thanks. Gotta go press my whites and shine my shoes."

"All this for that little blonde who sings in the choir, huh?"

Davis smiled and left the mess hall.

* * *

Ensign John F. Kennedy, USNR, was just arriving at Griffith Stadium in Washington D.C. to watch the Redskins play the Philadelphia Eagles. There was an anxious tension in the nation's capitol that had been going on for weeks regarding U.S.-Japan relations. Everyone was feeling it—civilian and military—especially with the heralded doings of the special envoys sent from Japan. Maybe the game would help everyone to relax and enjoy themselves. A game at the stadium was one of the few social moments where a young officer might run into the brass without an appointment.

* * *

The two-hour flight from the carrier *Shokaku* had been uneventful, and as Kasumi now gazed down at Pearl Harbor through the heavy glass of his cockpit, he positioned himself above and to the right of the flight of dive bombers, protecting them from any American aircraft that might get off the ground. Captain Mitsuo Fuchida, commander of this first wave of Japanese aircraft, had earlier signaled *"To, To, To"* ("Fight! Fight! Fight!") over his radio. Now as the American Navy and airfields stretched out below them, he gave the final signal, *"Tora! Tora! Tora!"* ("Tiger! Tiger! Tiger!"), which told his pilots and those monitoring the attack on the ships of the task force that they had surprised the enemy. The commander of the lead formation later recalled, "Pearl Harbor was still asleep in the morning mist."

Holding his position, Kasumi watched as the bombers began their runs, unleashing their cylindrical burdens of destruction. Ford Airbase had the exact configuration that he had seen on the charts—even better! All the aircraft were lined up on the runways like a child's toys on a game board. As he passed over, watching the bombs tearing apart the aircraft and the buildings, Kasumi knew he had little to fear from any American pilots.

Tiny figures ran from the buildings toward the aircraft as the explosions scattered them across the tarmac. Kasumi saw three men running toward an anti-aircraft battery and banked hard to his left, feeling the thrust of the engine. He straightened, going into a hard dive as he lined the figures up in his sights. Pressing the firing mechanism, he watched the heavy bullets tear into the men and fling them about the base of the anti-aircraft battery like puppets. He grinned widely as he went into a long turn out over the sun-spangled sea, setting himself for another run.

The airbase now virtually destroyed, he heard his commander's voice crackle over the radio, "And now—the big ships! After that—targets of opportunity!"

Kasumi lined his Zero up on Battleship Row, tracking the channel between Ford Island and the big island of Hawaii. The seven huge warships were lined up in a double row with the *Nevada* by herself on the far end, just off Ford Island. As he steadied himself on course, he clicked off the names of the big ships: *Maryland, Oklahoma, Tennessee, West Virginia, Arizona*, and finally the *Nevada*.

Kasumi began his long flat pass over the harbor, seeing a geyser of water and smoke shoot high into the air at the base of the *Nevada* as a torpedo hit it broadside. The Zero, responding to his slightest touch on the controls, dove toward the men scurrying about the deck of the wounded ship. Two men were manning a twenty millimeter gun mount. Kasumi turned loose a hail of heavy bullets, crumpling them like paper.

* * *

After Josh left the enlisted mess, Ben refilled his cup and returned to the table, leisurely sipping his coffee and listening to the conversations of two men sitting behind him.

"This is really the life, ain't it?" one of the bosun's mates was telling his friend. Like Tondi, he was from New Jersey and had the same accent. "Yes sir, there's nothing like the Navy life. Almost every weekend off and not much to do during the week."

"You're right there," his grinning buddy from Oklahoma agreed. "Long as nobody's shooting at you, it can't be beat. And the way they been givin' us all this free time, there can't be much danger of anything happenin.'"

"Where'd you go last night?"

"Went to see that new movie with Humphrey Bogart, *The Maltese Falcon*. Peter Lorre was in it, too. That little rascal's supposed to be mean, but he just tickles me to death!"

"I bet it was real good. I like Bogart, and Raymond Chandler's one of my favorite . . . was that thunder?"

"Couldn't be. I was just topside. It's a perfect day. Not a cloud in the sky."

"Well, anyway, the one I want to see is *Citizen Kane* with Orson Welles. It's gonna be playin' next weekend."

Ben listened to the noise from outside, an uneasy feeling working around in the pit of his stomach.

Finishing his coffee, Ben left the mess and made the short trip topside. As he stepped onto the main deck, the dull, distant thudding of bombs falling on Ford Airbase on the opposite side of the island caused a cold band of fear to tighten in his chest. He raced to the railing to get a clear view. The sky above Pearl Harbor was alive with enemy dive bombers and fighters. At that moment, the deafening klaxons sounded on the *Arizona* and most of the other ninety-five U.S. warships in the harbor, calling general quarters.

Ben grabbed a helmet and life jacket on the run, careening into his gun mount just as the cruiser *Helena* and the minelayer *Oglala*, down near the dry docks, were hit by torpedoes. He threaded the ammunition belt into the twenty millimeter cannon, jamming it. Josh Davis suddenly appeared at his side, unjammed the weapon, and fed the belt back into the breech, standing ready to handle the ammo when Ben was in poition to fire the cannon.

Thrusting himself into the shoulder rests, Ben looked down the barrel directly toward the cockpit of an incoming torpedo aircraft. He fired a long burst, the abrupt pounding of the cannon clearing the daze he found himself in. The aircraft, untouched by Ben's burst of fire, dropped its lethal burden from beneath the fuselage and climbed abruptly, barely clearing the lofty turrets of the *Arizona*.

Seconds later, a tremendous explosion rocked the *Arizona*, ripping apart its hull at the water line. Ben was slammed against the protective armor of the gun mount, gashing the left side of his head from temple to eyebrow. Davis scrambled up, grabbing Ben and pulling him to his feet. From the open hatchway, they could hear the screams of the wounded and dying below.

A torpedo struck the battleship *Nevada*, directly in front of them, the sound of the blast lost in the continuous, roaring reverberations of the explosions all around them. Regaining his balance, Ben saw a heavy wrench lying on the deck, snatched it up and, in a vicious backhand blow, sent the sight assembly clattering off the barrel of the cannon.

Ben saw Davis smiling at him as he held the ammo belt in both hands, ready to feed the shells into the breech.

"Blow 'em back to Tokyo, partner!" Davis yelled over the thunder of the bombs.

* * *

From the cockpit of his Zero, two thousand feet above, Kasumi had seen the *Arizona* rocked by the torpedo and the two American sailors battered by its concussion. He watched them regain the gun mount, one of them swinging a heavy object at the gun barrel.

He has lost his mind from fear and is attacking his own weapon, Kasumi thought. *It is time to send this American Imperialist to meet his ancestors before he can harm any of my comrades.*

Kasumi could tell the American battleship was mortally wounded, and he determined that he would destroy as many sailors as he could before it went down. He glanced at the tiny pair of baby shoes hanging to his left in the cockpit—saw the face of his wife again as she held his firstborn up toward him—his infant son reaching out as if he knew his father. *I will bring home honor to our divine emperor, our homeland, and to you, my dear wife and child when next we see each other.*

Dipping his left wing, Kasumi banked against the rising sun, dropping like a stone into a steep dive toward the *Arizona*. Behind the scream of the engine, he saw the bloodied sailor spot him, turning the long barrel of the gun toward the flight of his aircraft. Kasumi rode the screaming wind down into a shower of bullets streaking upward toward him, his hand gripping the stick, prepared to rip the American apart with his own storm of lead.

* * *

As Kasumi's Zero banked high above the surface of the harbor, the glass of its cockpit glinted in the high pale light. Catching sight of it, Ben leaned hard into the shoulder rests, staring down the smooth, clean length of the barrel. The aircraft slipped sideways, sliding down the long golden rays of sunlight toward the *Arizona*.

The world closed in about Ben; it was inhabited by a population of two—he and the Japanese pilot behind the two machines that other men of their separate nations had created for them to kill each other with. Ben heard only the high, hard hammering precision of the Mitsubishi engine—increasing in pitch with a dopplered whine as it plunged toward the *Arizona*.

Ben suddenly remembered his first hunt, the squirrel skittering at an angle through the trees. He let the cannon become part of him, its long barrel an extension of his arm, finger pointing toward the fighter as it sought a garden for its blossoming flowers of death. Leading slightly, he squeezed off a long burst, raking the aircraft obliquely from propeller across the cockpit to the rudder. It tumbled like a shot mallard, smoke billowing from the engine as it cartwheeled downward, sending up a geyser of water from the oil-slickened surface of the sea.

"Yeee—haah!" Davis gave a wild Rebel yell, lifting both fists in front of him. "That's *some* shootin'!"

Just as Ben swung toward an incoming aircraft, another torpedo hit the *Arizona*, lifting him from the gun mount and flinging him like a rag doll to the steel deck. Gray-black towering pillars of smoke were roiling upward among the masts of the ship—the bridges and tripod turret almost hidden in the billowing darkness. Lying on the deck, Ben came back into this roaring, shuddering hell from his own private darkness. He felt a warmth on his right side, a sticky flow, then a jagged shard of steel embedded in the flesh. Gritting his teeth, he gripped it tightly and pulled it free. His head spun as he almost lost consciousness from the pain that knifed through him.

"You all right?" Davis shouted through the clamor, helping Ben up for the second time.

Ben stared at Davis's left thigh. Blood, seeping from a deep cut, had soaked his trousers. "Yeah. How 'bout you?"

"Fine. Let's see if we can knock a few more down," Davis coughed, climbing into the gun mount.

Ben stumbled toward Davis, his vision clearing.

"Gotta give 'em some cover," Davis yelled, pointing toward groups of men who were trying to leave the ship.

Ben looked up at a sky crowded with Zero fighters, strafing the ships and the men already in the water. He manned his gun, firing burst after burst at the attacking planes as Davis fed the ammo smoothly into the breech.

"Three o'clock," Davis barked.

Ben spun to his right, staring directly into the flashing guns of a Zero roaring low across the water. He squeezed the trigger until he saw the propeller fly to bits, parts spinning off like shrapnel. The whirling aircraft blossomed into a brilliant red-orange fireball that struck the water three hundred yards from the ship.

Back to the left, Ben saw another Zero begin its run, pounding the deck with its heavy fire. Two men went down in a bloody heap before his eyes. Whirling the gun around, Ben aimed for the engine of the aircraft as it pulled up and away from the ship, riddling it with his second burst. Heavy smoke poured from the plane as it skidded into the waterfront at Ford Island.

Ben became a part of the gun, wedded to it in a ceremony of blood and fire. He knew it as one knows an old friend—all its moods and movements embedding themselves into his very being. Time no longer had any meaning—the old earth had passed away —the new one a roaring, blazing inferno of darkness and thunderclap death.

Davis grabbed Ben's shoulders, shaking him fiercely. "Ben! Ben! The ship's goin' down—!"

Ben came out of the darkness and the fog. "What?"

"The ship's capsizing! I think some of the men are trapped down below!"

They ran across the slanting deck toward the hatchway that led to the sleeping quarters below. Ben smelled the coppery scent of blood as he entered the smoky twilight of the cabin, awash with the foul waters of the harbor.

"Here's one!" Davis yelled. "I'm taking him up."

Ben found a young seaman lying on the floor, barely conscious enough to hold his head above the water. He lifted him over his shoulder, carrying him topside where a crowd of men were trying to get down the ladders into the boats.

"Hey—come over here and give us a hand!" Ben yelled.

Four of the men came running, lifting the two wounded between them and carrying them across the deck where others pitched in and helped.

After two more trips, Davis kneeled on the deck, coughing. He wiped the sweat and grease from his face with a white handkerchief. "I think that's all of 'em."

It hit Ben suddenly, like a sharp pain. "Where's Whitey? You see him come out?"

"No."

Ben ran to the group of men who were leaving the ship. "Anybody seen Whitey?"

No one had.

"I'm goin' back down, Josh."

The ship was listing dangerously. "I think we better get off while we can, Ben. I didn't see anyone else down there."

"You go ahead. I won't be long," Ben called back over his shoulder as he descended into the darkened ship.

Below as Ben sloshed through the knee-deep, oily water he heard the sibilant sound of broken steam pipes behind the bulkheads like a hundred locomotives firing up. He passed the sleeping quarters, entering the head where one of the explosions had torn through the shower stalls, breaking the sinks apart. Inside a twisted wash basin was someone's right shoe with all the black color scuffed off the toe. The foot and the bloody stump of an ankle were still in it.

"Whitey? Whitey?" Ben called out.

In the corner against a broken shower partition, he lay in a crumpled heap, blood staining a sock and handkerchief where he had managed to staunch most of the blood flow before he lost consciousness. Ben took off his shirt, wrapping it tightly around the ragged stump, and lifted Whitey gently onto his shoulder. Topside, four men carried him away with the precious few who would escape the *Arizona*.

Ben watched in horror as two of the men carrying Whitey collapsed, their bodies riddled with heavy bullets from the Zero that roared overhead. Ben ran for the gun mount, Davis two steps behind him.

"Get off this thing!" Ben yelled at Davis as he gained the gun mount. "It's gonna capsize any minute!"

Davis knelt beside the ammo crate, ready to feed the belts into the breech of the cannon. "Plenty of time," he smiled, pushing his glasses up the bridge of his nose. "Besides, this gun would jam in two seconds if I left."

Ben swung the big gun around just as another Zero was beginning his run across the deck of the ship. Letting loose a quick burst, Ben saw the aircraft explode instantly in an orange fireball. A cheer went up from the men on deck.

One more Zero tumbled into the rolling waters of the bay before it happened. Ben thought someone had hit him on the left shoulder with a baseball bat. He slammed against the gun, trying to hold on as he slowly collapsed on the deck. Through the gathering darkness—through the fading away of light and sound, he saw Josh Davis kneeling next to him over the ammo crate, as though in an attitude of prayer. Three ragged, gaping wounds across his back looked like they had been made by railroad spikes.

Oh, God—not Josh! Please, not Josh! He taught me about Jesus! He's the best one of us.

16

THE CONGRESSIONAL

On a Sunday morning in December 1941, some twenty-four hundred American fighting men lost their lives at Pearl Harbor. The battleship *Arizona* went to the bottom with most of her crew. The *Oklahoma* was sunk, six battleships were severely damaged, and ten additional ships were either sunk or badly damaged. The American fleet no longer existed as a viable strike force in the Pacific. Half the aircraft (Army, Navy, and Marine) on the island were destroyed.

* * *

Throughout the Eagles-Redskins game, Ensign Kennedy heard admirals and generals being paged through the stadium's sound system. He didn't know what had happened until he heard the news report on his car radio after the game. Kennedy requested sea duty as soon as possible.

* * *

A brigadier general at Fort Sam Houston was sleeping soundly after spending weeks in the field on maneuvers. His wife answered the phone quickly so as not to disturb him. Awakening him a few seconds later, she heard him say, "Yes? When? I'll be right down." As he hurried from their home, Dwight D. Eisenhower told Mamie that he was going to headquarters and had no idea when he would be back.

* * *

Sometime after the attack, Winston Churchill made a phone call. "Mr. President, what's this about Japan?" "It's quite true," FDR said. "We're all in the same boat," Churchill replied. "This actually simplifies things. God be with you." The British prime minister went to bed and slept soundly.

* * *

A seaman in a rescue party boarded the *Oklahoma*, which had taken six torpedoes below the waterline and was on the verge of capsizing. "I was terribly afraid. We were cutting through with acetylene torches. First we found six naked men waist deep in water. They didn't know how long they had been down there and they were crying and moaning with pain. Some of them were very badly wounded. We could hear tapping all over the ship—SOS taps, no voices—just those eerie taps from all over. There was nothing we could do for most of them."

* * *

Alvin Ditweiler trudged heavily across the stage of the Liberty High auditorium carrying a brown, cathedral-shaped radio under his right arm, his pudgy face lined with concern. A long black extension cord in his left hand trailed along after him from behind the curtains. He placed the radio on a wooden stool, plugging it into the extension cord. Taking a deep breath, he stepped before the microphone, one stubby hand positioning the heavy silver stand. He glanced over his shoulder at the band in their blue-and-white, gold-braided uniforms. They were seated in the small bleachers that pulled out from the rear of the stage, the director standing at attention in front of them.

When Ditweiler nodded his head sharply, the director made an about-face, lifted his hands from his sides, palms upward, bringing the band members to their feet. Using a small baton in his right hand, he led them in the national anthem. The students rose to their feet, placing their hands over their hearts, some singing—some standing at attention with tears in their eyes.

Tapping the microphone with the tips of his fingers, Ditweiler cleared his throat and began. "As most of you already know, the Japanese bombed Pearl Harbor yesterday. A lot of our boys died."

Rachel Shaw sat next to Ben's sister, Dinah, in a fold-out, theatre-type seat near the back of the auditorium. Her light brown eyes were puffy and slightly red from the hours she had spent kneeling by her bedside through the night, praying for Ben and for the safety of the other sailors and soldiers at Pearl Harbor.

Like many others in the town and around the country, she feared a Japanese invasion of the U.S. mainland. Rumors ran rampant, of Japanese warships south of them in the Gulf, of another sneak attack—this time on the West Coast—and the hundreds of other nightmares that war had thrust into the imaginations of the people.

Shafts of thin December sunlight through the high windows were filled with drifting dust particles, like snowflakes in a glass paperweight. Rachel sat among the familiar smells of old wood and books and floor wax, listening to the drone of Ditweiler's voice, but her heart was thousands of miles away. In her mind, she searched for Ben, wandering in a place that looked like the smoking ash dumps of the nether world—the blackened, burning tangle of wreckage and bodies that had been the Pacific Fleet.

Ditweiler was squatting down, trying to tune the radio, a bright trapezoid of sunlight lying against the unfurled American flag behind him. The static hissed and popped over the loudspeakers as he tried to find the station.

"You'd think he would have it on the right station before he brought the thing on the stage," Dinah whispered in disgust to Rachel. "We'll probably end up missing half of the president's speech!"

The static vanished as the clear, reassuring voice of Franklin D. Roosevelt filled the auditorium.

> Yesterday, December 7, 1941—a date which will live in infamy—the United States of America was suddenly and deliberately attacked by naval and air forces of the Empire of Japan. . . . Very many American lives have been lost. Always will our whole nation remember the character of the onslaught against us. . . . No matter how long it may take to overcome

this premeditated invasion, the American people in their right-
eous might will win through to absolute victory. We will not
only defend ourselves to the uttermost but will make it very
certain that this form of treachery shall never again endanger
us. We will gain the inevitable triumph—so help us God. I ask
that the Congress declare . . . a state of war.

A heavy silence fell over the auditorium, then Tom Shaw,
Rachel's brother, stood up from his seat on the aisle near the front.
His pale blue eyes held an intense light, his blond hair shining like
corn silk in the streaming light. "Mr. Ditweiler, I love this school
and this town, but I'm goin' to join the Navy right now!"

He turned around quickly and walked with long even strides
down the aisle toward the doors of the auditorium.

No one said a word, but all heads turned, following his
progress down the aisle.

Then a dark, heavy-set boy with straight black hair stood up.
"I'm going too! Wait for me, Tom!"

Two more followed within five seconds. With no prompting
from the director, the band stood and began playing "Anchors
Aweigh" as the four boys marched out of the auditorium. There
was a rousing cheer from the students.

Not to be outdone, two boys on the front row stood up—one
shouting, "We're joining the Marines! Anybody wanna go with us?"

One of their friends joined them, and they marched proudly
down the aisle, smiling and waving to their friends—the sounds of
"The Marine Hymn" bringing everyone in the auditorium to their
feet.

As the heavy doors closed behind the boys, a dozen more were
looking eagerly about them, picking each other out in the crowd.
"Who's for the Army?" a tall, gangly redhead shouted, punctuating
his words with a fist held high in the air.

Simultaneously, all twelve headed for the aisle, laughing and
shouting words of encouragement to each other. The "Caisson
Song" rang through the auditorium as they marched in ragged columns of two toward the exit signs.

Of the nineteen who left the auditorium that day to the cheers
of their classmates, seven joined the armed forces. The others slunk
back to school the next morning like twelve deserters, avoiding

their friends and flinching each time they heard remarks like, "Didn't take you very long to whip them Japs, did it?" or "Hey, I like that new navy uniform. I thought they wore bell bottoms though—not overalls."

* * *

Jewel Logan sat on one of the stools at Ollie's soda fountain, placing a tattered brown paper bag beside her. Her face was seamed with care, the skin having a gray pallor almost like it had stolen some of the color from her eyes. Debbie Lambert, Peggy Jackson, and Keith Demerie sat in the last booth near the jukebox. Dinah Shore was singing "Blues in the Night" in a sad, sultry voice.

"Oh, Mr. Caston? Are you back there?" Jewel called out weakly, leaning over the counter.

Ollie appeared at the door, wiping his hands on his apron. "Why, Mrs. Logan—if this isn't a coincidence! I was just about to send Jack Clampett out to your house."

Jewel's worn face held a puzzled expression.

Ollie walked to the counter, reached under it and took a letter from a cigar box. He handed it to Jewel. "This just came a few minutes ago. I guess because his allotment checks are delivered here, the Navy thinks this is where Ben's family lives."

Jewel stared at the letter on the counter. "The Department of the Navy" was stamped on the return address in bold letters. "Would you read it for me, Mr. Caston?" Jewel asked weakly.

Ollie slit the end of the envelope with a penknife, blew the edges apart, and took the letter out. Unfolding it, he read a few lines and smiled broadly. "Ben's fine, Mrs. Logan."

Jewel clutched her chest with her right hand, bright tears welling up in her eyes. "Oh, thank God! Thank God!"

"He was wounded and he's recuperating in a hospital near the naval base. This says he'll probably be home inside two months."

"Thank you, Mr. Caston! Thank you!" Jewel almost sobbed. She grabbed her bag and headed for the door.

"Mrs. Logan?" Ollie called after her.

Jewel turned at the door, the light in her eyes as bright as the afternoon sunlight through the plate glass window.

"You forgot your prescription."

"Land sakes," Jewel said absently. "That's why I come in here in the first place."

"It's on me this time," Ollie said, handing her the white bag and holding the flat of his hand toward her. "To celebrate Ben's coming through the attack alive and sound."

"Thank you so much, Mr. Caston," Jewel said, hugging his neck over the counter. "You always was so good to Ben. Many's the time he told me so hisself."

"Wonder what that ol' fanatic's carrying on about?" Keith Demerie said, watching Jewel Logan leave the drugstore as he ran the tip of his right forefinger along the thin purple scar on his upper lip. "She's nuttier than that son of hers."

"That's right," Debbie Lambert agreed, the light in her eyes as private as the diary tucked away in her dresser drawer. "At least Ben had better sense than to go to that insane asylum she calls a church."

Peggy Jackson smiled pertly, the freckles on her face almost as red as her curly hair. "My daddy says that religion is the opiate of the masses. Isn't that smart?"

"It sure is," Debbie replied, winking at Demerie. "Karl Marx said the same thing. Must have stolen it from your daddy."

* * *

The hospital was located on the flattened crown of one of the foothills that rolled upward from the harbor. It had massive off-white stucco walls and a red-tile roof. Palm trees were scattered about the grounds, and near the main building and in the garden area trellises were hung with purple wisteria. Flanked by banana trees, the leeward side of the hospital held a well-tended half-moon of periwinkle, dancing brightly in the sea breeze.

"Ben—I, uh—just wanted to tell you I'm sorry." After he had brooded for days over how he would say this, Bobby Lee Brannon felt like a complete fool, now that it was out in the open and he had made such a mess of it.

Lying on the crisp white sheets of the hospital bed, Ben stared at his friend, sitting in the wheelchair next to him, his hair and eyebrows so blond they appeared to be giving back light from the long window that opened onto a flagstone terrace. Confronted by a subdued and contrite Brannon, Ben was at a complete loss for words.

"I don't blame you if you don't want to see me no more," Brannon confessed, scratching the heavily bandaged stump of his right leg with his left foot. "Just had to tell you."

"You've got it all wrong, Whitey. Nothing's changed," Ben offered, trying to adjust his position in the bed. "Friends have falling-outs all the time, but that doesn't mean they're not friends any more."

Brannon turned toward Ben. "You saved my hide Ben—after the way I treated you."

"Actually, I just went back down there for my toothbrush. I couldn't find it, so I took you instead."

The corners of Brannon's mouth turned up slightly, then the smile came and the infectious laughter that told Ben that Bobby Lee Brannon was on his way back.

"Scratch my back, will you?" Ben asked, handing Brannon a length of split bamboo with two curved fingers on the end. "This thing's worrying me to death."

Brannon stood on one leg, balancing himself with his left hand as he probed down the back of Ben's body cast with the back scratcher.

"That's it. Right there. Ahhh—that feels great."

The two friends sat together looking at the harbor laid out below them—the docks, cranes, destroyer groups, and submarines. Wisps of smoke still rose from the shattered, half-sunk battleships. Twisted wrecks of aircraft littered the fields—hangars nothing more than blackened skeletons of buildings.

Ben and Brannon talked of the "old days," as they called them—of boot camp, seafaring, and Sydney. And they did seem like such a long, long time ago, although the two sailors had known each other less than two years.

"What's Meyers been up to?" Ben asked. "Tondi came by a few minutes the second day I was in here, but I haven't heard a peep out of that smart-aleck Yankee."

Brannon looked away in the direction of the *Dobbin*, his expression gone stony.

Ben followed his gaze, picked up the heavy binoculars an officer had loaned him to pass the time, and trained them on the *Dobbin*. It was facing him at a slight angle, seemingly untouched as he scanned through the heavy glasses that foreshortened it, giving it the appearance of a cartoon ship. Then he saw it! A twisted, blackened section of railing curved around the corner of the bulkhead—the small section of deck he could see blackened.

Ben dropped the heavy glasses, his eyes staring at something in the air six feet in front of his face. "Tondi told me Meyers was still sleepin' when he left the ship that mornin'. Said he stayed up all night writing."

"I thought you knew," Brannon mumbled toward the window. "A dive bomber in the first wave hit the fantail of the *Dobbin*."

"I didn't know. Guess Tondi didn't have the heart to tell me." Ben remembered the day Meyers had told them of their reassignments to the *Arizona*—all the times together at sea and in Sydney—that first night in boot camp when Perez had hung the nickname "Volunteer" on him.

Brannon never turned his head from the window.

"He always wanted to keep our little group together," Ben said absently.

"Yeah," Brannon agreed, watching a nurse push a wheelchair along one of the sidewalks. The man sitting in it wore a dark blue robe and the leg rests were folded up, almost touching his stump of a body. "Never could figure that. All of us was poor as church mice, 'cept him. He took to us though. You'd figure somebody with his sense and money would be an officer."

Ben stared at Brannon, slumped in his chair. The years seemed to be settling about him like drifting snow. As he turned his head, the light catching his eyes in a certain cast, Ben knew what he would look like as an old man.

"Friendship," Ben said cryptically.

"What?"

"That's what held us all together. Nobody plans it—figures it out—it just happens. And when it does, it's something special. That's what Meyers knew before any of us." Ben picked up the binoculars, looking out across the harbor toward the *Dobbin*, then placed them gently on the nightstand. "That's why he tried to keep us all together—because he knew how rare friendship is."

"Yep," Brannon remarked offhandedly in his own encapsulation of Abe Meyers. "He was a cutter."

* * *

"Morning, sailor," the commander said crisply, standing at the foot of Ben's bed. His iron-gray hair was close-cropped and bristly, appearing as though it would prick your finger if you touched it. "How're they treating you?"

Ben climbed slowly up from the subterranean country of his dreams. Noticing the insignia and gold braid, he sat quickly up in bed. He didn't know whether to salute or not. Encountering an officer, from a hospital bed, was omitted somehow by Perez in his endless discourses on military courtesy.

Ben started to salute, his hand pausing in mid-air, halfway to his head. "Uh—good morning, Commander."

Lawrence Phillips smiled at the young seaman's quandary, his teeth almost too white above the jutting chin. "Relax, son," he remarked, "they didn't teach me about hospital etiquette either."

Ben smiled uneasily, sitting up in bed, the pillow braced at his back. "Everything's fine, sir."

"Food OK?"

"Yes sir."

"Good—good!" Phillips said in an avuncular tone, sitting in the chair next to the bed.

Ben knew that full commanders didn't make calls on ordinary seamen just to pass the time of day. He tried to think of what he might have done wrong. The only thing that came to mind was that he had knocked the sight off the barrel of the cannon. *That's stupid! The Arizona's on the bottom of Pearl! What difference could it possibly make now? But with the Navy you never know.*

"Ben—you don't mind if I call you Ben, do you?"

"No sir."

"Ben, a lot of people saw what you did the day of the attack," Phillips continued.

Ben squirmed on the bed. He felt his throat constricting and coughed to clear it.

"I myself witnessed some of it."

Uh oh! Here it comes!

"Son, I've been in the Navy twenty-three years. What I saw you doing on that Sunday morning was the most courageous thing I've ever seen!"

Ben was certain he had misunderstood Phillips. "Sir?" He asked, pulling his knees up under the sheet.

"Come, come, my boy. No need for modesty," Phillips said reassuringly. I can still see you firing that twenty! The Japs blew you clean out of the gun mount, and what did you do? You got up and blasted some more of them out of the skies! Yes sir, if you're an indication of the kind of seamen we've got in this man's navy—why, this war'll be over in six months."

"It's not that, sir, its just that . . ."

"And—so I'm told by several members of the crew—enlisted as well as officers—you got the men organized to get the wounded off that ship. Went back down and brought the last one out yourself. Is all this correct, son?"

"Well—yes sir. I reckon so. Things got kind of confusin' there for a while." Ben had the feeling that none of this was really happening—that he had never awakened—that the voice he had heard was merely calling him from one dream into another.

"Let me summarize some of the statements for you, son," Phillips was saying, opening a manila folder he had laid on Ben's nightstand. "Now this first one . . ."

Ben heard a not unpleasant drone in the background, as Phillips spoke. In his mind he was watching a newsreel of the attack. It all seemed like it had happened yesterday and a thousand years ago at the same time.

The first frames were of Josh Davis's face as he knelt beside the ammo crate, refusing to leave the ship with the other men—staying with Ben until the last. He heard Josh's wild Rebel yell when Ben shot the first Japanese plane from the skies. In the oily, black smoke and the flames of war—with that same terrible thirst—Ben saw Josh kneeling next to him over the ammo crate, streams of blood flowing from his wounds.

"You all right, son?"

Ben felt like he was awaking for the second time that day, but the images were still flashing in the back rooms of his mind. Feeling the hot tears on his cheeks, he wiped them quickly away with both hands. "Yes sir. I'm fine."

Phillips put his papers away. "I'm not going to intrude on you much longer, Ben. I'm certainly not here to add to your pain. But there's some important business we need to take care of."

"Yes sir."

"I'm recommending you for the Congressional."

"Sir?"

"The Medal of Honor, son. Our country's highest award for valor under fire."

"But—I didn't do nothin' to get that. Everybody was helpin' out," Ben protested.

Phillips crossed his legs, hands folded on one knee. "Not everyone—not by a long shot."

"But look at all the men who were killed. Josh Davis did more than me. He . . ."

"Ben!" Phillips interrupted, leaning forward in the chair. "No one's saying they weren't brave men. No one's trying to diminish the other acts of heroism that took place that day—tarnish for one minute the deaths of those valiant men." Phillips took a deep breath. "Nevertheless, the Congressional is given for how much damage you inflict on the enemy—not for how much damage he inflicts on you. That's a general statement, but basically true."

"I don't know what to say—how to take all this," Ben murmured, glancing out the window.

Phillips gazed beyond the clean sweep of sunlight across the hospital grounds to the far horizon. A bright web of lightning flashed across some dark thunderheads rolling up from the sea. "There's another side to this matter that may seem even more confusing to you, Ben."

Ben stared directly into Phillips's lead-colored eyes.

Phillips looked back out the window. "Right now this country needs heroes, Ben. The president himself said that the nation needs flesh-and-blood champions of the common people to rally around. In the words of some speechwriter, to "Fire the spirit of patriotism."

From down the hall, where the burn ward of the hospital was located, Ben heard a scream of agony, rising in pitch like a siren—then fading away as if breath could no longer sustain it.

"There's little doubt you'll get the Congressional, Ben," Phillips continued after a brief pause. "Then you'll be sent on a tour of the country—selling war bonds."

"I wouldn't be very good at that," Ben mumbled, thinking of how much he wanted this officer to leave him alone with his memories—the only part of his life that seemed real.

"No, you wouldn't—you'd be great!" Phillips beamed. "You're perfect. Good looking—but not *too* good looking. A young man of humble birth—a man of the people. A hero that blasted the

'Yellow Peril' from the skies! Why, Ben, you're the Navy's answer to Sergeant York—Abraham Lincoln with a small nose. You're just what the country needs."

A flash of insight hit Ben. "Everything's already been done—hasn't it, Commander?"

Phillips rose from the chair. "Yes it has, son. Soon as you get that cast off and they fix up that scar on the side of your head a little. A hero's got to look bright and shiny—unsullied by the hazards of war."

Seeing no reaction from Ben, Phillips pressed ahead. "It's for the good of the country. Maybe it seems mercenary and callous to you, but sometimes that's the way governments are—even this one. And it's the best in the world!

Ben saw lightning flash in the distance, like faulty wiring somewhere in the heavens.

"Some of those words belong to the P.R. boys, Ben," Phillips confessed. "What I said about your actions on the *Arizona* though—that's the absolute truth. You deserve that medal as much as anyone who ever wore one. I'd be proud to have you as a son."

Ben could tell that he meant it. "Thank you, sir. Do you have any children?"

"One son," Phillips answered, walking to the door. "He was on the *Oklahoma*."

Ben wanted to tell him how sorry he was, but the commander had vanished into the hall. Bracing himself with his good right arm, Ben eased himself painfully over the edge of the bed. Standing barefoot on the cold tile floor, he saw the first heavy drops hit the window. He walked over and looked out at the rain-dented harbor and the white caps on the open sea beyond.

As he watched the storm roll in, Ben found himself back in Sydney harbor on the fantail of the *Dobbin*. He sat next to Josh Davis, their Bibles opened to what had become Ben's favorite chapter—the third chapter of the Book of John. He heard Josh's voice as he read it aloud. "Greater love hath no man than this, that a man lay down his life for his friends."

I'll never forget you, Josh—my friend. And someday I'll see you again.

17

HERO

Oh, my goodness! Just look how cute he is—and those muscles!" Debbie Lambert squealed as she sat at the last booth in Ollie's drugstore, staring at the cover of the latest copy of *Life* magazine. It was the picture Ben had refused to have taken until a direct order was given by Commander Phillips. In the picture, staged by the Navy P.R. unit, Ben stood shirtless and smoke-blackened at a twenty millimeter gun mount. In the distance, a Japanese Zero spiraled in flames toward the sea.

Debbie was bouncing gently on the springs of the seat, her blue eyes bright with wonder. "Oh—I just can't wait to see him."

"Let me see it, Debbie," Peggy Jackson demanded, her red curls flying as she grabbed for the magazine. "What do you care anyway? You went to the cast party with Keith here when you already had a date with Ben. You don't think he's gonna forget that, do you?"

"I can make a man forget *anything*, honey," Debbie said seductively, releasing the magazine.

Keith Demerie glared across the booth at Peggy, his square jaw jutting out more than usual. "Aw—Debbie's not interested in that white-trash, pulpwood cutter—are you, Debbie?"

Debbie gave Keith a surprised look, as if he were a child speaking out of turn. "When a man makes the cover of *Life* magazine, sweetheart—he no longer qualifies as white trash," she said coldly. At the soda fountain, Ollie Caston was trying to wait on customers while a reporter named Higgens from the *New York Times* interviewed him. Higgens wore a brown Fedora with a wide black band, a tan, double-breasted suit, and a brown necktie with a tomato soup stain at the very bottom. Both his eyeteeth were yellow, and he had a tic in his right eye when he got excited.

"You see this?" Higgens said, pointing to a picture of Ben shaking hands with the president on the front page of a crumpled copy of the *Times*. "That's yesterday's news! What I'm looking for is some human interest stuff—something fresh. Right now that boy's the hottest item in the country. Tomorrow—next week, who knows?"

Ollie took two fountain cokes to a couple at one of the tables, hurrying back to fix chocolate malts for Debbie and her friends in the booth. "What're you interested in?" Ollie asked, scooping vanilla ice cream into the tall, shiny metal cup.

"What kind of work did he do?"

"Delivery work on his bicycle, worked the fountain, stockroom—whatever needed doin'."

"Well, it's better'n nothin'," Higgens mumbled, scribbling in his steno pad with a stub of a yellow pencil. "What else?"

"He was honest, dependable, hard working, and—"

"Yeah, yeah," Higgens interrupted. "Ain't they all? Tell me something different."

"It's the truth!" Ollie said hotly, fed up with Higgens' big-city manners. "Maybe that's different!"

"What about a girlfriend?"

Ollie glanced over at Debbie. "The blonde in the last booth over there. She's probably the closest thing he had to one in Liberty. Here, take this with you," he ordered, handing Higgens a metal Coca-Cola tray with three malts on it.

Higgens frowned, but accepted the tray, carrying it over to the booth.

Ollie watched Debbie's face light up, turning on the charm when Higgens spoke to her. *She'll have Higgens believin' she stayed home every night cryin' for Ben Logan—the only boy she ever kissed.*

"Hey, Debbie!" Taylor Spain called out, stepping through the door of the drugstore. His acne was ridged with dull red blotches in the glare of the plate glass window. "Your daddy wants some help gettin' things ready for Ben's homecomin' down at the depot. All three of ya'll come on. The train'll be pullin' in real soon."

Debbie waved the fingers of one hand at Taylor Spain, holding on to Higgens's arm with her other hand. "Be with you in a jif, Taylor. This nice man's going to put my name in the *New York Times*."

At the train depot, there was bedlam among the towns-people. Limited space on the speaker's platform meant a battle to secure a chair in one of the exalted positions. Arguments were breaking out on the depot platform and all along the tracks.

Men, women, and children were putting up signs, banners, and streamers everywhere. As no one had been put in charge of decorations, the area around the depot looked like a cross be-tween a Fourth of July celebration and the New Orleans Mardi Gras.

Hartley Lambert, who owned the lumber mill and half the rest of the town, was butting heads with Calvin Sinclair, the mayor and owner of Sinclair's Real Estate, about who would in-troduce Senator Demerie, who would in turn introduce Ben.

"I don't care *what* you say, Calvin," Lambert bellowed from the platform, his blond hair and blue eyes a replica of Debbie's. "*I'm* the man to introduce Tyson. There ain't no loudspeaker sys-tem and your squeaky little voice wouldn't reach the front row!"

Calvin Sinclair wriggled his short black mustache, strutting like an aged penguin over to the steps of the platform in his black business suit. He looked like a slightly overweight Charlie Chaplin. People called him "Charlie" behind his back because he favored the "Little Tramp" character Chaplin had made famous in his silent films. "Let's get one thing straight, Hartley," Sinclair squeaked. "I'm the mayor of this town, and it's traditional for the mayor to make the introductory speeches. Now you just get on back to your lumber mill and cut up some two-by-fours or something else you got sense enough to do."

Big bear of a man that he was, Hartley Lambert gave in. He knew all too well of the little man's legendary tenacity. Once when an escaped convict had tried to steal Sinclair's car at Three Corners to get out of town, Sinclair had knocked him in the head with the nozzle of the gas hose, almost beating him to death with it before Ring Clampett could pull him off the burly convict.

That crazy little tyrant would climb right up me like a monkey and take the microphone away in front of everybody, Lambert thought. "All right, Calvin," he said. "I guess tradition wins out this time. Try not to sound too much like Mickey Mouse before his voice changed when you make the introduction though. This is the biggest thing to ever hit this town!"

Sinclair, who had long ago forged a shield impervious to insult, bounced up the steps to the platform. "You just make sure to comb the sawdust out of your hair before you sit down up here, Hartley. I'll take care of the rest."

Hartley spotted Debbie and Keith Demerie weaving their way through the crowd. "Hey, Debbie!" He shouted above the deep murmur of the crowd. "Get ahold of four or five more of your boyfriends and go bring some foldin' chairs from the high school. Everbody and his brother thinks they got to sit up here today."

*　*　*

"Ben, I owe you a debt of gratitude. You can rest assured, I'll never forget it, either," Senator Tyson Demerie said in his rich bass voice. "Nobody from Liberty has ever been invited to the White House before—not as far as I know anyway. Your bravery in combat really put our little town on the map!"

"You don't owe me a thing, Senator," Ben replied, leaning back in his seat, staring at the ceiling. "To tell you the truth, puttin' Liberty on the map never crossed my mind when them Japs started droppin' bombs and strafin' the ships."

"Well, your thoughts, like every man's, are private," Demerie assured him, running his hand through his thick, silver-gray hair. "The reasons a man does what he does, however, don't detract from the deed itself."

Ben knew he had put it off long enough—he had to do it, and for some reason it didn't seem so difficult now.

"I'll never forget that sight as long as I live!" Demerie continued. "FDR shaking your hand and presenting you with the Medal of Honor. And then he actually shook my hand! This has to be—"

"Senator," Ben offered, sitting up, placing his hands on his knees. "I'd like to apologize for what I did to your son. It was my fault, and I'm sorry for it."

"Oh, come, come, my boy, there's no need for that," Demerie said paternally. "After all, boys will be boys. Had a few scraps myself when I was your age."

"I'm gonna ask Keith to forgive me, too—soon as I see him," Ben continued.

Demerie flicked his hand as if he were dismissing a servant. "You don't have to do that for Keith. He's forgotten about it after all this time."

"Maybe he has, but I have to do it for myself, Senator," Ben said evenly.

"Well, if you feel that way. You know this reminds me of how politics and forgiveness . . ."

Ben knew that Demerie was launching into another of the series of political treatises he had listened to on the trip down from Washington, and he put his mind into neutral.

Sitting next to the window, Ben stared out at the stark February landscape. That morning the sky had been sealed with clouds like a gray cotton blanket stretching from horizon to horizon, but when he woke from his nap it was perfectly clear. The pale sunlight carried little warmth as it shone on the winter trees, their dark limbs leafless—filigreed against the hard blue sky.

Remembering how nervous he had been at the White House the day before, Ben knew, like Demerie, he would never forget. Franklin Roosevelt's smile had been like a balm to him. Immediately he felt at ease in the presence of this greatest of the world's leaders. He had felt the terrible burden the man carried, had noticed his battle against physical pain, but most of all, had sensed a courage and an iron will that overshadowed everything else.

"Well, here we are, son," Demerie said, laying his hand on Ben's shoulder.

Ben had dozed again, and when he looked out the window he hardly recognized his hometown. Red, white, and blue bunting was strung from virtually every building and pole in sight, even the street signs. Streamers of crepe paper fluttered in the breeze along with hundreds of flags. "Welcome Home Ben" signs were tacked everywhere, with people holding aloft or waving other signs and banners carrying the same or similar message.

"Looks like one of them bombs landed on a ribbon factory," Ben observed, turning to Demerie.

Demerie chuckled. "Well, they're all excited about a hometown boy making the big time. This ain't like that Fifth Avenue parade you got in New York, but the feelings are real."

The first thing Ben saw when he stepped off the train in his dress blues and pea jacket was a big bouquet of roses thrust at him by Debbie Lambert. "Oh, Ben, I've missed you so much," she said breathlessly, putting her arms around him and the roses, kissing him warmly on the mouth. As Ben felt Debbie's lips on his, he was lost in the scent of roses and perfume and the smooth, soft pressure of her kiss. All the long nights in boot camp—even in the clamor and smoke and whiskey-numbed barroom nights, her face would flash before him unexpectedly.

He opened his eyes when she stepped back, drinking in the sight of her. He was lost for a moment in her intense blue eyes, her fine blonde hair flowing about her face in the afternoon breeze. Like he had been told in the Navy—maybe this was indeed the reason they were willing to risk their lives—just to be able to come home to a girl like Debbie, or a hundred thousand other versions of her.

The first thing Senator Demerie saw when he got off the train was a sign that said, "Ben Logan for State Senator—He's One of Us." And then he saw some more of them. *Good Lord! This thing's gotten out of hand!*

Hartley Lambert was right behind his daughter. "Ben, Ben— you've made us all so proud." He grabbed Ben's hand in both of his and shook it firmly.

What happened to "See my daughter again and I'll have you locked up," Ben wondered, remembering the message Lambert had sent him the last time he was home.

At the back of the crowd, Ring Clampett was talking to a man holding a "Ben Logan for State Senator" sign. "You know what?" he drawled, popping a stick of Doublemint chewing gum in his mouth to suppress the whiskey smell. "I took a real interest in that boy 'fore he left for the Navy. Sort of helped him be what he is to-day—you know?"

In the press of the crowd and the forest of waving signs and banners, Ben was looking for his family. He finally spotted his mother and father on the platform, seated in folding chairs on the back row at the far end. He tried to get to them, but Lambert and Demerie had him by the arms, escorting him to the position of honor at the front of the platform.

Calvin Sinclair opened his arms as if he were greeting his long-lost son. "Ben, Ben—a true Son of Liberty. Welcome home!"

First time he ever said a word to me, Ben thought, half expecting him to tell someone to go and kill the fatted calf.

Ben sat between Demerie and Lambert in a plush leather chair someone had brought over from Rev. Thad Majors's study at the First Baptist Church. Rev. Majors was almost six feet tall and wore a dark brown, vested suit. With his crinkly eyes and wholesome smile, he had the appearance of Roy Rogers turned businessman. After giving his usual lengthy invocation, he took his place in a folding chair at the end of the single row that faced the audience.

Calvin Sinclair walked briskly to the lectern. Taking a crumpled sheet of paper from his inside jacket pocket, he began in his sharp little voice: "Fellow citizens of Liberty. Today I have the pleasure of presenting the first true hero of the war against tyranny— one of our own sons. Taking no thought for his own life, he put himself in harm's way to protect and defend our freedom against the cowardly and treacherous tyranny that threatens freedom everywhere in the world today. I am proud to say I watched this young man grow up right. . . ."

Tyson Demerie fumed as he watched Sinclair standing on tiptoe to see his notes. *That little sneak! He knows I'm supposed to introduce Logan. Stealing all my best lines too!*

Ben smiled at his mother—and his father. He searched the faces in the crowd for Rachel, but couldn't find her. Dinah and Micah were at the foot of the steps, smiling up at him. He gave them a quick, little wave and a wink. They waved back and began talking excitedly.

Ollie Caston, wearing his usual white shirt and black bow tie, stood next to Leslie Gifford near a corner of the depot. Gifford, in his ancient tweed jacket, was beaming—so proud of Ben that it was even reflected in his strange, sad eyes.

As Ben let his eyes roam over the crowd, he noticed the "Ben Logan for State Senator" signs scattered among the "Welcome Home Ben" and "Ben Logan—Jap Killer" banners and signs. He also noticed that the political slogans were not lost on Senator Demerie, who squirmed uncomfortably every time he forced himself to glance at one of them.

When the interminable speeches were over, Ben was completely engulfed in the press of the crowd. People were shouting his name, reaching out to shake his hand. Cries like "Way to handle them dirty Japs, Ben!" and "Shoot one for me, Ben!" rose above the tumult.

Trying to reach his mother and father, Ben was blocked by Hartley Lambert. Debbie stood smiling brightly at his side.

"Ben," Lambert shouted above the din. "We've fixed up a room at our house so you can be available to the press or any of the elected officials or the military. I know Debbie would be thrilled to have you come visit us for a day or two. Or, if you prefer, I've arranged for the hotel to reserve their best suite for you."

Ben glanced at Lambert, then at Debbie. "I—I don't know, Mr. Lambert. I haven't even thought about it."

"Well, you should, Ben," Lambert insisted. "There's a lot of important people who're gonna want to see you. You're a public figure now. I'm afraid that little house of your daddy's just won't do. Besides, it's way out of town."

Ben felt Debbie holding tightly to his arm. The touch and scent of her was something he dreamed about during those nights on the open sea, as he lay on his cot under the star-crowded tropical sky. Now that she was here in the flesh, it all seemed too easy somehow, too accessible. Part of him was still drawn to her—to the fulfillment of fantasy, while part of him knew there was decay at the center of his desire.

"I reckon the hotel will be just fine then."

A look of disappointment crossed Lambert's face. "We'd be glad to have you at the house—but whatever you say. The suite's all ready when you are."

Pushing through the crowd toward his parents, Ben shook hands and greeted people along the way. When he finally reached her, he put his arms around his mother, hugging her tightly.

Earl Logan held out his scarred, work-hardened hand to his son, an awkward smile on his face. Ben ignored the hand, taking his father in both arms and hugging him as he had his mother.

Earl Logan felt an unexpected rush of emotion. His throat tightened as he stammered, "I—I missed you, son."

"Me, too, Daddy," Ben smiled, turning back to his mother.

"Oh, Ben! Thank God you're home safe!" Jewel Logan cried, the bright tears beginning to spill down her cheeks. "Thank God!"

Dinah and Micah managed to slip through the crowd. "Ben! Ben!" Micah screamed.

Ben squatted down and picked Micah up, holding him in one

arm while he put his other around Dinah, pulling her to him and kissing her on the cheek.

"This is my big brother!" Micah shouted to the world at large, his hand lifted high, pointing to Ben.

Wouldn't Pete have loved all this? Ben thought. *I can just see him now—wisecracking with everybody—trying to get in all the pictures. He'd have been a lot better at it than I am. Well, I'm glad I had him for fourteen years. Next time I see him, there won't be any more good-byes!*

Higgens tapped Ben on the shoulder from behind, his notebook poised and a white "Press" card stuck in his hatband. "Hey, buddy, I'm from the *New York Times.* Can we go somewhere and talk? The reading public wants to know all about you." The tic began in the man's right eye as he spoke.

"I haven't had any time with my family yet," Ben protested, looking about him for a way to escape.

"Look, Mac," Higgens announced, popping a stick of gum into his mouth. "You belong to the American people now." He pointed over his shoulder to the throng of reporters waiting at the foot of the stairs. "And we're the ones who tell them all they want to know about their heroes. Your life's not gonna be your own for a while."

Hartley Lambert stepped in and took charge. "All right, everybody! If you'll just follow us, we'll move over to the hotel, and you'll all have ample opportunity to interview Mr. Logan." He took Ben by the arm and started for the steps.

Ben shrugged, glancing helplessly at his family.

"It's all right, Baby," Jewel Logan called out to him as he was carried away by the throng. "We'll have plenty of time later."

As the crowd carried him along, Ben noticed Tyson Demerie rip a "Ben Logan for State Senator" sign from a tree, tear it into pieces, and fling it angrily to the ground.

* * *

"What's it like out there, Ben?" Ollie Caston asked, squirting chocolate syrup on Ben's sundae. "You think the Japs can whip us?"

After five hours of interrogation at the hotel by the reporters—and, later, people from all over the area—Ben had managed to slip out the back door for some time on his own. He went straight to Ollie's, where he sat at the counter with Leslie Gifford. Leslie sipped his coffee as Ollie set the sundae on the counter in front of Ben.

"'Course not," Ben said in answer to Ollie's question. Ben took the first spoonful of sundae into his mouth. The sweet, rich chocolate—the cold smoothness of the ice cream—were some of the things he thought about in those long nights at sea. "After the Japs hit so hard at Pearl, I was out of commission for a while. Seamen are the last ones to hear about anything in the Navy."

"Well, I know they hit Wake and Midway the same day as Pearl," Ollie offered, walking around the counter. "Our boys at Wake sunk two of their destroyers the first time they tried to take it, but they came back with carriers a couple of weeks later, and it was a different story."

"You think the Japs can take us, Mr. Gifford?" Ben asked, spooning ice cream into his mouth.

"No," Gifford replied cryptically. "After Hong Kong and Manila fell, that pretty well gave them everything north of Australia—the Dutch East Indies, Indo-China, the Phillipines, Malaysia—everything. Even the men on Bataan and Corregidor can't hold out much longer. But I think the war was lost for the Japanese when they backed off after Pearl. They missed their chance."

"Let's go sit in a booth," Ollie said, locking the front door and turning the *Closed* sign to the street. "Not going to be much business the rest of the day anyhow."

"Why do you think the Japs already lost the war, Leslie?" Ollie asked, after they were seated. "Everbody I know is scared to death they'll be walking down Main Street tomorrow."

"You sure you want to hear this, Ollie?" Gifford replied with a lean, wry smile. "I'm an English teacher, not a military strategist."

"You'll do until one walks in the door," Ollie laughed.

"Well, after the attack on Pearl, the Japanese had us back on our heels. The whole nation was in shock. That was the time to press the advantage. They could have brought troop ships and landing craft with them and taken the whole island chain—after that, who knows where it would have ended?"

"And now?" Ben asked, holding a spoon of ice cream and chocolate syrup in front of his mouth.

"Now the American war machine is going into high gear. The Japanese aren't in the same ball game with us when it comes to industrial output." Gifford sipped his coffee contemplatively. "It'll be a long, terrible war, but Japan can't hope to hold out."

"What about Hitler?" Ollie asked, eyes wide with interest.

"Hitler's insane—nobody knows what he'll do. The Russians and the British will keep him busy for a long time, though. Right now, it's the cowardly, slant-eyed Japanese that the American people love to hate. The Germans look too much like us to hate them like that," Gifford smiled ironically.

"I know what you mean," Ollie laughed. "I saw a sign on a car yesterday that said, 'Slap That Jap.'"

Ben took the last bite of his sundae. "Did you see the one in the barber shop? It says, 'Japs Shaved Free.'"

* * *

The pool area at the back of the Lambert mansion revealed an acquaintance with good taste—but only a nodding one. Most of the downtown decorations had been relocated there, with the exception of the political slogans, in deference to Keith Demerie, the senator's son.

There were long tables covered with white cloths and laden with food. Music was piped from the G.E. record player through the radio to outside speakers that had been installed for the occasion. The finishing touch was a yearbook photograph of Ben, blown up to life-size and tacked to a wooden stand at the far end of the pool.

"How do you like the party, Ben?" Debbie cooed, holding tightly to his arm as they walked through the crowd. "I planned everything just for you. All your classmates who matter are here."

Classmates who matter? I don't even know most of them, Ben thought. He was trying to answer two or three questions at once as they encountered people in their stroll around the grounds. "I think it's just like you, Debbie," Ben answered wryly. "And I appreciate all the work you put into it."

Sit down for a while," Debbie said, ushering Ben to a chair under a massive live oak. "I know you must be exhausted. I'll bring you some food."

I am exhausted—this is worse than boot camp! I've only been here two hours, and it seems like all night. Ben saw Taylor Spain and Keith Demerie crossing the patio area toward him. *Well, here's my chance.*

"How's the Sergeant York of the Navy?" Taylor Spain asked good naturedly.

"You saw that, huh?" Ben smiled. "That's Navy P.R. for you. I think they're all past champions of the National Biggest Lie contest."

Keith Demerie smiled. "From what I read, there's a lot of truth to it, Ben."

Ben looked at Demerie, thinking of the two fights they had had—both over Debbie. "Keith, I been meaning to talk to you. Now's as good a time as any."

"What'd I do now?" Demerie half-smiled.

"Nothing. It's what I did," Ben confessed. "I'm sorry for those fights I started with you. I was wrong."

Stunned into silence, Demerie stood there waiting for the punch line. "You're kiddin'!"

"No, I'm not. It was my fault."

Demerie smiled, shaking his head. "If this don't beat all. I'm just as much to blame as you, so let's just forget about it." He shook Ben's hand firmly.

Debbie returned with a plate piled high with food, handing it to Ben. "You've just got to try the shrimp, darling," she coaxed. "Daddy had them brought in all the way from Destin."

"We'll see you later, Ben," Demerie said. "Debbie, I'll pick you up at eight tomorrow night."

"You'll what?" she exclaimed, turning quickly around.

Demerie looked puzzled. "The country club dance. We've had the date for two months."

"Oh, don't be silly, Keith," Debbie said, dismissing him. "I can go to an old dance anytime. How many girls get to date a man who has his picture on the cover of *Life* magazine?"

Ben saw the sudden hurt on Demerie's face—remembered Debbie's doing exactly the same thing to him the night of the cast party. He looked around the party at the animated, smiling people —at all the trappings of wealth. *They're no better—no worse than anybody else,* he thought. *I just don't have much in common with them. Why did it seem so important to me to fit in?*

"Ben, you don't really have to go back to that old hotel, do you?" Debbie asked. She pressed against him, her body soft and yielding. "Daddy and Mama won't be back 'til morning. We can get rid of the whole boring lot of them if you want to."

Ben stared into Debbie's perfect blue eyes, looking for what lay behind them, but he couldn't see anything. "Will you excuse me, Debbie?" Ben asked politely. An intense desire to get away from all the glitter had taken him. He longed to be back with his people in the old house—just to *be* with them, in the old way.

Debbie frowned slightly, then gave him a firm kiss on the mouth. She whispered, "Ben—I've missed you so much! I can't *wait* until we're alone! Don't be long."

Ben walked through the crowd into the house, retrieved his hat and pea jacket from the hall closet and left through the front door. Walking through town in the damp coolness of the February night, Ben thought of his family, wondering why Rachel hadn't come to town with them yesterday. Later, pausing at the top of the little rise that looked down on his house, he smiled—then walked toward the light from the kitchen window, shining into darkness.

18

RACHEL

*B*en awakened at first light, in his cot, wrapped in the quilt his mother had made for him as a child. Lying there as the last thin webs of sleep faded from his mind, he heard the faint, distant sound of a rooster crowing. Sitting up slowly, he drew the quilt around his shoulders and looked at Micah snoring softly across the small room. The misty gray light through the single window outlined Pete's folded cot, stacked in the corner with Micah's toys.

Slipping his hand into the hiding place in the wall, Ben felt the money, rolled neatly and tied with a piece of string. *Three dollars—he did make it last a long time,* Ben thought, remembering what Pete had told him in the cold twilight of their living room the previous February.

After he had dressed, Ben walked the old familiar path to the well, his smoky breath drifting on the crisp morning air. As he drew the bucket, hand over hand from the bottom of the well, his left shoulder began a dull throbbing ache. *That's one Jap pilot I won't forget the rest of my life—even if I never did see him. Hope that doctor was right about the bones healing better in the next few months.*

A tilting shaft of light suddenly broke through the fine mist—the orange tip of the sun flaring softly as it topped the treeline. Ben poured the Mason jar half full of water from the long, narrow well bucket, pouring the rest into the bucket he had brought from the back porch. He sipped the clear water from the jar, taking pleasure in the cold, clean air—breathing deeply as the morning came to life.

The trees, becoming noisy with birds, gathered the gold light into their branches, tinting it with a pale green. Ben marveled at the beauty of the earth, at the creation wrought by his God. As the sun grew brighter, the words from Genesis seemed to him etched by some great hand across the morning sky.

In the beginning God created the heaven and the earth. And the earth was without form, and void; and darkness was upon the face of the deep. And the spirit of God moved upon the face of the waters. And God said, Let there be light: and there was light. . . . And God saw every thing that he had made, and, behold, it was very good.

Carrying the bucket up the path, Ben saw the kitchen light come on. He poured water into the pan on the back porch, washed his face, and combed his short hair.

"You'll catch your death, son," Jewel Logan chided gently, starting a fire in the stove as Ben came in the back door. "Why didn't you bring that water in and let me warm it for you?"

Ben kissed his mother on the cheek. "You spoil me too much, Mama. Besides, after two years in the tropics, a little cool weather feels good for a change."

"I heard you come in last night," Jewel said, stoking the fire. "Figured you could use a little time to yourself though, after that mob you had to put up with in town."

"Yeah, it was a mess all right," Ben agreed. "I got to visit with Ollie and Mr. Gifford a little while though. That was fun. I think Mr. Gifford's about the smartest man I know."

Jewel dumped flour into a mixing bowl and added baking powder and a pinch of salt. "Figured you'd be staying in town another day or two with all the plans I heard they had for you."

Ben smiled. "I was supposed to. Got tired of that 'Hero' business an hour after the train pulled in though."

"Hand me that milk out of the ice box, Baby," Jewel said, tearing off a piece of Cutrite waxed paper and laying it on the counter.

Ben handed the bottle of milk to his mother, watched her mix the heavy biscuit batter with her hands, tear off chunks of dough and form the biscuits. He heard the bedsprings creaking in the back bedroom, and a few seconds later his father appeared at the kitchen door, yawning and rubbing the sleep from his eyes. His hair was sticking out and his black beard showed two-days' growth, but there was no smell of whiskey on his breath.

"Morning, son," Earl said, sitting down at the table.

"Morning, Daddy."

Ben sat across from his father while Jewel poured them steaming cups of dark coffee. Spooning in sugar, Ben watched his father sip the coffee, noticing the scarred, calloused, work-hardened hands. The pine tar had been ground in so heavily over the years with grease and dirt that no amount of scrubbing could get them completely clean. *A man who works that hard's got to have a lot of good in him,* Ben thought. He tried to remember the good times before liquor ravaged his father's spirit.

"How we doin' in the Pacific, son?"

Startled from his reverie, Ben glanced from his cup to the face of his father. Earl Logan's dark eyes held a melancholy glaze, but there was also a hint of something Ben never remembered seeing before—a mildness, something like a gentle wind blowing through his soul. "Holdin' our own, I reckon. The Japs are pretty much doin' whatever they want to over in Asia right now from what I hear, but they missed their chance to take Hawaii."

"How much leave you got?" Earl asked, his eyes still heavy with sleep.

"Thirty days. Then I got to go on a trip around the country sellin' war bonds. I sure ain't lookin' forward to that," Ben answered gloomily, watching his mother put the biscuits in the oven.

"You just do what them Navy people tell you to, Ben Logan," his mother insisted, sitting with them at the table. "At least nobody's gonna shoot at you sellin' war bonds. Besides, you done yore part. Them Japs almost killed you."

Ben saw the fear in his mother's soft gray eyes—fear that she would lose him, now that Pete was gone. "Mama, none of us have done our part 'til the war's over. There's boys out there right now went through the same things I did—and they still got to fight when the time comes."

"He's right, Jewel," Earl agreed, holding his coffee cup with both hands. "Let's just be grateful that, for a while at least, Ben won't be goin' back into combat."

Ben smiled at his father, then his mother. "That's right, Mama. Who knows, I might just get to like bein' around all them movie stars and big shots. Maybe they'll put me in a movie with Judy Garland—or Rita Hayworth even. Boy, she's pretty!"

Jewel laughed softly. "You ain't the type, son. Now Pete—he'd have been right in the middle of 'em."

The three of them laughed, talking about some of Pete's antics for a while. Ben couldn't remember the last time he had sat with his mother and father, the three of them just enjoying one another's company. *This is almost as good as gettin' saved! When I get married and have a home, I'm gonna see to it that my family has some time together like this, no matter what.*

When the biscuits were done, they ate them with freshly churned butter and cane syrup, washing them down with strong, black coffee.

"Mama, did I tell you we had a Bible study on the ship?" Ben asked, biting into one of the big "cat head" biscuits, butter running from it down the side of his chin.

"You mentioned it in one of your letters, I believe."

"Yeah! It turned out real good. Three boys got saved. A whole bunch of 'em would come and go, so maybe it helped some of the others too."

Jewel looked at her son with a light in her eyes that expressed her great relief that he was still alive—her joy that he was becoming the man she always knew he could be. "It's a great blessin' to see how God works in people's lives, Ben. Only He can give 'em what really counts—joy all through the day and peace when they lay down at night."

"That's the truth," Ben said, seeing in his mother's face, in spite of Pete's death, a lifting of some great burden. "I thought one time if I had enough money I'd be happy as a pig in slop. Sure didn't work out that way though. All it got me was Ring Clampett's baseball bat upside my head, a night in jail, and run out of the town I'd lived in all my life."

"Wasn't all your fault," Jewel protested, shaking her head.

"Every bit of it was my fault, Mama," Ben disagreed. "Nobody made me do anything I didn't want to."

Ben noticed that his father had gone silent, staring into his coffee cup, but he knew he was listening to every word.

"I think maybe God used all my mistakes, though," Ben continued. "The Bible says that all things work for good to them that love God. I believe I always loved Him, but maybe I loved Ben Logan more. Gettin' saved was the hardest—and the easiest thing that ever happened to me. Sounds strange, but that's the way it was."

Earl Logan looked at his son with a puzzled expression on his face. *Takes after his mama.*

Jewel Logan felt a warmth flow through her as she listened to her son's testimony for the first time.

Ben took a sip of coffee, smiling at his mother and father. "It was so hard because I knew I had to give up everything Ben Logan wanted —money, a special girlfriend, fancy clothes—everything. Even though all I did was make a big mess of my life, never got all those things I thought mattered so much, it was still hard to do. Give myself completely to Jesus—give up everything I thought was so important. Just trust Jesus! And when I did! When I just let go of Ben Logan completely—I fell right into the arms of Jesus. I could almost feel it happening just that way. That's when I realized how easy it was."

"Well, I reckon I better get to workin' on that ol' truck," Earl said, taking his cup and plate to the dishpan. "It ain't gonna fix itself."

"Need some help, Daddy?"

"Naw. You set and visit with your mama some. It's kinda a one-man-job anyhow. Won't take long."

Later that day, as Jewel was sewing and listening to the radio in the front room, she glanced out the window. Ben and his father had gone to work on the Model T. They were leaning over the fenders of the old car that had sat rusting in the yard for years. Both of them had grease on their hands, arms, and faces. Their clothes were dirty and grimy, but she forgot about the hours it would take to wash them clean when she saw the smiles on their faces as they worked together.

*   *   *

Ben sat on his cot, looking out the window. The afternoon sunlight lay softly across the backyard, creating a tableau of brightness and deep shade. In the shadow of the well, a cat squirrel was scooting across the bare ground on his belly, clawed forefeet in front of him, looking for buried acorns. Finding one, he sat up quickly on his back legs, his tail a fuzzy question mark behind him. Holding the acorn with both front feet he gnawed away at it, stopping every few seconds to glance quickly around him for danger.

Reaching for the .22 rifle that leaned in the corner at the head of his cot, Ben unwrapped the scrap of old bedsheet that he kept it covered with. He lay it across his lap, the burnished oak stock gleaming in the light from the window—the blue-steel barrel, a slight scarring where the sight had been filed off—giving off a dull sheen, and the faint smell of Three-in-One oil. Pulling back the bolt, he saw that the receiver was clean. With the bolt open to let the light in he looked into the barrel.

Picking up his hunting bag from the floor, Ben slung it over his shoulder and went to the kitchen. "Mama, I think I'm gonna get a few rabbits for supper."

Jewel was listening to the familiar opening lines of "Lum and Abner": *And now—let's see what's going on down in Pine Ridge at the Jot-Em-Down Store.* "That's fine, son. It might be a good idea to take them over to Pastor Shaw's, though. They been havin' a pretty rough time lately. People in the church ain't got much to put in the offerin' plate. He works all the time he ain't pastorin', but it's still hard."

"Guess I'll do that then."

"Ben?"

"Yeah, Mama?"

"You seen Rachel since you been home?"

"No ma'am. I didn't think she wanted much to do with me, after the way I treated her when I was on liberty. Except maybe as a friend. We did write some."

Jewel smiled, shaking her head at the folly of her son. "Men!" She sniffed disgustedly. "Sometimes I think you're all just little boys with whiskers. You visit with her awhile when you drop them rabbits off. You might want a *friend* like her one day."

Twenty minutes later, Ben stood on a slight rise looking down at a frost-withered briar patch at the bottom. He had seen the flash of a white tail as the rabbit, disturbed from its feeding, bounded to the safety of the briars. Patches of sunlight formed pale yellow pools on the hard ground beneath the live oaks near the briars. The sky was a vaulted dome of blue.

Wish I still had my dog, Ben thought. He picked up a stick and flung it at the briars. Nothing. Walking closer, he found a longer limb and began poking around in the dessicated briar patch, gray as the bark of a cedar tree.

With a flash of white—a heartbeat-hammering of its feet on the hard ground, the rabbit bolted up the hill. Ben whirled the rifle around one-handed, still holding the limb. The smooth, clean barrel of the rifle seemed drawn to the fleeing rabbit as if it had a will of its own, holding steady to its flight. For an instant, Ben saw the tropic sun glinting off the cockpit of a Zero as it banked sharply against the high white clouds, roaring down the tilting shafts of sunlight toward his gun mount—and a grave at the bottom of the sea.

Another instant and Ben saw the rabbit gaining the top of the hill, moving as if in slow motion, the muscles of its hind legs working smoothly under the skin. He looked as big as a white-tailed deer to Ben, and he knew the rabbit was his. As he squeezed the trigger, he heard the report of the rifle as if it came from the other side of the hill, the rabbit's front legs crumpling under him as it tumbled over and over on the hard, dry winter ground.

* * *

"Well, if it ain't Ben Logan!" Samuel Shaw was washing his hands in the blue enameled pan on the shelf. "Good luck huntin'?"

"Four rabbits. You can have 'em. Mama said we got plenty," Ben replied, leaning his rifle against the wall.

"'Preciate it. Esther can fry 'em up with a brown gravy. You'll have to help us eat 'em." Shaw dried his hands on a tattered piece of towel. "You doin' all right?"

"I'm doin' real good now, Brother Shaw," Ben replied, setting his sack of rabbits down on the porch. "Like every sailor on liberty."

Shaw laughed, his blue eyes bright in the shadowed porch. "Come on in and we'll get Esther to make us some coffee."

"No coffee, Samuel," Esther Shaw smiled, as they stepped into the kitchen. "We're all out. I do have some of them tea bags that Sister Jacobs gave us at the last pounding."

"Reckon that'll have to do then," Shaw said, pulling out a chair from the table. "The sacrifices I make for the Lord, son! Drinking hot tea like one of them Englishmen with lace cuffs and buckles on his shoes!" He sniffed in disgust, then added, "Grab a chair, Ben. You can suffer with me."

Ben laughed as he sat at the table, watching Esther Shaw prepare the tea. There was barely room to squeeze her plump body between the table and the cabinet as she reached for the cups. *Rachel's short like her mother, but slim like her father—thank goodness it's not the other way around,* he thought.

"Rachel tells me you wrote her about startin' a Bible study on the ship. That right?" Shaw reached for one of the cookies his wife had set on the table.

"Yes sir. Kind of—anyway," Ben replied, taking a cookie from the plate. "A good friend of mine really headed it up. He taught me a lot about the Bible."

"That's the real heart of Christianity, Ben. One Christian talking to one other person, or maybe a small group like your Bible study, about Jesus." Shaw's blue eyes were intense as he spoke. "Preachin's got its place, but there's nothing like Christians sharing their faith on a personal basis. Jesus did more of that than He did preachin'."

Ben sensed a warmth and strength of purpose in the words of Samuel Shaw. "You remember that brush arbor meetin' the night before Thanksgivin', Brother Shaw?"

Shaw looked pensive. "That was Thanksgivin' two years ago, wasn't it? Yes, now I remember. Your brother Pete got saved. There was a mighty move of the Spirit that night, praise God!"

"Well, I never forgot your sermon. It was from the Book of John," Ben continued, remembering that long night on the fantail of the *Dobbin* in Sydney Harbor. "I was all by myself readin' that book and before I finished chapter fifteen, I accepted Jesus as my savior."

"Praise God!" Shaw exclaimed, his eyes bright with joy. "Rachel told me you wrote her you got saved, but it's sure good to hear it from your own lips. There's power in the gospel, son! Hallelujah! Us poor ol' preachers sometimes get to thinkin' that we got somethin' to do with people gettin' saved, healed, their lives changin' from night to day. But that ain't so. It's all done by the power of the gospel of Jesus Christ! God help us *never* to forget that!"

"You're preachin' again, Samuel," Esther Shaw smiled, setting the cups of tea on the table. "When God calls a man to preach, Ben, his pulpit is the whole world."

"I do tend to get carried away sometime," Shaw confessed. "Preach a sermon when a simple word or two would do just as good—or maybe better."

"We're so happy for you, Ben," Esther Shaw said. "Rachel just couldn't wait to tell us when she got your letter. I can see the difference in your life all over your face."

Ben smiled. "By the way, where is Rachel?" he asked, looking toward the front rooms.

"I think she took a walk down by the river," Shaw answered for his wife. "Well, I got to go visit Brother Westcott. His pneumonia's not gettin' any better I'm afraid."

"At least change your clothes, Samuel," Esther Shaw warned.

"No time to change. I washed up. That'll have to do for now." Shaw kissed his wife and turned to Ben. "Good to see you, son. You come back and visit any time."

"Thank you, Brother Shaw," Ben replied as Shaw left the kitchen.

Ben finished his tea, pushing his chair back from the table. "Guess I'll be goin'. Thanks for the tea, Sister Shaw."

"You're more than welcome, Ben."

Ben stood up to leave, pausing at the back door. "You reckon Rachel would mind if I walked down to the river and visited with her for a little while?"

"I think she'd enjoy that just fine, Ben," Esther Shaw replied. "She's been kind of moody lately. Takes these long walks a lot. You might be just what she needs to cheer her up." As Ben left, she watched him go and said a quick prayer under her breath for her daughter's happiness. *He's a good boy, Lord, and she's a good girl—if it's not against your will, let them find each other!*

* * *

The clear, green water of the river splashed over the rocks and trunks of fallen trees, making a small almost tinkling kind of music as it flowed through the shadowed woods. Above this miniature rapids, there was little current as the water was deep, moving almost imperceptibly between a beach on the near side—where you could stand and see the sand-and-gravel bottom eight feet down when the sun was overhead—and a twenty-five-foot rocky bluff on the far side.

A large irregularly shaped boulder had moved upward through the earth's crust thousands of years ago, a part of its surface protruding from a sandy slope at the upper end of the beach. The boulder curved smoothly upward, flattening near the base of a massive, spreading live oak. It almost touched the trunk, forming a bench-like surface where several people could sit with the tree trunk and parts of the boulder acting as backrests. In the summertime it would be crowded with swimmers, resting from their watery pleasures. On this late February afternoon it was host to a single seventeen-year-old girl.

Ben saw her in the sun-dappled shade, her curly brown hair shining in a swatch of light. It was even longer than he last saw it, pulled back and held behind with the same silver comb. He could see the clear light in her hazel eyes, but he was too far away to pick up the tiny flecks of green in them. Wrapped in a coarse, dark coat, and wearing heavy shoes, she looked fragile and defenseless.

Rachel heard the *scrunch-scrunching* sound of Ben's boots as he walked across the sandy beach toward her. Framed by his shiny black hair, his light gray eyes had an almost silver tint to them, against the dark tan of the tropic sun. Rachel sat with her feet together, her hands clasped in her lap, her back against the smooth stone. Ben sat beside her, leaning back against the trunk of the live oak.

"Your mama told me I could find you here," Ben said, clearing his throat.

Rachel watched a leaf turning slowly on the surface of the dark water as it moved downstream.

Ben shifted in his seat, leaning forward, elbows resting on his knees. "She said you wouldn't mind if I came down here to see you. You don't, do you?"

The leaf hit the beginning of the rapids, careening through the white swirling currents and green eddys.

Ben began a tuneless humming, tapping his right hand on his thigh. He fidgeted on the cool stone, smelling the water and the damp sand at the river's edge. Clearing his throat again, he asked softly. "Rachel? You all right?"

"Your *friend?*"

"What?"

Rachel spun around, facing Ben, a dark anger smoldering in her eyes. He remembered seeing it once before. "That's the way you signed your letters to me. 'Your *friend.*' Is *that* all I am?"

"Well, what's the matter with—"

"Oh, hush up, Ben Logan," Rachel snapped. "If you want a *friend*, go buy yourself another *coon dog!*"

Ben waited in silence for another tirade, even more confused when it didn't come.

Rachel sat with her arms crossed, staring out over the still water. At that instant a yearling white-tail deer appeared at the top of the bluff. He stared back at her, then snorted explosively, and with a quick turn and a single bound, disappeared into the underbrush.

"I guess it was kinda stupid at that," Ben muttered. "I—I just thought you wouldn't want nothin' much to do with me after the way I treated you that summer I was on liberty. I'm sorry—I really am."

Rachel relaxed, uncrossed her arms. Turning to Ben she said sedately, "Well, you're a man—I guess that gives you a right to be stupid."

Ben was caught off guard, then he saw the warm smile on Rachel's face. "You really had me goin' there for a minute," he laughed. "I thought you was serious."

"I was serious," Rachel said, the smile no longer on her face. "Till you apologized."

"You know, Rachel, I think maybe we'll be seeing a lot of each other," Ben ventured. Then hastened to add, "That is if it's all right with you."

"It's all right with me, Ben," Rachel smiled.

"Well then, don't you think it'd make things a lot better if you just come out and tell me when something's bothering you?"

"No."

"No? Well, why not then?" Ben asked, believing the issue to be a simple one.

"Just doesn't work that way."

"What do you mean it doesn't work that way?"

Rachel looked at Ben as a mother might look at her three-year-old, explaining why he shouldn't play in the street. "It's just not that simple between men and women. But then you're only nineteen. Maybe you're not old enough to understand."

"Not old enough?" Ben almost shouted, then caught himself. "I'm old enough to go to war! I'm old enough to get invited to the White House! They want me to sell war bonds for this country! What do you mean, I'm not old enough? Besides, you're only seventeen!"

"It's different with women," Rachel said enigmatically.

Ben took a deep breath. He got up slowly and walked down to the river's edge. Finding a smoothly rounded stone in the sand, he picked it up and threw it with all his might. It sailed over the water, further and further out, until it bounced off the rocky bluff.

"I'm glad you came down here, Ben," Rachel admitted, standing beside him.

Ben looked down at her, as she slipped her soft hand into his. "Rachel, there's something I want you to know."

Rachel pressed against Ben, placing her other hand over his.

"When that first Jap plane was comin' at me, I was scared to death. Didn't even come close to shootin' it down. He hit the ship with a torpedo that knocked me clear out of the gun mount."

Striated light through the trees was fading as the sun dropped behind the trees, its pale light vanishing from the pewter surface of the river.

"I just wanted to lie there and die!" Ben continued, filled with a sudden fierce emotion. "But something happened! I could almost hear you saying, *God told me I'm going to be your wife!* I knew then I was going to make it—you couldn't marry a dead man!"

Rachel turned to Ben, pressing herself to his chest, her arms around his waist. "Oh, Ben will you have to go to war again? Won't it be over soon?"

Ben put his arms around Rachel, holding her tightly against him, lost in the softness and scent of her hair. "I believe it's going to be a long, terrible war, Rachel. The little bit of it I've seen is nothing. It'll touch everybody in Liberty before it's over."

Rachel looked up into Ben's eyes, thinking they looked like clear silver in the dark air. As he bent to kiss her, she came up on tiptoe, her mouth opening slightly, feeling warmth like a current passing through her body as they joined together.

"Oh, Ben—I've loved you for so long! I can't lose you to this war!"

Ben didn't think of the war any longer. He realized that it was only a part of a much greater warfare that had begun with the first Adam. It was enough being here with Rachel—enough that they had found each other. He felt her warm and soft against him—felt a joy and peace with her as deep as his heart's blood.

"The sun's almost gone," he whispered into her ear.

Rachel gazed upward into Ben's face and he saw the pure, clear light in her eyes.

"We'll go home together then, Ben."

They left the river and walked down the narrow path away from the gathering darkness.